When seventeen-ye  scholarship to a tо _____ ___ool, he thinks maybe his no _____ ___ck nas finally ended. With a hearing for ...s legal emancipation on the horizon, he dreams of getting scouted and securing a place on a D1 college team. There's only one problem: Roman has serious beef with his new winger on the team, Damien Bordeaux. They're supposed to be perfectly in sync on the ice. But Roman, with his buzzcut and tattoos, has nothing in common with trust-fund-kid Damien, his floral scrunchies, and designer T-shirts that cost more than all of Roman's secondhand hockey gear combined.

When eighteen-year-old Damien Bordeaux starts his senior year, he tells himself he's going to focus on hockey and school. No more making out in the stacks, no more dorm parties. He needs to decide what his future will look like. Does he pursue his long-held dream of becoming an author? Or stay in his lane and do what he's good at: hockey. Regardless, he's not going to let any pretty boys distract him from figuring his shit out. Except his new center, Roman, is possibly the most beautiful boy Damien has ever seen. And his hockey— the way he moves on the ice—might be even more beautiful. Too bad he's also probably a homophobic, racist asshole.

But their antagonistic beginning turns into an unlikely friendship and then turns into something much scarier for them both. Navigating relationships is hard enough for normal teenagers. It's a lot harder when contending with lawyers, NHL scouts, and mutual past trauma. Roman and Damien have to decide: What do they really want in life? Are they willing to fight for each other— including fighting against their own pasts and prejudices—so they can have a happy ending?

ALL HAIL THE UNDERDOGS

THE BREAKAWAY SERIES,

BOOK THREE

E.L. MASSEY

A NineStar Press Publication

www.ninestarpress.com

All Hail the Underdogs

First Edition, August 2023

ISBN: 978-1-64890-685-5

Also available in eBook, ISBN: 978-1-64890-684-8

CONTENT WARNING:
This book contains the discussion of child abuse by a parent (past, off page), search for birth parents; scenes of minors drinking/issues with drinking.

For my mom. Who has read everything I've ever written. Even when it was indecipherable scribbles. Even when it was not her cup of tea. Even when it was spicy fanfic with the chapter heading "maybe don't read this one, Mom." Thanks for everything.

CHAPTER ONE

PATRICK ROMAN HAS his mother's eyes and his father's nose, and on his face, they're still a family.

He considers his reflection in the filmy bus station bathroom mirror. He rubs his thumb down the raised line of scar tissue bisecting his chin: pink and new and only partially hidden in the drip-paint collage of his freckles, and then rubs harder, more habit than intention.

After spending the summer as a stern man on his uncle's crab boat—sorting, banding, baiting, resetting, trying his best to repair the limping hydraulic trap hauler that should have been scrapped a decade ago—layers of sunburn have turned into a tan, multiplying the pigment across his nose and cheeks and shoulders to a point where he looks constantly dirty. As if he'd been working in his other uncle's garage and absently smeared an oiled forearm over his face.

His cousin Saoirse once said that Patrick looked like a Jackson Pollock painting. He thinks she was trying to be mean. Or elitist. Or both. But he sort of agrees with her. He didn't know who Jackson Pollock was, at first, but when he went with his aunt into town the following weekend, he used the library computer to google him.

At thirteen, with new calluses on his palms from his first-ever crab haul, constant peeling skin over his nose and shoulders, and the kind of secret that scrapes your insides hollow, he'd found the paintings, grainy and pixelated as they were on the old computer monitor, strangely familiar.

Maybe he *is* like a Jackson Pollock painting: a dark, incensed, anxious spatter of reds and yellows and blacks and blues. Too much color for one canvas. Too much feeling for containment. *Too much*, maybe, in general.

Someone bangs on the bathroom door, and he stops glaring at his reflection because there's nothing much he can do about it.

He uses a paper towel to dry his hands, runs his fingers, still damp, over his buzzed hair, and shoulders his duffel bag.

St. James Academy is waiting.

He googled St. James when he googled the rest of the best hockey prep schools in the country.

Same library.

Same shitty library computer.

Initially, he wanted to try to play for a junior team;

he was good enough, he'd been scouted. But now, money issues aside, billeting would be all but impossible considering his legal situation. So he'd spent stolen hours at school and after work searching boarding schools with prep hockey teams, comparing stats and rosters and course offerings. He sent in his game tapes and paperwork with scraped-together application fees and letters of recommendation from his former and current coaches.

He applied to six schools and was accepted at two.

St. James was the closest, not that he really cared about staying close, but his lawyer said it would make things easier for possible future hearings if he was within a few hours' drive of Port Marta.

St. James was also the cheapest, which he did care about, and it routinely produced D1 prospects, which was his primary concern. A full scholarship with housing, a meal plan, and a chance to elevate his game to the point that maybe, next year, he could get a scholarship to college? An easy decision.

After getting a handful of salt-crusted hundreds from his uncle at the harbor early that morning as payment for his summer of work, he'd hitched a ride with another stern man from Port Marta to Brunswick and then took a Greyhound from there to Concord, and then a city bus to the station closest to St. James.

And now he's here, standing outside with a paper map from his library's equally shitty printer, a duffel bag from the army surplus store full of abused hockey gear, and an address written in permanent marker on his wrist. It's three miles away, but he's not about to waste money on an Uber.

He shoulders his bag and starts walking.

The campus looks exactly like the online pictures—sun-dappled and idyllic, with people lounging under trees and throwing frisbees and weaving colorful bikes in and out of foot traffic on immaculate sidewalks.

He's too hot in his leather jacket, and the strap of his bag is rubbing the side of his neck raw, but he walks with a purpose and doesn't make eye contact when people look at him.

And people *do* look at him.

He's six foot two, dressed all in black and carrying a bag over his shoulder that's nearly as big as he is. Doubtless, he stands out like some sort of hulking freckled raven among songbirds.

By the time he finds the administration building, his palms are so sweaty it's hard to get the stupidly ornate door open. Once inside, standing in line on the marble floors, looking up at the vaulted ceiling, the whispered assertion that's been following him since he stepped foot on campus gets louder: *You do not belong here.* He's felt that way for most his life, though, wherever he was, so it isn't that disconcerting.

He clears his throat when it's his turn, stepping up to the counter at the student center.

"I'm a transfer," he says. "Patrick Roman. I need to pick up my dorm keys."

Before the receptionist has a chance to answer, though, the person behind him speaks.

"You're our new center?"

He turns to look at the speaker and pauses.

Because he recognizes the boy's face.

He's seen it on rosters and game footage and even a few news articles.

During his research, Patrick memorized the names of three players at St. James Academy. Two players he thought were exceptionally good. *These would be your peers*, he told himself.

The first was Aiden Kane. Junior. Winger. Number 5.

The second was Justin Lefevre. Senior. Defense. Captain. Number 73.

Damien Raphael Bordeaux. Senior. Winger. Number 21.

What he didn't anticipate is that, off the ice, Damien Raphael Bordeaux looks a lot less like the goon he does on the ice and a lot more like the kind of boy Patrick's father warned him against becoming, sometimes with words, but sometimes with fists.

Because off the ice, Damien wears cuffed skinny jeans stretched tight over the bulk of his thighs and half-unbuttoned floral shirts and velvet scrunchies to hold back his long, curly hair. His dark skin is clear and pore-less, and the delicate gold chain around his neck should look out of place on someone so broad, but it doesn't.

He is irritatingly well-groomed.

He's also waiting for an answer.

"Yeah?" Patrick manages, and it maybe comes out more aggressive than he intended.

"I'm Damien," Damien Raphael Bordeaux says, extending a hand and smiling with straight white teeth and the easy confidence that comes with money. "I'm on the hockey team too."

He has the slightest accent that might be French. Of course, he does.

Damien's hand is warm and dry, and the torn calluses on Patrick's own chapped hand scrape jarringly against his palm.

"Rome," Patrick says. Because if there's one thing hockey has given him, it's a name that his father didn't.

Damien squeezes his fingers, holds on a moment past comfortable, grins wider so the skin around his eyes crinkles, and says, "Rome. Cool. Coach says you're going to be my new center."

And all Rome can think is:

Oh no.

*

LUCIFER WAS AN angel once.

That's what Damien thinks the first time he sees Patrick Roman.

The boy is beautiful even though he shouldn't be. Even though he's doubtless the kind of person who would punch you in the face if you said the words "you" and "beautiful" to him in the same sentence.

His skin is choked with freckles. It's potentially more freckle than skin. Not just his face, where his nose and cheekbones are so hyperpigmented they look tanned, but his collarbones and forearms and the knuckles of his callused hands. The close-shaved brown stubble of his hair should make his ears look too big or his mouth too wide, but instead, it accentuates the long curve of his throat and the cup of velvet skin between the tendons in the back of his neck. It makes his cheekbones sharper, his eyes—so light blue they look almost silver—more stark under dark spiky lashes.

He's wearing boots and jeans and a leather jacket that could either be beat to shit for aesthetic reasons or just beat to shit, and a permanent scowl that will likely give him wrinkles at an early age but right now is just terribly flattering.

It all adds up: the interesting face; the long, wiry frame; the taut, fight-ready stance—to create a body that casting directors for edgy photoshoots would salivate over. The sort of photoshoots that, if they involve teeth, it isn't because people are smiling.

The point is, he has a carefully curated look, and that look is *fuck off*.

Damien wants to touch him.

Damien has never touched someone with that many freckles before, and he doubts this particular someone would let him close enough to try, which is (he thinks a little despairingly of himself) perhaps why he finds the boy so damn compelling.

Damien reminds himself, as he stands in line at the administration office and tries not to stare at the freckled nape of the other boy's neck, that Damien is at St. James to focus on hockey and school. He's not here to admire transfer students who are undoubtedly straight and probably won't share a single class with him. Damien will likely only see the newcomer from a distance for the next year and then never see him again. And that's a *good* thing because he's here to *focus on school and hockey.*

Except then, the new kid steps up to the receptionist's desk and says in a rough, surprising drawl. "I'm a transfer. Patrick Roman. I need to pick up my dorm keys."

And Damien knows that name.

It was in the email that Coach sent out over the summer. It was the name of the video file attached to it. The footage was grainy, badly spliced together, and clearly shot unprofessionally from the stands, but it was enough. Roman was good. Tall, but fast. Aggressive, but smart. Together, Damien thought, they might be great.

So when Damien hears the name, he doesn't even think. He just speaks.

"You're our new center?" he asks.

And the boy turns around and considers him with what might be contempt, or what might only be the way his face looks, and says, "Yeah?" like it's a challenge.

And Damien thinks:

Oh no.

CHAPTER TWO

THE DINING HALL is overwhelming.

Damien pointed it out as they walked to the dorm and then invited Rome to join him for dinner.

Except now, Rome is uncertain where to begin because there is food *everywhere*. A salad bar to his right. Omelet station on the left. Pizza and hotdogs and burgers. Lasagna. Chicken. Meatloaf. Pasta. Juices and milks and sodas and a whole section for dessert around the corner.

He follows Damien, and he fills up his tray with all the same things Damien does: chicken, pasta, mixed vegetables, a fruit cup, a cookie.

Well. Rome gets two cookies.

He feels like he did the first time he ever left Port

Marta on a bantam hockey trip, and they'd stayed at a hotel and were allowed to eat as much as they wanted at the buffet for dinner. Rome gorged himself to the point that he nearly was sick. He reminds himself of that night as he carefully doles out the portions on his plate.

The dining hall isn't going anywhere.

He'll have these options *every day* now.

That realization is enough to almost make Damien's company bearable.

Almost.

Damien clearly has no similar appreciation for the embarrassment of riches before them. Once they sit and begin eating—Rome at a careful, measured pace—Damien cheerfully complains about the chicken being too dry and the vegetables too soggy, and the unacceptable fact that St. James doesn't offer organic salad greens. It's a good thing Rome's mouth is full and his hands are busy cutting his chicken because it distracts him from laughing. Or maybe punching Damien in the face.

"I'm getting milk," Damien says as he sucks cookie crumbs off his fingers. "You want some? Coach is probably going to give you hell about your weight, just so you know."

Rome does laugh then. A sharp, brittle thing that makes Damien frown at him.

"Yeah," he says. "Sure."

Every coach he's had since he was ten and on his first real team has told him he needed to gain weight.

"You're a tall kid for your age, son," his bantam coach said despairingly after nearly every practice. "But you're too skinny. Just put some weight on, and you'd be a more effective presence on the ice."

It sounded easy, like that.

Just put some weight on.

And then he moved up to Triple A, and the refrain continued. They gave him black-and-white printouts of recommended caloric intake and carb-to-protein ratios and portion sizes, and then later, they asked if he was keeping up with his meal plans and workouts, and he'd lie and say he was.

What they didn't seem to understand is that food costs money. And Rome didn't have any. His family lived off markdowns and seafood they caught themselves and WIC items his stepmother snuck past his too-proud father. He worked at the rink after hours to afford getting his skates sharpened, worked at his uncle's garage on weekends and his other uncle's boat during the summers to pay even discounted team fees. He could afford to eat more healthy shit or he could afford hockey, but he definitely couldn't afford both.

He doubts Damien Raphael Bordeaux, with his Ray Bans and designer shirts, has ever had that problem.

So Rome stayed skinny, and he made up for a lack of bulk with speed and aggression. He learned how to use the size he did have. He learned to intimidate without having to use his body at all.

And as long as his numbers stayed up, which they did, coaches wrote off his weight as a fast metabolism and his attitude as the kind of superiority complex that comes from being the best athlete on a small team.

So when Rome sits there with his tray full of food, *healthy food*, and Damien bemoans its quality—

He knew St. James Academy would be full of rich kids, but he's never really been around rich kids before.

Even on Rome's last team, the spectrum ranged from desperately poor to sort of poor to not poor. *Rich* is a whole new thing.

And apparently, that thing is disdainful of perfectly good, fully cooked, within-date chicken.

"Hey!" Damien says, flailing a little and nearly knocking over his glass of milk. "Olly! Justin! Kaner! Come meet the new guy."

Rome recognizes only one of the three people who approach. Justin Lefevre, his new captain. Blond hair. Green eyes. Perfect teeth. He looks just like his father, and he'll probably go on to be just as famous if his hockey career continues on its current trajectory. The other boy is brown-haired and olive-skinned and has the general look of an athlete about him. The girl's face is vaguely familiar, with sharp features and dark hair, but he can't place her. She also holds herself like a person used to using their body like a tool.

"This is Justin," Damien says. "Our captain, defense." He points to the second boy. "Olly, goalie. And—" He points to the girl. "Kaner, the other winger on our line."

"But you're a girl," Rome says before he has the chance to stop himself.

"I am," Kaner says. "Thanks for noticing."

Weirdly, it doesn't sound sarcastic.

"Kaner is special," Justin says.

"Kaner is trans," Kaner says. "Let me know if that's going to be an issue for you."

Rome has no idea what that means in this context, but he also knows, from the way the other boys are all looking at him, that he needs to tread lightly. "No issues here. I'm Rome."

"Sweet," Justin says, offering him a closed fist. "Thought your name was Patrick though. Hockey nickname?"

Rome bumps their fists together and then shakes Olly's and Kaner's outstretched hands. "Yeah. Started with Romer. Turned into Rome. Doesn't feel right to answer to anything else now."

It isn't 100 percent true, but they don't need to know that.

"There are worse nicknames," Olly agrees. "Brian Campbell graduated last year. His was 'Soup.' And one of our D pairs is 'Jeeves' and 'Wooster.' But Coach's email said you're from Maine, right?" Olly has a southern lilt to his speech that makes Rome take a second, closer look at him.

He's wearing a black shirt, jeans, and scuffed brown boots. While none of his clothing is threadbare or patched, none of it looks name brand either. Not like the others who, even in athletic gear, wear wealth like a habit. Olly's not poor, Rome assesses, but he's not rich either. It's enough to give Rome a little bit of hope. *Not poor* is better than whatever the hell Damien, Kaner, and Lefevre are.

"Yeah, Maine," Rome says, and then, because he knows it's expected, "up the coast."

Olly makes a noise of agreement and says, "You look like someone who's actually worked a day or two in your life," and, oh, Rome likes him already. "Any chance you know your way around washing machines?"

"Some," Rome says.

"Well, neither of the two in the basement of our dorm are working, and maintenance can't come until next week. I was thinking YouTube and I might go have a chat with them. You care to join me?"

Yes. Please.

"Sure." Rome stands, remembers to tip his head to the others, and picks up his tray. He follows Olly back to the lobby, depositing his dirty dishes in a bin by the exit.

Olly touches his arm to point out the plasticware and takeaway boxes in case he ever needs one, and Rome flinches. Just a little.

Olly doesn't say anything, but he does withdraw his hand.

"You here on scholarship?" Olly asks once they're outside.

"Yeah. You?"

"Yessir. And I gotta say I'm happy to have you with us. When Leefer graduated, I thought I was going to be the only scholarship kid on the team. I love these guys to death, but sometimes—" Olly sighs. "You know, I was complaining about the laundry situation on the way over here, and Kaner offered to just buy us new washing machines rather than wait for maintenance to show up? Whole ass. Brand new. Washing machines. Like that's a thing that people do?"

"Rich people," Rome says.

"Lord, don't I know it," Olly agrees.

CHAPTER THREE

WITHIN FORTY-EIGHT HOURS, Damien decides he does not particularly like Patrick Roman.

Within a week, he decides he might hate him.

He tries to be friends, harder than Rome deserves, frankly, but nothing *works*.

The first night, when he gets back to the dorm, he walks into the common room to the sound of Olly and Rome in the kitchen. Rome is a little less...whatever he was before. He's not holding himself like he might need to engage his fight-or-flight reflex at any moment. And his face has settled into something that might be called a neutral expression, which progressively gets softer as Olly, nearly choking on laughter, tries to finish a story about Justin having absolutely no concept of what a single roll of toilet paper costs.

By the end of the story, Rome is smiling.

It's a good look for him.

"And so—" Olly laughs. "Kaner and Justin go off into town on some sort of toilet paper crusade and come back with the entire back of Justin's car full of different brands."

"Seriously?" Rome says.

"Seriously. He kept a journal as he worked his way through them all, broken down by brand, price, comfort, company policy, and environmental impact. He has a lot of opinions about toilet paper now. Don't get him started on it unless you want him to get out the journal and educate you."

Rome doesn't laugh, but it's a near thing.

"That kid is going to do great things one day," Olly finishes fondly. "He's petitioning the school board to change the dress code and hygiene rules so seniors are allowed to have facial hair. He's arguing that the rules infringe upon his bodily autonomy."

"Can he even grow facial hair?"

"Shut up," Olly says, too delighted to mean it. "He'd sure try if it was allowed. He says his face is made for a playoff beard."

Rome studies the latest team picture on the refrigerator. "You know, I can see that."

"I can, too, unfortunately— Oh, hey, Damien. We've got the left-side washer working, but the right is still refusing to cooperate."

And any new softness sitting on Rome's features evaporates the second Damien rounds the corner from common room to kitchen. He straightens, wiping his hands on the towel by the stove, and nods toward the stairs.

"Oh," Olly says. "You don't want to stay? I was about get out the controllers for FIFA."

"Nah," Rome says. "Gotta unpack. You know who my roommate is?"

"No one," Damien supplies. "Jeeves decided not to board last minute. His parents' house is twenty minutes away."

"And he has a girlfriend now," Olly adds helpfully. "And Brass—that's our house dad; you'll meet him later tonight—he'll look the other way for parties, but he's a stickler about overnight guests."

"And Jeeves's parents travel a lot," Damien says.

Olly rolls his eyes. "Jeeves's parents wouldn't notice if there was an extra person in their maze of a house even if they were home."

"Fair."

Rome nods toward the stairs.

"Well," Olly says, "thanks for your help, man."

Rome retreats.

Olly frowns after him for a moment before taking a breath, pivoting to smile at Damien, and offering him water like he's not perfectly capable of getting out a glass from the cabinet himself. Southern hospitality is something else.

Damien watches Rome's back, the way his long fingers curl around the handrail on the banister, the way his battered jeans stretch over his thighs to accommodate taking two steps at a time up the stairs.

There's a poem in that, he thinks. Something about freckled knuckles and sun-bleached oak wood. Something about shifting muscle and torn denim.

Rome's eyes meet his just as he turns to go out of sight at the first landing, and if his expression isn't outright hostile, it's something close.

Damien is baffled.

Things don't exactly improve over the following days.

Their rooms are right next to each other, so he has plenty of opportunities to invite Rome to grab coffee or froyo; to hit up the movie theater after practice; to breakfast and lunch and dinner at the dining hall.

Almost every time, Rome says no, if he says anything. Unless it's to the dining hall, and even then, the others are usually there, and he mostly ignores Damien. Not that he's super talkative with anyone else either. But still.

The following week, Damien steals Rome's phone at practice one day and adds him to the group chat. Which backfires spectacularly, though he has no idea why.

When he knocks on the door to Rome's room that evening to let him know that they ordered pizza and are skipping the dining hall, Rome is lying on his stomach on his still-bare mattress surrounded by still-bare walls with a chemistry book open in front of him and a pen clenched between his teeth.

"What," Rome says flatly.

"Hey. We got pizzas downstairs. Olly added jalapeños. Kaner is crying but still eating it. Did you get my text?"

"No," he says. "And stop adding me to your group chat."

"It's team bonding, asshole," Damien says. "And you're, like, three years behind. Embrace it."

"No. I have to pay for every shitty meme you post."

"So just get unlimited texting like a normal human being."

"Right, because that *doesn't* cost money."

Damien rolls his eyes. "Come on, man. We're your team. We're worth it."

Rome just looks at him blankly. "Get out of my room."

"What?"

"Get out. Of my room."

"Seriously?"

Rome slaps his textbook closed and stands up. "Fuck. Off."

Damien fucks off.

He doesn't try to add Rome to the group chat anymore.

The following night, after listening to a combination of Fall Out Boy, Paramore, Panic! at the Disco, and 30 Seconds to Mars bleed from the room next door for over an hour, Damien bangs his fist against their shared wall.

"Hey, Rome. Could you maybe relive the '90s a little quieter?" he yells.

"Try early 2000s, asshole," Rome yells back.

The music gets louder.

Chai, Damien's roommate, sighs from his bed on the other side of the room. "Don't," he says.

But Damien is already halfway into the hallway.

He knocks on Rome's door because they're practically adults, and they can talk about this face-to-face like reasonable human beings. Except when Rome opens the door, he's wearing the kind of expression that says this will probably either end in Damien giving up or in Damien getting punched.

"Hey," Damien says because he's already committed. "Have you ever heard of headphones?"

"I don't have any."

Damien checks his watch. "Bookstore is open until 9:00. If you hurry, you can go get a new pair before they close."

"No."

"*Jesus.* Why not? I'll give you a pair of mine, then. What is your deal?"

"Fuck off. I don't want your headphones."

"Then turn the damn music down. I'm trying to read, and your angst is harshing my vibe."

Harshing your vibe, Rome mouths, one eyebrow arched with infuriating condescension.

And Damien is readying a cutting retort, except that's not going to get them anywhere.

"Look," he says, palms up, not like he's begging, but...okay, maybe a little like he's begging, "You may not care about your grades, but I care about mine, and I can't concentrate on Pablo Neruda with your angstfest music coming through the wall."

"I care," Rome says, firm and grating like that somehow wins him the argument.

"Okay," Damien says slowly. "Then turn down your shitty music or let me give you some headphones."

Rome doesn't take the headphones. But he does turn the shitty music down.

After a few weeks, and a few more doorway stand-offs, they have a tentative truce on the music front, and Rome starts talking a little more. But rather than ignoring Damien or giving him short responses that usually contain the words *fuck* and *off*, now, he's added in being a sarcastic little shit as well. He rolls his eyes through conversations about gay rights or economics and straight-up leaves the common room when Damien and Brass get into a friendly debate about racial inequality in the Ivy League.

Damien probably shouldn't be surprised. So Rome is a little homophobic. A little racist. A majority of St. James Academy students are. And he's not even as vocal about it as some—like Chad in his poli sci class, who likes to sit behind him and quietly refer to Damien as *Affirmative Action* when the teacher isn't in earshot. It sucks, but it could be worse. He knows from experience it could be worse.

Regardless, after two months, Damien can solidly say that he and Rome are not friends.

To make matters worse, for all his terrible personality traits, Rome is still entirely, unfairly, attractive. And Damien sees him naked on a near-daily basis in the locker room.

So now he knows that the freckles really are *everywhere* and well—

There are the tattoos to consider.

And Damien does. Consider them.

The first day of practice, Damien was studiously

ignoring Rome in the locker room when Justin whistled something about *wicked ink, bro,* and then everyone was crowded around Rome, and Damien had to look.

Rome has four tattoos.

The largest, a series of grayscale interconnected Celtic-looking knots, forms a band around his right arm, high up, nearly to his shoulder. It's just high enough that the sleeve of a T-shirt would cover it—clearly professional work with sharp lines and beautiful shading.

Equally beautiful is the rose under his left collarbone: black and white, fully bloomed, the outside petals just starting to curl with rippled darkened edges.

The third, a date, looks far less professional and hugs the curve of his ribcage.

The fourth is a small, chaotic mess of wobbly, faded, blue ink on the top of his right foot.

"A rabbit," Rome said when Olly asked, as if it should be obvious.

"Bless its heart," Olly said.

"You're seventeen," Damien said faintly, like maybe if he protested with the semantics of age and legality, the ink would somehow disappear.

Rome didn't say anything.

That's a habit of his.

So. The tattoos, even the shitty ones, round out the unfairness of the Patrick Roman situation. Because Damien has a type, and that type is apparently *terrible.*

The worst thing though. The *worst* thing is that they play really good hockey together.

He knows some players just click; he's seen it on television and in person during NHL games and, to a degree, with Jeeves and Wooster. But he's never personally experienced chemistry like this before. He has a weirdly innate knowledge of where Rome is at all times on the ice. And once they've played a few games, it's clear the coaches will be keeping them on the same line. They're just *good* together.

Not that you'd know it from the way Rome treats him.

Off the ice, Rome is still mostly quiet and reserved, if occasionally condescending and nearly always profane. On the ice, he's abrasive and opinionated and even more profane.

Which would be a problem if he was that way with everyone, but he's not. He immediately defers to Justin, carries on actual conversations with Olly at the net, trades sarcastic quips with Kaner, ducks to make himself smaller around the freshmen, listens intently when Coach gives advice, and even playfully roughhouses with Chai.

But with Damien?

Criticism. Always.

He criticizes Damien's puck handling during tracking drills, his back-checking during neutral zone drills, and his ability to be clairvoyant during zone breakout drills.

Where were you? Rome snaps after one of the rare instances when his pass had just missed Damien's stick. *Why weren't you there?*

And he wants to say, "I'm not a fucking mind reader, *Patrick*," except he's learned not to use Rome's real name unless he's really spoiling for an argument. Rome, for some reason, absolutely hates his name.

Justin frowns at them a lot as the season progresses, Kaner has perfected the art of rolling her eyes at them, and the coaches give each other a lot of "we're having entire conversations without speaking" looks whenever he and Rome snarl at each other in the locker room, but—

No one says anything.

Because Damien is playing some of the best hockey of his life, and Rome probably is too, and the coaches *love* Rome.

Rome is the first one on the ice and the last one off. He never goes out on school or game nights. He follows his meal plans and his workouts to the letter. He never has cheat days and always goes back to the dining hall right before it closes at eight to have a last protein shake every night. Why he doesn't just keep milk and powder in the dorm kitchen like everyone else, Damien doesn't know, but even he has to admit it. Patrick Roman is the perfect athlete and a near-perfect center.

If only he wasn't such a dick of a person.

CHAPTER FOUR

ROME LOVES ST. James Academy.

The teachers and coaches are top quality, the resources at the library are frankly a little overwhelming, the food is fantastic, and the grounds—well. There's a reason St. James is usually listed as one of the most beautiful boarding schools in the US.

The classes are difficult, especially since his previous school district wasn't exactly top tier, but between their house dad, Brass, looking over his homework and the student tutoring center, he's making A's and B's. And he's managed to get a part-time job from an aging mechanic named Benny, picking up slack whenever he doesn't have practice or a game or tutoring, which isn't that often. It means he has to skip pretty much any extracurricular hangouts the rest of the team invites him to, but it isn't like he can afford to go to the arcade or theater anyway. Benny also loaned him a shitty bike for the semester that Rome enjoys riding along the twenty-minute stretch of back roads into town.

He also likes the work. It's usually pretty easy, monotonous, stuff Benny has him doing: oil changes and detailing, helping him as a tool lackey, and cleaning up around the garage. But it pays well, and Benny is soft-spoken and kind. It's a nice escape to familiarity from all the newness of St. James Academy.

The hockey though. Hockey is the best thing about St. James.

The team has grown up together, so there are a hundred inside jokes about superstitions, from special tape jobs and skate-lacing rituals to a decade-old water bottle Olly claims has magical powers. But they fit Rome in seamlessly, including him on pranks and warning him not to interfere with Jeeves and Wooster's very specific warm-up routine.

The first time he plays in the St. James igloo, on a team full of college, if not NHL prospects, in front of shouting fans all decked out in green and black, he feels settled, maybe. Like he finally belongs to something bigger than himself. Like it isn't him against the other team, it's his *team* against the other team. He never really enjoyed being the best, as hard as he fought for it. So being here—on a line with Kaner, who's the fastest goddamn skater he's ever seen, and Damien, who stickhandles like he was born doing it—he feels like he can exhale. Like winning or losing won't come down to him. It's a good feeling.

He scores his first goal three minutes into the first period after Kaner steals the puck from a defenseman, sends it to Damien behind the net, and Damien passes it between the second defenseman's legs straight and flat and right onto Rome's tape, where he's perfectly positioned front and center of the crease.

It's an easy top-shelf goal. A snap of his wrist and the puck is in the net just above the goalie's right shoulder and just below the crossbar.

And then Kaner is slamming into him, yelling *fuck yeah* around her obnoxious sparkly mouthguard, and Damien throws his arms around them both a second later. Justin and Chai crash into them as well, with enough force that they all end up in a pile on the ice.

The physicality of joy is something Rome has always loved about hockey. It's brief—the euphoria that comes from a goal—but it's visceral and honest and real in a way he's never experienced off the ice. And sometimes, if he's lucky, if the goal matters, he earns colliding bodies and helmets pressed together and incoherent screaming. It's as physical as affection can get, and it's excused by adrenaline and the triumph of the effort succeeding, and *god*, he loves hockey.

"Nice steal," he says to Kaner as they're hauling themselves upright.

"Nice goal," she answers.

"Damien also had a nice pass," Damien says.

Rome ignores him.

Kaner rolls her eyes.

"Hey, Rome," Damien says at the next line change,

spinning into a one-legged hockey stop and swinging his other foot around to dust Rome with ice.

"Damien," Rome says, stopping like a normal person before climbing over the boards and onto the bench.

Damien slides next to him. "I got a hat trick my first game here."

"Did you," Rome says.

"You know. If you want something to aspire to."

"Dunno," Rome says. "Three goals just don't feel like enough. I think I'll go for four."

"Four," Damien says disbelievingly.

Rome holds up four fingers. "That's this many."

"All right, asshole—"

"HO-KAY," Kaner interrupts, shoving her way between them. She spits out her mouthguard and then waves it at the scoreboard. "Let's focus on getting a second point for now, yeah? We'll talk three versus four after that."

Rome doesn't get four goals. But he does get two. And two assists. Both for Damien's goals, which he can't be bitter about even if he'd like to. He may not like Damien, but their chemistry on the ice is undeniable. They win the game handily. And Rome can't wait for the next one.

On the first of October, Rome is included in a *USA Today* article about promising prep school NHL prospects. It focuses mostly on Justin, but they do have a rather nice picture of Rome scoring top-shelf and a solid paragraph that declares that while "unknown until this season," he's an adept center whose impressive stats may elevate him to become a "dark horse" in the upcoming draft. Olly and Damien get mentioned in the article as well, but only mentioned. Chai won't be eligible for another year, so that's not too surprising, but Rome is a little shocked Damien doesn't get more attention. Because he's good. *So* good. And he's no small part of the reason Rome's performance is through the roof. Kaner doesn't get mentioned either, even though she should. Rome still doesn't really know what her deal is. Only that she used to be a boy, or people thought she was a boy, but she's not anymore. And even though her stats haven't changed, she's stopped showing up in top prospect reports. She says she doesn't care, that she just plays for the love of it or whatever. But Rome is pretty sure he would care if it were him.

After that, he starts googling his name every few days, and it keeps...showing up. In things. Nothing big. Nothing noteworthy aside from the fact that it's his name and it's being included in lists of players who will likely get drafted.

He's gotten used to the occasional scouts or visiting GMs sitting in the stands during games and practice. Justin is, after all, the second coming of hockey Jesus. But twice now, instead of shaking Justin's hand after a game, the men in suits have sought Rome out and asked him about his future plans. Could he see himself on the East Coast? Does he want to play D1 or go straight to the NHL?

It takes him several nights of loud music—*fuck you, Damien; I'm having a crisis*—to wrap his head around how those are both potential options for him now.

So the hockey is good.

Damien though. Damien Raphael Bordeaux is a problem.

Because he doesn't make *any* sense.

At first, Rome thought he was your standard douche-bro athlete with muscles on muscles and an Insta full of shirtless pics. But now he knows that Damien also gets his eyebrows threaded and has a skincare routine, that he's a hard worker, is fiercely protective of his teammates, makes all A's, listens to weird instrumental music, and lets Kaner paint his nails. He swears like a sailor on the ice and has no problem getting physical in games, but spends his free time on Sundays off setting up a hammock by the lake, reading poetry, and writing in his leather notebooks.

And the poetry is...a thing.

Damien is taking poetry as an elective and apparently has even published a few pieces he's written, not that Rome looked them up in the library or anything. And according to Olly, he goes to open mic night at a coffee shop in the city sometimes. Rome has caught him, every now and then, getting teary, maybe, over a book, sometimes murmuring the words, sometimes in *French*, and that's—

But Damien Raphael Bordeaux is also a moron when it comes to things like money and any concept of how people who don't have trust funds live.

Like the time they were all in the common room watching the Sharks play, and Olly asked at intermission how Damien's monthly talk with his grandmother went. And Damien said fine, but she'd spent most of the call complaining about how her house in California was under water restrictions due to a drought, and since she obviously couldn't *stop* watering the impeccable landscaping, she was having to pay fines.

Rome hadn't meant to say anything, but he couldn't really stop himself. "So what happens when the city runs out of water because too many people are just paying the fines? Fines don't do shit for the actual problem."

Damien shrugged. "Start buying bottled water and wait for a hurricane? My uncle was suggesting she drill for her own water. Because there's an aquifer under the property."

"Okay," Rome said tightly. "But what about normal people?"

"Normal people," Damien repeated. "What do you mean?"

Olly laid a hand on Rome's arm before he could answer. "He means," Olly said, far more gently than Rome would have, "people who can't afford to drill their own well."

"Or buy bottled water," Rome had to add. "The kind of people who don't have lawns in the first place."

"Oh." Damien looked suddenly uncomfortable. "Well, shit, that's fucked up."

That was something.

Even though, in many ways, Damien is the exact sort of cavalier rich kid Rome expected him to be, often carelessly, infuriatingly, wasteful...he's still nice.

Not to Rome, probably because Rome is admittedly an asshole to him, but he's not the entitled dick Rome initially assumed he would be. He does little thoughtful shit all the time, like running errands and staying after practice to help the coaches with gear. He sneaks Chai coffee in the computer lab when he knows he's going to be working late on a project and lets Kaner use him as a live model for her drawing class assignments. He helps the rookies with their homework and watches tape with Justin when he's stressed, and he always washes dishes in the dorm kitchen after they've eaten something.

So Rome, maybe, has some reevaluation he needs to do.

Especially when it comes to race.

Rome has never had a friend who wasn't white before. Not that he's ever had *friends*, per se, and definitely not that *Damien* is a friend, but his hometown is overwhelmingly white, so race was never a thing that got talked about unless it was in history class about the Civil War.

Rome remembers on his second day at St. James, walking into the common room to Damien and Kaner talking about white privilege, and Rome made a disgusted sound and turned right around and left because in no world did *Rome* have more privilege than Damien Raphael Bordeaux. Sitting on his naked mattress, sewing up a tear in the collar of one of the three shirts he owned, Rome stewed in frustration and embarrassment, adding the words "white privilege" to the annoyance he felt toward Damien after the whole food-in-the-cafeteria thing. And it all just sort of spilled out on the ice at practice the next day. And the day after that. And...and then it was just habit. Even though he knew it wasn't really fair.

Except then, the thing with the cop happens.

It is, actually, the first time Rome has ever been in Damien's car. Olly needs more jalapeños for pizza doctoring, and Damien volunteers to go pick some up. But Rome also needs some half-inch screws to fix one of the sagging light fixtures in the second-floor bathroom, and he doesn't trust Damien to find the hardware store, much less the correct screws once he gets there. So they go together. In Damien's beautiful white exterior/brown leather interior Porsche Cayman GT4. Because, naturally, that's what Damien Raphael Bordeaux drives. Like some sort of douchebag in a teen movie.

Rome feels a little like screaming when he eases into the passenger seat. But the car is clean, well-kept, and clearly loved, and Damien shifts with the smooth, habitual grace of someone who's been driving a stick since well before it was legal for him to do so.

Rome closes his eyes and listens to the engine hum and lets the cool wind from the open windows push against his face.

And then they're pulled over.

Damien wasn't speeding. Rome knows this because Rome was judging Damien a little for his strict adherence to the speed limit. It was an empty road at almost 7:00 p.m., and he was sitting on 385 horsepower. Live a little.

So Rome honestly has no idea why a cop idling at an intersection pulls a U-turn to follow them for a mile and then turns on his siren.

Damien pulls over to the side of the road with studied care, both hands on the steering wheel. Ten and two.

Rome reaches for the glove compartment. "Is your

insurance here?"

"Don't," Damien says. "Just sit there. Please."

It's the *please* that gets to him. Rome doesn't think Damien has ever said *please* to him before. He considers the tight clench of Damien's fingers on the steering wheel, the smear of red and blue in the rearview mirror, and obligingly goes still.

Damien slowly reaches for his wallet only after the cop asks for his license, but he hands over his student ID before anything else.

"This isn't your license, son," the man says, and then a second later, in a completely different voice, "Oh, you go to St. James Academy?"

"Yes, sir," Damien says. "We both play on the hockey team there. Sorry about that, sir. Habit. Here's my license."

The cop ducks a little to get a better look at Damien and then Rome, his posture suddenly a lot more friendly, and asks for proof of insurance.

"Can you tell us why you pulled us over?" Rome asks and adds, "Uh, sir?" when Damien hisses *Roman* under his breath.

The man tells them to "sit tight," and walks back to his squad car.

"What part of 'just sit there' did you not understand?" Damien says, sharp and low once the man is out of hearing range. "Jesus Christ. Please don't say anything else, okay?"

And Rome looks at him, baffled, because a docile, compliant Damien kind of freaks him out.

After several minutes, the cop comes back and says

something about thinking the registration was expired—which is stupid; the windshield is crystal clear—with a *sorry to bother you, boys,* and *have a nice evening.*

Damien pulls back onto the road, going even slower than before. Once they get to the hardware store, he just sits there for a minute after taking his seatbelt off, hands on his knees.

"So what the fuck was that?" Rome asks. "Are you afraid of cops or something?"

He knows Damien gets upset about news stories where police shoot unarmed Black people, but Damien isn't anything like those people on the news. Some guy living in the projects selling individual cigarettes or stealing shit from a convenience store is about as far removed from Damien and his Cayman GT4 as you can get.

Damien shifts, pulls his phone out of his back pocket, and scrolls through his photo reel for a second before shoving the phone in Rome's face.

Rome takes it from him, holding it far enough away that he's not cross-eyed, and pauses.

It's Damien, smiling, in a suit that's clearly tailored to fit him. On either side of him are two blond, middle-aged people whose clothing combined is probably worth more than tuition for a semester at St. James Academy. The man has very white teeth and his arm around Damien's shoulder. The woman holds Damien's hand, leaning into him.

It takes Rome a minute to figure out what he's looking at. "Are these...your parents?"

"Yeah."

"They're, uh…"

"White," Damien says flatly. "Yeah. I know."

Rome doesn't know where to go from there.

"I was adopted," Damien says.

"Oh."

"I was arrested when I was twelve."

Rome isn't sure if he'll recover from the conversational whiplash. "What?"

"When I was twelve. I was arrested. See, a lot of non-white parents, they give their kids—especially their boys—a talk. Even when they're little. They tell them to be careful with police. Respectful. Calm. Even if they think they're being treated unfairly. Except my parents never gave me that talk. They didn't know they needed to. So when I was twelve, and we were staying in New York for the summer, I took the subway to meet up with a friend on the Upper East Side, and the police stopped me and wanted to search my backpack because I matched the description of a *twenty-three-year-old* suspect. I didn't stay calm or respectful. I was charged with resisting arrest and police battery, and they didn't let me call my mom for *five hours*."

The cracked way Damien says "mom" makes Rome's stomach go heavy and sour with something he can't put a name to. He wants to respond *that's not fair* but doing so seems both painfully obvious and horribly trite.

"My parents threatened to sue the shit out of them, so charges were dropped, and the guy ended up losing his job. But I had nightmares for over a year afterward. So yes. I *am* afraid of cops."

"Damien," Rome says, but Damien keeps talking.

"My parents have three houses. Paris. Manhattan. Telluride. I haven't been arrested since that day, but do you want to know how many times I've been stopped in my own neighborhood or hotel, not because I was doing anything wrong, just because I 'might be lost' or they wanted to make sure the car I was driving really belonged to me? You want to know how many times I've had the cops called on me because someone saw me through the window of a penthouse or on the balcony of my *own goddamn bedroom* and thought I was stealing shit? How many times I've been stopped and questioned while waiting in lobbies? How many times I've been followed around high-end stores or exhibits? Money is— I realize I'm crazy privileged when it comes to money. But no amount of money can change the fact that I'm *not white.*"

Rome swallows. He feels like maybe Damien isn't just talking about the police thing anymore. "I didn't know," he says.

"Yeah, well. Now you do."

Damien turns off the engine abruptly and opens the door.

Rome scrambles to follow him.

They go into the store.

The rest of the trip is silent.

They kind of avoid each other for the following week because that last conversation was dangerously close to a heart-to-heart, and Rome is vehemently opposed to those, and Damien seems embarrassed, maybe, and Rome definitely is. But Rome also starts paying more attention to Damien, who, he's already started to realize, is more than just a pretty boy with money. Maybe a lot more.

Rome realizes there is a distinct possibility that he's fucked up in a major way.

The problem with paying even more attention to Damien (intentionally sitting closer to him in their shared classes, actually listening to his discussions with Kaner and Brass and Chai) is that he starts noticing even more things about him. Things like the way, off the ice, Damien has turned nonconfrontation into an art form. Sometimes, other students say terrible things to him, like Chad in their poli sci class. But Damien doesn't draw attention to their shitty behavior, or if he does, he offers slanted rebukes, which are kind enough that the perpetrators aren't embarrassed. Rome notices that sometimes girls—rich, beautiful girls—talk about Damien as if dating him, sleeping with him, would be something to check off a list or use in an argument with their parents. And people call him things like "exotic" as though it's a compliment and ask what kind of "mix" he is like that's an okay thing to ask another human being.

Rome can't believe he hasn't even noticed it was happening until now, but he also sort of can because Damien talks about *big* injustice with Kaner and the guys all the time. News stories and protests and worldwide phenomenon. But the little things, the daily things, the things that happen to him? Apparently, he just deals with them with wan smiles or gentle, humorous criticism as if it's normal. And it probably is.

Rome also notices other things. Like how Damien

talks to the plants in the kitchen window, how he's especially gentle when he waters them, lifting their leaves and testing the soil with his pinky finger. Rome notices the way he handles his books just as gently, never folding back the front cover or splaying them facedown. The way he chews on his bottom lip when he's concentrating and touches his throat when he's uncertain and absently plays with whatever scrunchy is on his wrist when his hair is down.

Rome notices the way he flirts, bashful and wide-eyed at the secret post-game parties the team hosts in their basement. Rome doesn't think they're all that secret since Brass isn't an idiot, but they don't play music very loudly, and if people drink, they're all just walking to whatever dorm they live in at the end of the night anyway.

Unlike some of the other seniors, who will occasionally disappear with a girl, Damien never does. He dances with them and seems to enjoy it, but his hands never wander, and he never seems interested in taking things further though the girls often clearly are. Rome makes assumptions about that, but doesn't get confirmation until the Halloween party.

Rome refuses to wear a costume and sits on the stairs, watching rather than participating. Watching Damien, mostly, because that's what he does now.

Except, instead of demure flirting with pink-lipped girls, a toga-clad Damien is dancing with a boy in leather pants and no shirt.

Close.

Head ducked into his neck.

Mouth against his ear.

And the other boy's hands are in Damien's back pockets, and his thigh is —

Rome leans his head back and closes his eyes.

He sets his cup aside because he's done with alcohol for the night.

It isn't a big deal.

So Damien is gay.

That's fine. That's whatever.

Except now, he's thinking about it: Damien being gay. Like, with other boys. Maybe leather-pants boy, even. Which is possibly why Rome doesn't notice that someone is approaching him until a hand wraps around his wrist.

"Rome," Damien says, his smile wide and broad, and he's definitely drunk. "Rome, you should dance with me."

Rome is so shocked by the invitation that he doesn't turn it down.

Damien takes his silence as acceptance and pulls him up and out to a clear pocket of space by the washing machines. Christmas lights hang from the basement ceiling, but the color-spangled, undulant crowd of teen-agers make the space look otherworldly, a tide of bodies moving with the pulse of music, heads thrown back, teeth white in the black light, their skin slick with sweat. Couples lean against the walls and one another, hands spanning backs, mouths to ears, lips to throats. The room is a study in unrestraint.

Rome can feel the bass in his lungs.

He doesn't know what to do—how to orient his body

or move it, or—anything. And Damien keeps trying to show him, clumsy but enthusiastic, with a hand on his hip or his shoulder or his back, and he can't—

Rome pushes away and flees up the stairs, except Damien follows him, laughing.

"You're about as bad at dancing as you are good at hockey," Damien shouts, louder than needed in the comparative quiet of the second-floor hallway.

It takes him a minute to parse that. "That's really bad, then," Rome says.

"Yes," Damien agrees somberly.

"Fuck you," Rome says because he feels like he should.

"I mean, it was a compliment." Damien reaches for Rome's wrist again. "Because you're really good at hockey. Your hockey is nice. Pretty."

"You think my hockey is pretty?"

"Yeah. It's like..." Damien absently pets the back of Rome's hand with his thumb, tracing the cordillera of Rome's scarred knuckles. "It's so smooth. And delicate. Elegant. But also rough. Aggressive. Angry. But also, like, happy? Your hockey is a paradox."

"Jesus," Rome says. "I thought you were a poet."

"I do sometimes."

"You do what?"

"Write poetry about you. Because you're so...you could be so much, I think. If you weren't—"

Damien sighs. "It helps...to write about you. Sometimes."

Rome suddenly feels a lot more sober, standing

there in the hallway, for all intents and purposes, holding hands with Damien Raphael Bordeaux. "Yeah?"

"Yeah," Damien sighs, letting go of his hand. He stumbles a little, and Rome catches him before he can topple back down the stairs.

"Don't tell, okay?" Damien says, leaning into him. "About the poetry."

"Don't tell who?"

"Rome."

"Okay," Rome agrees. "I won't."

CHAPTER FIVE

DAMIEN WAKES UP in his bed with no recollection of how he got there.

He remembers drinking. He remembers getting the text from his dad: *I just don't think it's going to happen this year* and the text from his mom: *but we'll see you at Christmas!* and thinking: fuck it.

He remembers things going warm and hazy and a little maudlin. He remembers dancing. With a boy. He remembers Rome watching him. He remembers expecting disgust and not understanding why he didn't receive it. He remembers thinking it was a shame that Rome was so Rome. Sitting on the stairs. Watching rather than participating. He remembers thinking, at the height of drunk logic, that maybe if Rome did less stair-sitting and more dancing, he wouldn't be such a dick. Maybe Damien could teach him to dance, and things would be better.

And that's about where his memory ends. With—

Warm skin.

Uncertain hands.

Freckles spilling over parted lips.

White teeth.

Wide eyes.

There's a cup of water on the windowsill by his head, a package of peanut butter crackers, and two Advil liquid gels. He doesn't know if he should be thanking his drunk self or someone else, but damn, does he appreciate whoever it was.

"Ugh," Chai says from his bed.

"Ehgh," Damien agrees.

He lies there for another hour, waiting for the painkillers to take the edge off, and then squints his way to the bathroom for a shower. When he gets downstairs, wearing sunglasses and feeling accomplished, Brass is sitting in the common room looking annoyingly chipper, eating a sandwich. There's one boba tea in front of him and another one sitting invitingly next to him.

"The bubble truck just made its rounds," Brass says. "I got you green tea mango."

Damien is too hungover to find this suspicious until he's already sitting down.

"Bro," Damien says. "Did you know I love you?"

Brass hums, taking another bite of his sandwich.

"So," Brass says after a leisurely chew. "You know how we were talking the other day about you getting pulled over? With Rome?"

Damien takes a minute to swallow.

"Yeah?"

"You have any idea why Rome came and asked me about my feelings on white privilege this morning?"

Damien nearly chokes on a boba pearl. "What?"

"He was stress-cleaning when I got downstairs. Did you know the grout in the kitchen is actually white?"

Damien did not.

He stands to lean around the corner to see for himself.

Huh. So it is.

"And the minute I came in, he asked if he could talk to me about 'race stuff' because I'm Black and an adult, and the next thing I knew, I was trying to explain the difference between privilege in general and race-related privilege, and how discrimination and oppression are different from racism before I even had a chance to get coffee."

"Well, shit," Damien says. "How, uh, how did that go?"

"Good, I think. Not bad. He didn't really say much of anything in response."

"Shocker," Damien mutters.

"But he did ask questions, mostly about my personal experiences, and he didn't argue. When I asked him why the sudden interest, he just said he was trying to figure some things out."

Brass is looking at him in a way that is probably meant to be significant.

"Okay?" Damien says.

Brass sighs. "So, did anything happen last night to prompt this? Or is the fact that you two left the party together just a weird coincidence?"

"What party?" Damien says, out of habit.

Brass doesn't even dignify that with a response. Instead, he says, "I had initially assumed a fight, except you didn't immediately start your standard *I need to vent about Rome* talk track when you walked in just now. So now I'm afraid it was a drunk hookup, which is even more concerning than a fight, just FYI."

"I don't..."

He remembers then. Standing in the hallway. Holding Rome's hand, and Rome letting him. Rome cursing at him but helping him into his room. Rome taking off his shoes, complaining about what a disaster he was. Rome leaving water and Advil and crackers from Rome's own room on the windowsill and making him promise he'd drink at least some of the water before he went to sleep or Rome would murder him.

Deft fingers, slipping the scrunchie off his wrist.

Gentle hands tying back his hair.

A palm pressed to the sweat-cooled skin on the back of his neck.

A soft exhale.

A whispered apology.

"Uh," Damien says.

Brass sighs again. "I'd tell you not to fuck up your friendship in case it affects your hockey, but you two seem to function best on dysfunction anyway."

Damien shrugs. It's true.

"That being said, if you're thinking about starting

something with him, maybe talk to a professional first. Because whatever you two have going on is not healthy. Hockey aside, adding sex to that shit show would probably be a personal disaster."

"Oh my god," Damien says. "I didn't—*we* didn't—and I don't want to start anything with him. Please stop talking."

"What are we not talking about?" Kaner says, coming down the stairs. "Damien's hate boner for Rome?"

"Not the way I would have termed it," Brass says. "But yes."

"Probably not healthy," Kaner supplies. "One cannot subsist on hate sex alone. You also gotta get that tender lovin', bro. And I don't know if Rome does tender."

"That's what I said," Brass agrees, bumping fists with her.

Damien picks up his boba tea with as much pride as he can muster while wearing sunglasses indoors. "You're both terrible, and I'm leaving," he says.

"Make a therapy appointment!" Brass yells after him.

Damien does the next best thing: he goes to the rink.

It's maybe not the healthiest coping mechanism. But stickhandling drills require just enough of his concentration that he can't get stuck in his head thinking about Patrick Roman and his rough hands and his pale eyes and the dark velvet stubble of his hair where it cups his freckled ears.

What are you, Damien thinks, *and why can't I stop asking?*

The rink is cold when it's empty. It's cold and

echoey without bodies in the stands and on the benches, and the skinny little windows above the bleachers make stretched rectangular shadows that move and change color, thinning out as the sun rises higher in the sky.

After an hour, Damien picks up all the pucks he's littered across the ice and works on footwork. He starts with iron crosses—forward, quick stop, back, cross step to the left, cross step center, backward, center, cross step right, cross step center. And again. He follows that with sprints into backward crossovers and then cross-side pokes and then—

"Hey," Kaner yells, leaning over the boards. "You trying to kill yourself?"

He careens to a stop, all flying ice and hard breathing, and then realizes that, yeah, maybe he is a little dizzy. He leans over, hands on knees, and tries not to gasp too loudly in the silence. He definitely has not hydrated enough since waking up.

Kaner swings her legs over, and he isn't really surprised that she's wearing her skates, looking innocent in leggings and an oversized hoody that he's 90 percent sure is Olly's.

"You want to talk about it?" she asks, patting an only slightly judgmental hand to his hunched back.

"Not even a little," he says, straightening.

"You want to take some very slow, not-potentially-fatal laps around the rink with me and talk about something completely unrelated?"

"So much," he agrees.

"Great. So I've been brainstorming for my end-of-semester showcase, but I want to get your thoughts. And by brainstorming, I mean I've settled on a vibe. An aesthetic. A feeling, if you will. My remaining struggle is translating the vibe into a description of the physical painted object I intend to create. Which is due tomorrow."

Relieved, Damien tosses his stick and moves to follow her. "What struggles artists must endure," he says.

"Truly," she agrees.

"So what's the vibe?" Damien asks.

She tells him.

*

FOR THE NEXT week, Rome is weird.

He seems to be actively trying to be nicer to Damien and mostly failing. He'll be halfway through a muttered snipe about Damien's inability to keep up with line changes, and then his eyes will go kind of wide, and he'll just...stop.

"Oh my god," Damien says after the third time it's happened in a one-hour period. "Would you just say it? You're going to give yourself brain damage if you keep suppressing your angst."

"Fuck you," Rome says. But he goes back to criticizing Damien's slapshot with a sharp smile, and Damien cheerfully points out that Rome's passes are looking particularly sloppy today. The guys are all giving them looks that are different than the usual looks they get, but whatever. Their hockey is fine. They're fine. Everything is fine.

"Hey," Rome says later as they're changing after

practice. "Does anyone have an electric razor? Mine broke, and I need to do my hair."

Damien is in the habit of not looking at Rome in the locker room, but he allows himself a quick glance at his hair which, yeah. It is getting a little long, comparatively, especially now that it's wet and sticking up a little from the shower. And there might even be a subtle wave happening.

"Bro," Damien says before he can stop himself. "Is your hair *curly*?"

"Fuck you," Rome says.

So that's a *yes*.

Damien tries to imagine it: Rome with little ringlets. Rome doing the same multistep routine that Damien does to keep his curls defined and frizz-free. It makes his head hurt.

"You can borrow my clippers tonight," Jeeves says. "If you need help, you should ask Wooster. He does me—"

"We suspected as much," Chai says.

"—every two weeks or so," Jeeves finishes, rolling his eyes at Wooster.

"I can do it myself," Rome says. "But thanks. I'll borrow them tonight."

They go swimming at the lake after practice because they're gluttons for punishment, and "It's basically the same thing as an ice bath, guys," Olly says as they shiver their way out into the water. "Good for our muscles."

While it's been strangely temperate the past few weeks, the lake is still cold.

The sun also sets early this time of year, so the trees

around the lake are dropping fire-colored leaves into water that reflects the same palette from the sky.

It's breathtakingly beautiful, and Damien stands there, knee-deep on the sand bar, forgetting to shiver, appreciating the view until someone hooks a foot around the back of his knee, and he's suddenly face-first in the water.

He surfaces with a very manly shriek and a rush of adrenaline. He thinks he may never sleep again.

"Olly, I swear to god—"

Except it wasn't Olly.

It was Rome.

Rome, who has never joined them for a swim, now stands waist-deep in the water next to him. His freckles are stark against the canvas of his pale chest, against the backdrop of dark water and fall colors and sunset.

He looks weirdly uncertain for someone who's just committed an act of lake warfare.

"Rome," Damien says dumbly.

"Damien," he agrees.

"You," Damien says, "are a dead man."

And Rome's mouth curves up, wicked and happy.

Rome doesn't smile often, but when he does, it exposes his crowded upper teeth. His canines slightly overlap the incisors next to them on either side of his mouth, which makes him look a little bit wild. Like a predator, maybe.

It's a well-matched fight that follows. It might not have been, back at the beginning of the semester, but Rome has gained weight and learned quickly how to use it. His stomach is lean now, rather than concave, his chest defined, his shoulders even broader than before.

Eventually, Rome gets Damien in a headlock, not really trying to choke him, more just letting him stumble around while Rome clings to his back like a large, warm, slippery leech. Damien lets him for a while before pretending to faint, then dumps them both in the water, where they float around, slapping ineffectively at each other before eventually crawling out to join the others on the beach, coughing.

They all watch the sun finish setting, teeth chattering, and walk barefoot back to the dorm. Standing in the hall, they shout at Kaner for using up all the hot water, then, when she's finished, crowd into the bathroom to shower themselves.

Later, as Damien leaves the bathroom with his toothbrush, he runs into a shirtless, boxer-clad Rome holding Jeeves's razor and its accompanying kit. He's looking down at it with a baffled distrust that Damien does not in any way find endearing.

"You need help with that?" Damien asks.

"No," Rome says. "I've got it."

"I think you're going to need help," Damien says.

Rome's shoulders go a little tight. "I've been shaving my own head for the last ten years. I think I can handle it."

"Well, sure. But that's not just a standard razor. It's a needlessly fancy sci-fi razor with twenty buttons and Bluetooth connectivity, and I'm sure it will offend your utilitarian sensibilities."

"So your help would be useful how?"

"Because, as you may have noticed, I also occasionally enjoy needlessly fancy things. And generally know how to operate them."

"I noticed."

"Great." Damien reaches to take the razor and kit out of Rome's hands. "Let's do this."

Rome lets him.

Within a few minutes, it becomes readily apparent that Damien did not think this through.

Helping Rome shave his head means: A. Standing Very Close to Rome, and B. Touching Rome while Standing Very Close to Rome.

Neither of which he is adequately prepared for.

Rome is just as physically compelling as he's always been, but now, he's also been kind to Damien several times since the Halloween party. Objectively, Damien knows that brief moments of decency don't negate two straight months of malice, but—

Rome sits on the counter, elbows on knees and eyes on Damien.

"So," Damien says, and he's definitely not stalling. "How do you usually do this?"

"I usually do an eighth of an inch, but, whatever."

"Right. An eighth, then." Damien turns the razor in his hand, pops off the current guard, and unzips the case to find the correct one.

"Unless—" Rome bites his lips, rolls the bottom one between his teeth. "Do you think longer would be better?"

Damien pauses. "Um."

One of Damien's favorite things to do in Telluride when he was a kid was to walk on the metal guardrails that hugged the mountain curves leading down from their house and into the city proper—arms out, the sun on his back, his balance the only thing between happiness and potential disaster.

He feels a little like that now. Like he has to be cautious, or he may suddenly tip from exhilaration to catastrophe.

"I think," Damien says slowly, "that one quarter would look good. Still short, but long enough to hold a little more heat as it gets colder?"

"Okay," Rome says, and the acquiescence feels a little like victory.

"Okay," Damien agrees.

He fits the two guard to the razor, scrolls through the settings, and steps forward between Rome's splayed legs, pale and long and so damn freckled. His toes, curled a little, seem strangely noteworthy. More vulnerable, even, than the bowed curve of Rome's neck as he offers Damien the crown of his head. Rome's skin is warm under his palm as Damien steadies the side of his face.

"Okay," Damien says again and then turns the clippers on and, starting at his left temple, makes the first slow pass.

It doesn't take long.

Within a few minutes, Rome slides off the counter and turns so Damien can finish the back of his head and even up his neckline.

Afterward, Damien runs his palm, lightly, over his work, then does it again under the guise of brushing off wayward clipped hair. He does it a third time without excuse, but Rome lets him, unmoving, and it's like petting the spring-felted antlers of a wild deer. *A holy, quiet thing. A thing that is allowed rather than taken.*

He stops, thumb trailing down the nape of Rome's neck to the bumps of his vertebra where neck meets shoulder, rubbing a little, like he can feel the freckles there if he tries, and then makes himself take a step back.

"Done," he says, too loud.

There are fragments of a poem struggling to assemble themselves in his hindbrain. Something about feral creatures and trust. Something about crooked teeth and vulnerability. He can't tell if meeting Rome's pale eyes in the mirror helps or hinders the process.

Rome straightens, leans forward to consider his reflection, and runs his hands over the crown of his skull. He pulls the tips of his ears down to check his temples, fingers resting, maybe a little distractedly, at the nape of his neck.

"Looks good," he says.

Rome takes the razor from him. He cleans the guard and packs everything back into the little case. And Damien doesn't know why he just stands there, watching, why he doesn't leave, job completed, except that he feels like he can't.

"Well," Rome says. "I need to shower again to—" He gestures at the dusting of clipped hair on his neck and shoulders.

"Right," Damien says. "I'll just...go...then."

"Goodnight," Rome says, stilted and nearly inaudible, as he pushes open the door to the hallway.

It isn't a *thank you*, but it's something.

CHAPTER SIX

ROME PROBABLY SHOULDN'T have let Damien cut his hair.

It was stupid.

The razor was needlessly fancy, but it wasn't exactly complicated. And Rome— He enjoyed it a little too much: Damien touching him.

Rome is still getting used to touching in general. And he thinks he might not ever get used to how much the St. James boys touch one another on a regular basis. Not even in a hockey-celly, backslapping way, but in a hugs-for-no-reason way. A piggyback-ride-to-the-cafeteria kind of way. A shoulders-pressed-together-on-the-couch way.

He thought, before, that physical affection was

something people grew out of. Something for small children and maybe rare happy couples. He's starting to realize he was wrong.

The thing is, he *wants* to be touched, now. He thinks he might even deserve it. But trying to reevaluate the various ways that his past has fucked up his understanding of interpersonal relationships is hard. Does he like Damien's hand on his neck because it's Damien's hand? Or because it's a modicum of physical kindness?

He handles this confusion like any well-adjusted teenager by avoiding Damien entirely. Which also helps with the whole "not being a dick to Damien anymore" plan.

Problem solved.

Until his lawyer, Elle, calls unexpectedly two days later—before Damien has probably even realized Rome is avoiding him—and ruins everything.

After Rome hangs up with Elle, he seeks out Olly in the common room and stands awkwardly in the stairwell for several minutes trying to psych himself up.

"Hey," he says finally, adept, as always, at gracefully starting a conversation.

"Hey. You all right?"

"Um. I have kind of a weird favor to ask, actually."

"Okay," Olly says slowly.

"Can I borrow some things from your room tomorrow? Just for the afternoon. I'll give them back after dinner."

"Things from my room," Olly repeats. "What things?"

This is the hard part.

"I have someone visiting from home. And I want my room to look—" *habitable* "—nice."

"Okay," Olly says, even more slowly.

Rome swallows, sitting on the couch. "Like...your sheets and duvet?"

Olly blinks at him. "Well, sure. But what's wrong with your sheets?"

Besides the fact that he doesn't have any?

"What about Rome's sheets?" Damien asks, coming through the front door. He throws himself onto the couch next to Rome, feet pushing into the meat of his thigh, groaning something about the audacity of French philosophers.

Fuck.

"Actually, Rome," Olly says, stupidly kind and completely unaware he's ruining everything, "if you want to impress someone, Damien has much nicer stuff than I do."

"I do," Damien agrees, like an asshole. "Who are you trying to impress?"

"Rome is trying to impress someone?" Chai asks, coming down the stairs with Kaner.

"Apparently," Damien says, "he's trying to steal Olly's sheets for whoever it is, so—" He wiggles his eyebrows.

"Damn, Rome. Who is she?" Kaner asks.

"No one. I don't have some girl coming over."

But it's too late because they're off, speculating, and Chai is hypothesizing that Rome would only want to impress someone if she herself was very impressive. A six-foot-tall Amazonian queen? A small but terrifying Irish woman?

Jeeves suggests booking the rink after hours to show off his skills, and Chai is saying, "Can we meet her? When will she be here?"

And Rome just—loses it for a minute. "She's my fucking *lawyer*, okay." He shoves Damien's feet away as he stands. "And no, you can't meet her. Look, just. Never mind."

He's standing, and they're all looking at him in confusion. And now he's going to have to explain why he has a lawyer and why she's coming to visit him. This is why he tries not to talk too much.

"Why won't you all just leave me the fuck alone?" he says.

He goes upstairs with as much dignity as he can, being that he's essentially just thrown a tantrum because his maybe-friends care about him.

He is a disaster.

He's lying on his stupid naked mattress, staring at the ceiling and regretting his life choices, when someone knocks on the door.

He's expecting Olly when he gets up to open it.

It's Damien.

"Really. They thought *you* were the best choice?"

"Well," Damien says, pushing past him into the room. "I'm used to you yelling at me anyway, so."

That hurts. It's true though. Which is maybe why it hurts.

"Right," Rome says.

Damien sits and nods to the space next to him as if Rome needs an invitation to sit on his own bed.

He does anyway.

"I have to point out that was a dick move," Damien says.

"I know," Rome mutters. "Sorry."

Damien looks delighted. "But we didn't know it was a personal thing, so... We're sorry too. Olly said he'll leave his key under your door in the morning, and you can take anything you want from his room. But, um...you can also use any of my stuff that you want. I could even move some things over in the morning for you since I have a free period before lunch. When is she coming?"

"Three thirty," Rome says. "And my last class gets out at three, so that would be..."

"Yeah?"

"Yeah." He swallows. "But none of your floral shit. Or fairy lights. Or any of that girly stuff, okay?"

Damien inhales, a crease between his stupidly perfect, carefully sculpted eyebrows, and Rome stares at him, daring him to start up a new lecture about gender or some shit. He can't deal with that right now, not on top of all of this. Damien just exhales, closing his eyes for a minute as if Rome physically pains him.

"Okay," he says. "I can do that."

"Thanks."

It's uncomfortably silent for a minute.

"So," Damien says, attention on his hands. He moves his ever-present scrunchy from one wrist to the other. "Can I ask about the reason you have a lawyer coming? And why she needs to see your room?"

"Will you tell the others?"

"I won't if you don't want me to."

"No," Rome says. "I mean, I don't want to have to tell them. So if I tell you, can you make sure they know, but I never have to talk about it again?"

"Oh. Yeah, I can do that."

"Okay, well." Rome stalls out, uncertain where to start or how much to say.

Damien shifts, bumps Rome's shoulder with his own, and keeps the point of contact between them.

"This isn't a heart-to-heart or some shit," Rome clarifies. "Just me giving you information, okay?"

"Okay," Damien agrees, but he doesn't move away.

Rome takes a breath. "I'm in the process of petitioning for legal emancipation. My court date is next month. My lawyer wants to come take pictures of my dorm to prove that I'm a functional human, or whatever. To include with my petition."

Damien glances around the room. The bare mattress. The bare walls. The bare shelves above his desk. The only signs of life in the room are the crushed pillow behind Rome's back, the blue tartan throw blanket in the corner at the foot of the bed, a short stack of library books, and a slightly taller stack of pucks wrapped in masking tape and badly labeled in sharpie—first goal, first hat trick, first shootout win—on the windowsill.

"Don't say anything, asshole," Rome says.

Damien doesn't say anything.

"She just called me today. I would have made it look like I was happy and comfortable and shit last weekend if I'd known."

"You've been here for nearly three months,"

Damien points out.

"Yeah?"

"So, were you ever planning to get stuff? Not because you have to prove you're happy and comfortable here but because you *are* happy and comfortable here?"

Rome is exhausted, so he answers truthfully. "I am. You have no idea how happy I am here. But I haven't been able to work as much as I'd planned. And I spent nearly all the money I made over the summer on new skates last month. I got the pillow and blanket from the Goodwill in town, but that was the most I could fit in my backpack. I don't know if I'll be able to afford textbook fees next year, much less better equipment, so sheets and posters are pretty far down the list of things I need to worry about right now."

"Oh." Damien doesn't say anything for several seconds, and Rome doesn't look at him. Then, he asks, "You're working?"

"Yeah. Garage in town. Changing oil and shit. I pick up hours whenever he needs help, but with practices and games and homework—"

"So that's where you go on weekends when we're not traveling?"

"Yeah."

Damien goes quiet again for a moment, frowning a little. "So the group chat thing. You weren't bullshitting. You really didn't have the money to pay for all the stuff we were texting you."

"Yeah."

"And that's the reason you don't ever go out with us. Because you're at work. Or can't afford it."

"Yeah."

"And why you won't use headphones. Because you don't have the money to buy any."

"*Yes*. Jesus."

"So you don't actually hate me," Damien says like it's a revelation. "You're just poor. Like...not Olly-poor. Really poor. And I keep rubbing your face in it."

"Fuck you. But, yeah. Mostly."

"Well, that's bullshit."

"I'm *sorry*?"

"No, I mean, you should have just said something. Do you know how much money I have? How much money Justin and Kaner and Jeeves and Chai all have? Like, we cover Olly almost all the time whenever we go out. Because we're a team. And we're *your* team. You think we're going to leave you behind at the arcade when some of us have trust funds so massive that they'll get passed down to our grandkids? Even if you have some sort of hang-up about me covering you, Kaner already has Olly on her cell plan. If she knew you weren't in the group chat because of money, she'd have added you too."

"Oh."

"And we all have old equipment. Probably go through it faster than we should because we're entitled divas who would rather buy a whole new chest protector than fix a fraying strap. Well. Except Chai. But he's weird about his hockey stuff. I think he's been using the same cup since freshman year."

"I've noticed."

"My point is you don't have to worry about that. Not with us. You need equipment or help with fees or whatever, we got you. And it's not charity. Because it's not a big deal for us. It doesn't count unless it would be...an imposition."

Rome opens his mouth to protest, but he doesn't get the chance because Damien just keeps talking.

"And if you *do* want to keep track and pay us back some day with your stupid huge NHL salary, then that's fine too but, like... I could buy you a car, and my parents probably wouldn't even ask about the charge, okay? A one-hundred-dollar health center fee is nothing. I have significantly more than that in my wallet right now."

And that kind of makes Rome want to punch him, but— "Okay."

They just sit there for a minute, leaning into each other.

"Hey, Damien."

"Yeah?"

"About what you said earlier. About me not hating you, just being poor?"

"Yeah?"

"I do hate you; I'm just poor too." He nudges him a little, just to make sure Damien knows he's joking.

Damien laughs softly, more exhalation than sound. "You don't hate me." He sounds confident.

"I do," Rome protests.

"You don't. It's okay."

Rome thinks it might be.

CHAPTER SEVEN

DAMIEN MAYBE GOES a little overboard with the whole "make Rome's room look habitable" thing.

Maybe.

But it isn't like anyone dissuades him when he asks them for help, so they're complicit.

He and Olly make a Pinterest board over breakfast.

Kaner makes a trip to Kinkos during her free period, while Damien is at his 10:00 a.m. class, and by the time it's 11:00, a whole stack of donated items from various people has accumulated in the hallway outside Rome's room.

Olly, only a few paces behind Damien on the stairs, bursts out laughing when he rounds the corner. Apparently, Olly showed up for his study hall period with donuts, sweet-talked the teacher for three minutes, and got a free pass to return to the dorm until after lunch.

Damien needs to learn how to sweet talk.

"He's going to kill you," Olly says cheerfully, surveying the cascade of textiles, small pieces of furniture, and decorations.

Damien, filling his arms with freshly laundered sheets, is too committed to back down now though. "You gonna help me or not?" he asks.

Olly scoffs and whacks him with a curtain rod.

They sort through things in silence for a few minutes as Damien tries to work up his nerve to speak.

"So," Damien says finally, "Can I ask you a few questions about, um—" He tries and fails to think of a better way to say *poor people*. "—poor people?" He grimaces.

"I'm not exactly poor," Olly says. "Compared to you, sure. But my family is solidly middle-class. If you have questions about living in actual poverty, Rome's not exactly forthcoming with personal information, so I don't really know what his situation is like, but he's probably who you should talk to."

"No. Well, I mean, yeah. I'm starting to get that, now. But that's why I have questions. Because I think I've been fucking things up with Rome, and I didn't even realize it."

"Oh," Olly says. "I see."

What he sees, with an expression like that, Damien isn't sure.

"You know," Olly says slowly, "Rome has a lot of— It hasn't been *your* fault. The way you two are. He's a good kid, but he still has a lot of growing to do."

"Oh. Yeah. I know." He appreciates hearing it none-theless. "But I think I've accidentally made things worse sometimes. And he's been trying to be better lately. So I can try too."

"Well," Olly says. "All right. Speaking of, it might be good to get Chai's input."

"Chai? His parents are almost as loaded as mine."

"Yeah, but he put his foot right in his mouth a good amount of freshman and sophomore year with Sasha. Remember? He might have some tips for you there. Mis-takes he made. Arguments they had. Maybe even things in general about wooing someone when there's such a huge difference between your income brackets."

"Wooing," Damien repeats, a little strangled. "I'm not—I don't want to *woo* Rome."

"Whatever you want to call it, man. Now, what ques-tions do you have?"

*

FOUR HOURS LATER, Damien has let himself back into Rome's room after class to vacuum the rug when several pairs of feet come clambering up the stairs. He turns off the vacuum, spools up the cord, and rubs the back of his forearm over his face.

"Wow," Brass says, leaning in the doorway. "It looks like HGTV up in here."

Damien glances around the room with something like dawning horror.

"It's too much," he says. "Oh god, he's going to kill

me. Why did I think this was a good idea?"

"I think it's great," Chai says. "I think he's going to like it."

"Nah," Wooster says. "He's going to kill you. It does look hella nice, though, brah. You should come do our room next."

The guys head back downstairs, talking about food, and Damien pushes the vacuum into the hall before returning to the doorway. Just standing there a minute.

Dark gray sheets and a light gray duvet that had been Damien's backup set cover Rome's bed. Two pillows. The matching curtains and black metal rod are also from Damien, but the fluffy charcoal rug that stretches from the window nearly to the door is from Chai, as is the wire trash can with the little wooden basketball headboard and hoop attached to it. The bungee chair by the window is from Kaner. The scuffed-up, sticker-covered blue steamer trunk next to the chair, taking up the awkward amount of empty space from removing the other bed and desk, is from Justin.

Damien's not sure who the dartboard came from, but it hangs next to the door.

Olly's utilitarian lamp is on the desk, and above the desk, the first shelf holds Rome's library books. On the second shelf, Damien has draped a strand of fairy lights—which, yeah, Damien *is* a dead man—but the lights illuminate all of Rome's pucks, so maybe he won't be too pissed.

But the big thing, the best thing, in Damien's opinion, is the empty opposite wall.

Except it isn't empty anymore.

Thanks to Kaner's habit of always taking pics for her social media and, subsequently, the trip to Kinkos, the wall is now full of regimented rows of pictures.

Pictures of the rink. Of campus. Of the lake. The lake at sunset. And the team. Not any of their faces, but a pyramid of pucks stacked on the boards backgrounded by indistinct figures on the ice. A long stretch of night-darkened bus seats and the silhouetted backs of heads wearing headphones and resting on neighbor's shoulders. A pair of freckled, scarred hands lacing new skates. Another set of hands—Damien's hands—taping a stick.

He doesn't know how Rome is going to feel about that. But his attention, at least, is stuck on the two final pictures, right next to each other, of their hands. The contrast is compelling.

Damien also doesn't know whether or not he was overstepping when he added some things to Rome's closet.

His things.

And maybe a few new things. Just a few.

Because he realized when he went to hang up the hoodie draped over the back of Rome's desk chair that Rome owned very little in the way of clothing. Rome's meager closet offerings brought the grand total of items he owned to less than two dozen. Which was probably about the number of items Damien had in his *hamper*.

Damien just assumed, until that point, that Rome had an aesthetic. That his closet was full of identical black T-shirts and torn jeans and maybe even several battered pairs of checkered Converse and dark, thick-soled boots. It occurred to him, only then, that Rome didn't have an aesthetic. The few clothes he did have looked similar intentionally, so people would make the same assumptions Damien had.

Damien didn't mean to, really.

He was thinking about his closet full of shit he didn't wear, some of it brand new. And then he was arranging pucks. And then he was thinking Rome was broad enough in the shoulders that Damien's shirts would probably almost fit him. And then he was hanging pictures. And then Damien was hastily shoving T-shirts and hangers from his own closet into his arms and furtively crossing the three feet of hall space between their doors. And then he was shoving shorts into the dresser and hanging up shirts and folding a couple flannels to put on the shelf—and a cable-knit forest-green sweater that would probably be a little big on Rome but look nice with his coloring.

Jeans though. There was no way any of Damien's jeans would fit Rome.

So he may have left class early to go to Target, and he may have called Coach to get Rome's measurements on the way, and then he may have gone a little overboard and bought not only three new pairs of jeans but also some socks and boxers and two knit hats because it was getting cold and Rome's ears were constantly pink.

Now, Rome's closet looks a little more full, and Damien is standing in the doorway of his room, not even looking inside the closet but knowing what's in it, wondering if he has time to pull everything back out again before Rome gets there because this *is* overstepping. This and the fairy lights combined might ruin the tenuous friendship-like thing they have going on now.

But he doesn't want to take the clothes back. He wants Rome to wear them.

Especially the green sweater.

And then he hears Rome's voice downstairs.

Too late.

Damien closes and locks the door, shoves the vacuum inside his own room, and casually descends the stairs.

In her heels, Rome's lawyer is nearly as tall as Rome. She's wearing black slacks and a white blouse that shows off Michelle Obama–level biceps, and she's holding a camera. When Damien reaches the bottom of the stairs, she's eyeing their couch with disdain and telling Rome he looks much healthier than the last time she saw him but to please wear some *color* when they're in court, for the love of god.

If Damien were straight, he may have immediately fallen in love with her.

"Hey, man," Rome says in what may be the most polite greeting Damien has ever received from him.

"Hey." He holds out Rome's key to him like they planned. "Olly said to give this to you."

"Did he get the book he needed?"

"Think so."

"This is Elle," Rome says, pocketing it. "Elle, this is my teammate, Damien."

"Elle?" Damien repeats, one eyebrow up. "Elle the lawyer?"

"Yes. And if you make a *Legally Blonde* reference,

no one will find your body."

"Hey," Damien says. "*Legally Blonde* is the shit. It focuses on, like, strong interpersonal female relationships instead of heterosexual romance, and Elle doesn't have to give up any of her feminine-coded personality traits to be successful. Yeah, it could use some diversity, but for 2001, it was pretty damn progressive."

Elle blinks at him. "Well, shit."

"What?"

"Now, I'm actually going to have to watch the movie."

"You've never seen *Legally Blonde*?"

"Even *I've* seen *Legally Blonde*," Rome says.

"Do not start with me," Elle says.

She considers Damien for a moment. "So, Damien. You do...hockey things...with Rome, right?"

"Yes," he agrees, trying very hard not to laugh. "Yes, I do."

"Are you hoping to play hockey professionally or collegiately as well?"

"I've been talking to college scouts, yeah."

And he should leave it at that, but for some reason, he doesn't.

"But I've also been accepted to a writer's workshop based in New York. A program that focuses on poetry. And I'm pretty sure I want to do that."

He waits for the shock—the confusion over why he would choose to do something like poetry when he has clear physical talents that could lead to a lucrative career—but she merely looks impressed.

"Wow," Elle says. "Programs like that are very

difficult to get into, I understand. Good for you."

"Thanks."

He very carefully does not look at Rome, though he can see, from the corner of his eye, that Rome is staring at him.

"Speaking of," Damien says, gesturing toward the door, "I need to go hit up my poetry instructor before her office hours end. It was nice meeting you."

"You too."

"Hey, Damien," Rome says. "Elle is going to drive me to work in a few minutes so she can take a statement from my boss. You mind picking me up after?"

Damien is so shocked that Rome is asking him for a favor that it takes him a beat to answer.

"Yeah, for sure. What time?"

"Nine? I can text you when I'm finishing up."

"Cool." He fist-bumps Rome because it seems like the thing to do. "Later," he says and escapes.

*

DAMIEN WAITS, A little anxiously, to get a text from Rome that says he's going to kill him but receives nothing until 8:45, and then it's only an address.

Damien assumes that means he should leave.

It's raining when he gets there, a modest garage with three bays, a gated lot, and an attached office. Only one of the bays is open when he pulls up front. The light coming from inside spills gold over wet, stained, concrete, bright where it reflects on puddled water.

"Hey," Rome calls, bent over a workbench as

Damien jogs inside, head ducked against the rain. "One minute."

"No problem."

Unlike Damien, bundled up against the chill and the wet, Rome wears navy coveralls—the top unbuttoned, sleeves tied around his hips—and a black tank top.

It's humid in the garage, the dry warmth from a space heater mixing with the moist, rain-heavy air from outside. Rome, when Damien stops to stand next to him, smells like sweat and gasoline. Like salt. Like the damp soil of just-watered plants in the sun. Organic. Alive.

Rome is writing something in a well-worn ledger on the work top, one hand braced beside it, the other carefully handling a tiny stub of a pencil. Blacks and browns streak his fingers. His nail beds are dark charcoal outlines.

Under the halogen lights, with the sheen of sweat on his freckled skin, his bottom lip tucked between his teeth, his bicep flexing as he writes in the ledger, Rome looks like he could be a Garin Baker blue-collar painting: a romanticized version of himself.

Looking at him, something in Damien's chest feels unmoored.

He wants to touch him.

He wants to *write* him.

I wish I was smaller. I wish I was a tidy thing I could place in your hands.

He has to look away, for a moment, to get the words in his head to quiet down. He can't get his phone out and start composing a poem on the spot. That would be weird, even for him.

Rome doesn't notice Damien's existential crisis. He closes the book, ducks into the office for a moment before stepping out again, hands empty, and locks the door. He turns off the space heater and uses a rag slung over the corner of the work bench to scrub at his fingers.

"Let me change and lock up," he says, attention still on his nails. And it's strange, the way Rome is standing: Shoulders curved in like he's trying to take up less space. No eye contact.

There's a pink flush on his neck that Damien had initially assumed was from exertion, but— Is Rome embarrassed?

"You look good," Damien says because *what the fuck his brain is the actual worst.*

Rome is startled enough to look up at him. "What?"

Everything is terrible.

"You look good. Like this. Like you know what you're doing. Competent. Like you are on the ice."

It isn't what he meant, but it is true, and he can't say what he meant, so.

"Oh," Rome says.

And then he nods jerkily toward a set of lockers at the back of the garage and walks away.

Perfect. A-plus work, Damien.

The drive home is quiet and dark, the blur of trees outside as lulling as the soft, rapid, movement of the windshield wipers.

There's something...a feeling like promise, maybe, like inevitability in the darkness. They aren't touching; several inches remain between Damien's hand on the gear shift and Rome's stained fingers, picking at a tear in the knee of his jeans, but Damien can smell him. Feel the heat of him. The preternatural awareness he has of Rome on the ice seems to have followed them into the small cab of the Porsche.

Rome doesn't say anything for the duration of the drive, and Damien doesn't either. Their silent pocket of warmth seems too intimate to disturb with words.

Back at the dorm parking garage, they each take a microfiber towel from the trunk and wipe the damp seats down, working with the same parallel precision they often have on the ice, which is a form of communication, in its own way, and one that doesn't lead to arguments.

They're already soaked through, so they don't bother running to the dorm, just duck their heads and cram their hands in their pockets and let the cold rain hit the backs of their necks. Damien, at least, has a hood.

At the dorm, Rome is immediately pulled upstairs by a tutting Olly who promises to take care of his leather jacket. *Don't waste time on that now, just get in the shower before you catch your death.* Damien pulls off his jacket in the kitchen, rubs a hand towel over his face, and leans back against the counter for a moment, feeling unsettled.

Brass comes to stand beside him. "Hey," he says.

The team sometimes jokes that Brass really is their substitute dad, but it doesn't feel so much like a joke now, the way Brass is looking at him.

"Everything okay?" he asks, nudging their shoulders together.

Objectively, yes.

Everything is fine. More than fine. Rome and Damien are coexisting. They managed to spend twenty minutes alone together without arguing, and even when they do argue these days, it isn't really arguing. That's good. That might qualify as "great," even.

But not so objectively, Damien has no idea.

He takes a page out of Rome's book and shrugs.

Brass sighs at him. "You going to shower?"

Damien swallows. He thinks about Rome already in the shower, probably alone upstairs.

"I think I'll wait," he says. He goes to his room and fishes his journal out of his bag.

He thinks:

> *You don't realize how much power you have.*
> *I hope you never do.*
> *I hope you're careful anyway.*

He writes:
I would give too much to touch you.

CHAPTER EIGHT

WHEN ROME BRINGS Elle up to his room, he isn't sure what to expect when he opens the door to his dorm, but it isn't...this.

It looks like something out of a catalog. Or a TV show. Still minimal and clean in grays and blacks and blues, but in an intentional way.

"Wow," Elle says beside him, rocking back on her heels. "This is not what I expected."

"The guys helped me," Rome says because it's true, and he can't really think of anything else to say in the face of—this.

"It's...really nice," she says. "I was preparing myself for teenage boy entropy. I didn't even want to hold out hope for a made bed. But you went full Pottery Barn in here. It's nicer than my *college* dorm."

Rome doesn't say anything.

He's too occupied, staring at the wall of photographs and trying not to look like he's staring at the wall of photographs. Because, ostensibly, he looks at this wall every day. And should not be feeling weird feeling-y things about it. The back of his throat starts to feel a little too hot and tight for comfort.

His team cares about him.

Damien, despite everything, cares about him.

Cares enough to do...all of this.

And yes, Damien included a string of fairy lights, despite Rome's edict against them. But they're snaked around the shelf over his desk, now displaying his pucks, and illuminating the whole little study nook with soft, sepia light. He can't really be mad about it.

Elle shoos him into the hall so she can take pictures.

Rome pulls out his phone, opens a new message to Damien, and then just stands there, thumbs poised over the screen, stymied.

Does he pretend to be mad about the fairy lights?

He should say thank you, is what he should do. He should fucking apologize too.

Why is that so hard?

He shifts from foot to foot, uncertain, for so long that Elle finishes her pictures.

He pockets his phone again, no message sent, and manages to sneak his key to Olly. He pulls his phone back out, still just as lost, as they walk to the visitor parking lot.

"You're really happy here," she says, "aren't you?"

"Yeah," he says. "I am."

"Good."

*

WORKING CLEARS HIS head.

By 8:00 p.m., he's detailed three cars and sweated through helping Benny finish the rebuild of an engine. After Benny leaves him to clean and lock up, he loses himself to the steady rhythm of the push broom, to putting away the tools scattered on various surfaces, to rolling up air hoses and turning off lights. By the time he's nearly finished, updating the ledger from the office because Benny refuses to use a computer, the world seems nice and orderly.

And then Damien arrives to drive him home and fucks everything up again.

He's wearing tight dark jeans and floral Doc Martens, a green anorak and some sort of chunky cable-knit, cream-colored sweater underneath it. He looks soft and touchable. Like something to be held.

Rome realizes, just as quickly, how very much he does not look like that.

He curls his stained fingers a little tighter around the pencil in his hand and carefully redirects his gaze. He has a brief moment of thankfulness that his shirt is black, so it isn't readily apparent exactly how smeared with oil he is, followed by fierce fury at himself for caring. He's dirty because he has a job. Because he's good at his job. And there's nothing shameful about that.

Except then Damien says he looks good.

Good.

And Rome can't seem to focus on anything else for the duration of the drive home. As they're wiping down Damien's leather seats. As he's stumbling up the stairs, teeth nearly chattering. As he's scrubbing his nails in the shower and trying to decide if he's disappointed that Damien didn't follow him.

You look good, Damien said, eyes dark and liquid and earnest.

You look good.

When Rome makes it back to his room, towel around his waist, wet clothes bundled under one arm, he feels along the top molding. He locates the key and opens the door, expecting the riches of its previous state to be gone—shuttled back to their respective owners now that Elle has the pictures she needs.

But it isn't empty as expected.

The chair and the trunk and the refrigerator and snacks are gone, but in their place is a squashy tartan chair, clearly stolen from the rarely used upstairs lounge, draped with a blanket and holding a box full of unopened jars of peanut butter and Nutella. A whole case of protein powder. Beef jerky.

The pictures are all still there. The rug and the lamp and the wall hanging. The fairy lights and the pens and highlighters on the desk.

Rome is okay with it.

He realizes his team cares about him, and this is the way they've chosen to show it, and he can appreciate that. He can accept the kindness.

He'll have to thank them tomorrow though. With

words.

What he can't accept is that his bed is still fully made with butter-soft sheets, two pillows, and a thick quilt, not to mention the blackout curtains that still hang over the window—all things he recognizes as Damien's.

It's a hugely disproportionate donation compared to everything else, which makes his stomach hurt, considering he's been disproportionately cruel to Damien.

Rome opens his closet to get some clothes because obviously he's going to need to talk to Damien, and he can't do that naked. He pauses again.

Rome touches the green sweater before he processes his closet full of clothes. It's soft. Softer than anything he's ever owned, and he's tempted to pull it off the hanger and over his head so he can feel that softness everywhere.

Except it isn't his sweater.

And those aren't his jeans.

And the shirts...

He carefully releases the sleeve of the sweater, pulls on a pair of shorts that he knows are his, goes to sit at his desk to do some homework, and waits.

Thirty minutes later, ten minutes after he hears Damien greet Chai next door, Rome steps into the hall and knocks on Damien's door. "Hey," he says. "You need to come take your shit back."

Damien, in a hoodie and boxers, rumpled and warm-looking, slides off his headphones. "What?"

"Your stuff," Rome repeats. "You need to take it back."

Damien follows him back to his room and waits

until the door is closed before saying, "I don't want it back."

"Damien," Rome sighs.

"The quilt isn't my color; it washes out my skin. Can't take any good shirtless pics with that backdrop. And the sheets are the worst. I accidentally ordered 200 thread count instead of 400. I was going to throw them out anyway. If you don't want to keep them, just toss them in the dumpster."

"Uh-huh. And the pillow?"

"Too lumpy. Hurt my neck."

"The fairy lights?"

"Too bright."

"The curtains?"

Damien thinks for a minute.

"Smelly," he decides finally.

He's lying, and Rome lets him.

He's not sure why.

"Hey," Damien says, and then—

Damien is touching him.

Two fingers, pressed to the hot skin of his upper right arm.

"Are you sunburned?" Damien asks, baffled.

"Oh," Rome says. "Yes?"

"How are you sunburned? It's November. And *raining*."

Rome stands very still, overly aware of Damien's hand, now fully cupping the ball of his shoulder.

"I detailed some cars outside when I first got to work before it started raining. Took off my shirt when I got hot. It was only for an hour, but I burn fast."

"The high was, like, forty-five today."

"I'm from Maine," Rome says. "And I was working."

Damien rolls his eyes. "Do you not have sunscreen?"

Rome would shrug, but that might dislodge Damien's hand.

He doesn't want that.

"Sunscreen doesn't really work on me. I just burn. Regardless. So."

"What do you mean it doesn't— What kind do you use?"

Whatever was on sale, right up until my mother left, and then no one cared.

"Dunno," he says.

"Well, you're probably not using the right kind. Or I read this article the other day about how a bunch of brands aren't actually the SPF they say they are. I could find it and let you know what kind you should be using."

"Why?" Rome says.

"Because...sunburns aren't healthy?" Damien seems confused by the question. "They can lead to skin cancer. And wrinkles. And your skin is so nice. I would want to take care of it. If it was me."

You look good, Damien said.

Your skin is so nice, Damien said.

"Oh," Rome says.

Damien's hand is still on his shoulder.

Damien seems to realize this.

He takes a step back.

"Anyway. I'll go find that article for you."

Rome clears his throat. "What about the clothes?"

Damien goes very still. Like maybe if he doesn't

move, Rome might forget the question.

"Clothes?" Damien repeats.

If there was any doubt previously about who was responsible for the state of Rome's closet, there certainly isn't any now.

Rome nods toward the open closet door. "Did you think I wouldn't notice all the shirts and sweaters and three new pairs of jeans with the tags still on them?"

"Dammit," Damien says. "I forgot about the tags."

"Take them back to wherever you got them."

"I can't," Damien says stubbornly.

"Yes, you can. As we've already established, the tags are still on them."

There's a short, heavy moment of silence, Damien frowning at Rome and Rome frowning at Damien.

Rome realizes what Damien is about to do a split second before he lunges into the closet. Damien takes out the whole tension rod in his haste and starts furiously sorting through the cascade of clothes around him, tearing off tags.

"Oh my god," Rome yells, "why are you like this?" and tackles him.

Damien is triumphant in his task by the time Rome, trying very hard not to laugh, manages to pin him down, hands around his wrists, thighs clamped around his waist, both of them breathing hard, surrounded by the victims of their battle.

"Uh, guys?" Chai says from the hall, hesitant through the half-open door, "Is everything okay?"

"Fine," Damien says cavalierly from the floor, a sock draped over one eye.

"Fine," Rome agrees.

"Ohhhkay," Chai says and slowly lets the door slide closed again.

They both start laughing then. The kind of laughing that's hard to stop. The kind that goes on until it hurts and then keeps going. Rome slides off Damien to lie next to him, breathless, ribs aching, trying to remember the last time he felt this happy.

He can't.

"I'm sorry for being a dick," he says quietly, once their laughter has petered out to occasional little hitches of breath. He says it to the particleboard ceiling, lit in long, wavy, shadows by the fairy lights above the desk. Both ordinary and ethereal.

"It was pretty shitty," Damien says. "I didn't know what I'd done wrong."

"Nothing," Rome says, even quieter. "Nothing on purpose. Just dumb shit. Rich kid shit. But all the guys do the same stuff. You were just an easy target because you were the first person I met. And not my captain. And I didn't understand before—I shouldn't have—"

He swallows, so much honesty all at once making his throat feel tight. "I shouldn't have. I'm sorry."

"Apology accepted. Also, I'm sorry if I ever made you feel shitty about money stuff."

Rome nods. He's just about out of words.

Their arms are touching.

"Here," Damien says finally. He sits up, trying to right the mess of his hair. "Let me help clean this up. We should go to bed."

They put the closet to rights again, elbows bumping,

the silence companionable. Then, Damien slips out the door with a nod and a lingering look that Rome can't interpret, and Rome goes to brush his teeth.

He realizes he's smiling when he sees his reflection in the mirror.

When Rome goes to sleep that night, he strips down to his underwear and pauses, standing in the door of his closet, fingers inexorably drawn again to the soft cable-knit fabric of the green sweater, a little wrinkled now from its involvement in the previous ordeal. He pulls it on before he can think too much about it.

Aside from the sweater, the sheets are the softest thing he's ever felt. He doesn't know anything about thread count, but he finds it hard to believe that something better than this exists. He revels in all the softness for a few minutes, shifting his legs back and forth, rubbing his cheek against the pillowcase.

He doesn't know why he does it, but he reaches up one hand and knocks his knuckles against the wall. Two times.

Thank you.

After a period of quiet:

He gets two knocks back.

He goes to sleep more comfortable than he's ever been in his life, trying not to think about how the quilt around his shoulders smells like Damien Raphael Bordeaux.

And he likes it.

CHAPTER NINE

PATRICK ROMAN WATCHES *Deadliest Catch* like it's a spectator sport.

If he's in the common room in the evening and he's yelling at the TV, it's usually over the Discovery Channel, not hockey.

He has favorite crew members and gets all bitchy about incompetence, and he croons over machinery with an adoration that most people reserve for small animals and infants.

It's adorable, is the point.

Damien very carefully does not mention how adorable he finds it to anyone ever, but he does download several episodes to his laptop for their next roadie and asks if Rome wants to watch them together on the bus.

Rome, after several seconds of baffled silence, agrees.

Damien decided after the whole dorm room thing that he was going to start being nice to Patrick Roman. Aggressively nice. Just to see what happened. He leaves a bottle of 50 SPF outside Rome's room. He saves the last pudding cup for him at lunch. He offers to drive him to and from work once the first snow hits. They don't talk about these nice things, and they still bicker constantly, but there's no longer a malicious edge to it like before. They smile, sometimes, when they're growling at each other on the bench. Sometimes, they yell nice things now too.

Being nice to Patrick Roman is strange, mostly because Patrick Roman is not nice at all, except—

Except maybe he is.

He's changed after the Halloween party or even after the cop, maybe. But once Damien starts being obviously, intentionally nice, it's like Rome decides it's a competition. Rome starts sitting next to him in their shared classes. Walking with him to lunch after third period. Saving him a seat by the window during their Friday study hall. He brings Damien succulent cuttings and little chipped pots from the garden store next to the garage—*they were free, Damien; it's not like it's a big deal.* And sometimes, when Rome comes back from a snack run to the caf, he'll bring up a few cookies or a slice of pie to Damien. He won't say anything. Just knock on the door, push it into his hands, and then disappear again.

Over Thanksgiving break, when he and Rome are some of the few people who stay on campus, Rome helps him cook an anti-Thanksgiving dinner of fish and chips that they eat together in the common room. They split a pie between them for dessert—lemon, because pumpkin would be giving in to the man. Rome lets Damien rant about what a dick Christopher Columbus was for twenty minutes on the roof afterward, wrapped in blankets and leaning into each other.

There's also the knocking.

The first night after Elle's visit, Rome knocked twice on the wall between their rooms—quiet enough that Damien wasn't sure, at first, if it was intentional. Sitting in bed, suddenly very aware that Rome was lying less than a foot away from him, Damien knocked back. And then he forgot about it until the following night when, shortly after he heard Rome return from the bathroom for his evening toothbrushing, the two quiet knocks happened again. And he knocked back again.

It's a thing, now. Every night. The knocking.

What's also a thing is Rome trying to understand the nuances of race and privilege or even how to have a conversation about understanding the nuances of race and privilege. Damien is trying to understand what it's like to be a teenager with no parental support and a history of poverty—the extent of which he still doesn't really understand. On most days, that's good enough to maintain their strange dynamic of happy antagonism that might even be friendship. The others continue to look at them weird, but the looks are more endeared than concerned these days.

The week of finals, most of the team is crammed onto the common room couch, celebrating. They're all done, or nearly done, with exams. They're watching the original *Rudolf* on TV, drinking hot chocolate, when Olly shoves his way inside the foyer, shedding several layers of clothing and kicking off his snow boots.

"I have had the strangest day," Olly says, moving into the kitchen to unload a grocery bag full of sriracha bottles.

"Why's that?" Justin asks.

"You would not believe the number of girls who tried to talk to me today. I was given numbers by four different people I've had classes with for three years who have never once spoken to me unless it was for an assignment. *Stacy Morrison* just cornered me at the grocery store, asking if I wanted to go out with her this weekend."

"What did you say?" Kaner asks. She seems to be holding her mug a little more tightly.

"No. Obviously."

He comes back into the common room, cheeks flushed with cold, and burrows between Kaner and Justin on the couch. "I have absolutely no idea what's happening."

Damien notices that Rome, on the other side of Justin, is very quiet and very red.

Jeeves does too.

"Rome?" Jeeves says. "You have something enlightening to add to the conversation?"

"Um," Rome says.

So that's a yes.

Brass pauses the TV.

"It might be my fault," Rome says.

Olly scoffs. "How, exactly, is my sudden popularity with the ladies your fault?"

Rome glances at Damien, then Wooster, and goes a little more red.

Everyone continues to stare at him.

"They were talking about Damien's dick!" Rome says, well, yells, really. "Damien and Wooster," he corrects at a slightly more normal volume.

Uh, Damien thinks. *What?*

"Uh," Olly says. "What?"

"Who?" Kaner asks.

"When?" Justin asks.

"How?" Chai continues. "Why? To what extent?"

Justin slaps the back of Chai's head.

"I was at the tutoring center this morning," Rome says, "And the front window looks at lake quad. And you guys"—he gestures to Damien, Olly, Justin, and Wooster—"were running around the lake, and there were these *girls*—"

"Which ones?" Kaner asks.

"Blonde?" he says. "Well, I think one of them was a brunette."

"Helpful," Kaner says.

"Go on," Olly coaxes.

"They were at the window. Talking about the hockey team. And who they'd want to date. Or, uh—"

"Bang," Kaner supplies.

"And a few of them were fine; they were saying nice shit about, like, how Justin is smart and hardworking, and Wooster is sweet and probably treats the person he's dating like a queen."

"True," Wooster agrees.

"But then one of them was like—" He stalls out, glancing between Damien and Wooster again.

Oh, Damien thinks. *Of course.*

"I'm guessing she said something about Black dudes having big dicks?" Wooster says helpfully.

Rome exhales. "Yeah. But also some other things? Like, pretty fucking racist stuff. About not knowing if Damien was—"

"Black enough to qualify for the big dick genes?" Damien offers.

Rome points at him. "And the other girls didn't even call her on it. And then two of them were trying to decide who they thought was—"

It's weird, seeing Rome, who has no problem with profanity, get tripped up talking about sex.

"More endowed?" Kaner suggests.

"Yeah. And they figured it was Damien."

"Wait, what?" Wooster says. "Why? By their own shitty logic, that doesn't make sense."

Rome ignores him. "And I was so pissed that I went over and just...told them that Olly has the biggest dick."

Olly chokes on his hot chocolate. Or Kaner's hot chocolate, which he has stolen.

"You did not," Olly says.

"I did. I'm sorry. But I was so mad, and I didn't—I'm not like you guys with a damn file of memorized elegant speeches to give when people are saying fucked up shit. I improvised."

"I still want to know why they thought Damien had a bigger dick than me," Wooster says, mulish.

"Does he?" Kaner asks.

"Yes," Damien says.

"No," Wooster says.

"I cannot believe," Olly says faintly, handing Kaner back her mug, "that this is going to be my legacy. And it's not even true. My dick is average. Maybe even below average. Which was something I wasn't even worried about until now that the entire school apparently thinks I have some sort of *monster cock*. Oh my god."

"Your dick is perfect," Kaner says, and all the little side conversations in the room come to a screeching halt.

Kaner's eyes go wide. "I meant— Not— I just mean, it's...proportional?"

"There's no way to recover from that, Kaner," Justin points out gently.

The redness on Olly's face quickly surpasses the redness on Rome's.

Chai clears his throat, and Olly throws him a grateful look.

"If you were really trying to fight racist stereotypes," Chai says to Rome, "you should have told them it was me. And it also would have been the truth."

"It would not," Wooster says.

"Would too."

"It's not like we've ever actually measured," Damien feels it's necessary to point out.

"We could," Chai says.

"No," Justin says.

"How would we determine the parameters?" Damien asks. "Like, what's the standard? Is it by length?

Circumference? Flaccid? Erect?"

"Better do all of them," Wooster says.

"No," Justin says again.

"Mama was right," Olly says. "Yankee schools are full of heathens."

*

THE FOLLOWING DAY is Damien, Rome, and Justin's poli sci exam. Nearly all the other guys finished the semester the day before and are packing up to go home as the three of them leave the dorm. The campus, in general, seems quieter, probably because of a new heavy blanket of overnight snow but also because the tracks through that snow are much more sparse.

"Just think," Damien says as they enter the classroom, shedding their coats, "In two hours, we'll be free for an entire, glorious week. And then, it's just hockey for two weeks after that."

Justin makes an affirmative noise and goes to find his normal seat on the far side of the room. Rome and Damien retreat to theirs, where Chad, despite looking end-of-semester exhausted, maintains his usual cruel smile.

"Morning, Trailer Trash," Chad greets them quietly. "Affirmative Action."

The girl next to Chad gives him a disgusted look, but doesn't say anything.

Damien and Rome ignore him.

The first time Rome ever sat next to him in the class, Damien had to grab his arm and pull him back down into his seat when Chad greeted Damien in his customary manner.

"The fuck is your problem," Rome said, knuckles pushed white against the skin of his hands.

"Oh," Chad said to Damien, "how cute. You've found yourself a pet."

And then, Damien had to struggle to keep Rome from launching himself over the back of his chair.

"What the fuck," Rome said, red and furious as Damien forced him into his seat. "Why do you let him talk to you like that? He's, like, half your size. Punch his stupid fucking face in."

"Because," Damien said tiredly, "first, his dad is on the school board, and second, his dad and my dad are sort of friends. Or the business equivalent of friends, anyway. I'm not going to be the reason their business partnership falls apart. Third, I'm pretty sure if I hit someone, I would be expelled. Violence is never the answer."

"Right," Rome snarled, "but sometimes violence is the question, and the answer is *yes*."

"That was almost poetic," Damien said, his hand still wrapped, restraining, around Rome's elbow. "I'm proud of you."

Later that night, Rome asked if Damien wanted to go for a run, and Damien agreed with a pretty good notion of what Rome wanted to talk about.

It took Rome three miles to finally say: "I don't understand. You call me out on little shit all the time. Stereotypes or, like, unintentional bias. But I'm not trying to be mean. Why do that with me and not people who are intentionally being shitty? Shouldn't people like

Chad be the ones getting your lectures about systemic racism?"

Damien took a moment to frame his answer.

"When I was little, I didn't notice. Or maybe it wasn't so bad. I was in a private school in London that had a lot of diversity and international students. And since my parents are white, I didn't get a lot of— Well, coming here was a culture shock. So I did call people out at first. Except if you embarrass people, they tend to not want to be friends with you anymore. And..."

Damien sniffed against the cold, rubbing his nose on the back of his gloved hand. "I'm big. Intimidating. Even as a freshman, when I'd get angry, people would flinch away from me. And I don't like that. People being afraid of me."

"So you just stopped?"

"No. I try to be gentle about it. Turn things into jokes. Point out fucked up ideas people have without causing a scene. But doing that all the time is exhausting. Making sure I'm not stepping on people's toes while trying to advocate for myself...it's easier to just let it go. Especially when you don't think it will have any effect anyway."

He sniffed again. Decided to be honest. "Kaner. The guys. You. I know you'll listen. Someone like Chad..."

"Lost cause?"

"Not worth my time or energy."

"That's fair."

Toward the end of the run, Rome asked, "Why don't you just move seats, then? In poly sci."

"Can't give Chad the satisfaction. I was there first.

He's not making me leave."

"Competitive asshole," Rome said, more fond than anything else, and Damien just raised an eyebrow at Rome, who laughed because, yeah, there's no way Rome would move either if it was him.

After that, Rome didn't bring Chad up again or even show any ire when Chad dubbed Rome "Trailer Trash."

Until, of course, they take their seats for the final class.

"You're an asshole, Chad," Rome says conversationally after Chad has greeted them. "Has anyone ever told you that before?

Chad laughs. He turns to address Damien. "Maybe tighten the leash a little."

Damien doesn't know what Rome is doing, but it doesn't seem like he's about to kill Chad or anything. He's just turned in his seat, hands in the pockets of his jacket. Casual.

Damien says nothing.

"I've been wondering," Rome continues, "why it is you treat us like shit. Me? Sure, I'm an asshole too, but him?" He nods to Damien. "He's nice. He's a good student and a hard worker. He's never done anything to you except, apparently, exist as a person who isn't white. I just don't get it. Why do you act like you're better than him?"

"Because I *am* better than him," Chad says, easy, like it isn't even malicious, like it's just fact. "He wouldn't be here if his parents could've had a real kid. He doesn't belong here. And neither do you."

"Interesting take," Rome says. "Thanks."

And then he turns around in his seat and gets out two number two pencils.

Damien is baffled. He doesn't look at Chad, but he's pretty sure Chad is baffled too.

"You wanna explain what that was?" he murmurs, leaning into Rome while he finds his own pencils.

"One minute," Rome says.

And then he stands up and goes to the front of the classroom.

"Mrs. Jamison?" he says, loud and clear. "I think there's something you'd be interested in hearing."

"I'm sorry?" she says.

And then Rome pulls his phone out of his pocket.

"All semester, Chad has been saying classist stuff to me and racist stuff to another student, who'd like to go unnamed. The other student didn't want to make a big deal about it, but this school prides itself on inclusivity. I'm sure faculty would want to know if someone enrolled here might tarnish that reputation."

Damien nearly chokes. Because that is not Rome talking just then. That is pure Brass.

"I'm not sure I understand," Mrs. Jamison says.

"Oh, here," Rome says and proffers the phone to her. "You'll see from the time stamp this was recorded just a minute ago. It's representative of Chad's comments throughout the semester."

He presses play.

In the sudden, curious, silence of the room, everyone can hear with perfect clarity the exact conversation that just took place between Rome and Chad starting with, "Morning, Trailer Trash, Affirmative Action."

It's obvious Damien is the "other student" being talked about, even if his name isn't said, and Mrs. Jamison looks right at Damien, eyes wide and furious.

But Rome reminds her quietly, "The other student would like to remain anonymous."

She considers that for a moment and nods.

Rome and Chad are escorted out of the classroom to the principal's office shortly afterward.

Rome returns within five minutes.

Chad does not.

And then Rome slides into his seat without looking at Damien, and their exams are distributed. Damien has to sit there and focus, in silence, thrumming with curiosity, for an hour.

"I didn't use violence," Rome says, warily, as they leave the lecture hall.

"You didn't," Damien agrees.

"And it was my fault Chad got in trouble," Rome continues, words sort of running together in his haste to get them out. "My name is the only one on the incident write-up, and Chad actually seemed relieved about that. You're just referenced as a 'student of color' in the report. So it shouldn't fuck up your dad's business partnership or whatever."

"Oh," Damien says. "Who thought of that?"

Rome makes a face. "You don't think I could have come up with it by myself?"

Damien bites his lip.

"Kaner and Brass," Rome mutters, shoving his hands in his pockets. "I asked them to help me figure out how to make sure Chad got what he deserved"—he pitches his voice higher, mocking—"without violence," like an insufferable ass. "But I also wanted to make sure it wouldn't be a problem for you."

Damien doesn't know how to show appreciation that Rome will accept.

He lets their elbows knock together. "Why did you wait until the last day of class though?"

Rome shrugs, grinning down at the snow.

He's wearing the green sweater under his leather jacket and one of the hats Damien got him.

He looks good.

"I wanted to make sure he still pulled an all-nighter studying for the exam. Feels better, doesn't it? Knowing he put in a full semester of work before he failed the class."

And that is so marvelously spiteful, so—so *Rome* that Damien could kiss him.

And—

Oh.

Oh *no*.

Damien wants to kiss him.

With, like, feelings.

The attraction to Rome isn't new. But the feelings. The feelings are new. Or maybe they aren't. Maybe the honest realization of the feelings is new.

"So you're not mad?" Rome asks, looking at him sideways.

"No," Damien says faintly. "Why would I be mad?"

"Because I was doing the—what did you call it the other day?—the white savior-ism thing?"

Damien thinks about that for a second. "Nah. You

were interceding where I couldn't. Using your powers for good and not evil for once."

"I'm not sure if that's a compliment or not."

Damien nudges him with his shoulder, pushing him into the snowbank a little. "Thank you."

"Whatever."

The dorm is empty when they get back.

Justin is taking Kaner to the airport and won't fly out, himself, until the following afternoon. Damien plans to drive home sometime afterward. Rome is staying at the dorm for Christmas.

And Damien thinks about how Rome will be here, alone. While Damien is in New York City, alone. And he thinks about Rome defending him in his own Rome way. How Rome's recent actions might even be construed as affectionate. And he does something very, very stupid.

"Hey," Damien says when Rome opens the door to the dorm. "Why don't you come home with me? To New York. For Christmas."

Rome laughs.

"I'm serious."

Rome stops laughing. "What? No."

"Why not?"

Rome rolls his eyes, dropping his backpack onto the floor. "Look. You don't need to thank me or anything. We're good."

"*Thank* you?"

"And I get that you probably enjoy going to balls and charity events and shit with your family. But I have no desire to spend Christmas doing whatever the hell rich people do to celebrate holidays, trying to fit in with your relatives and remember which fork to use. You do your suits and champagne. I'm good here."

"Right," Damien says. "Yeah."

The warm clutch of fondness in his chest from earlier has gone cold and icy. Like he's been outside for too long and his lungs are considering whether or not he deserves to acquire a cough as punishment.

"Yeah," Damien says again. "You're right. Stupid idea. I'm gonna—" He nods toward the stairs.

"Oh," Rome says. "Did you not want to go get food?"

"You go. I'll get some with Justin later."

"Okay."

Damien heads upstairs to pack.

He leaves before Rome gets back from dinner.

CHAPTER TEN

WHEN ROME GETS back from dinner, the dorm is quiet.

There's light coming from under Justin's door upstairs, but Chai and Damien's room is dark.

He doesn't think much of it until he's coming back from brushing his teeth and there's still no light under Damien's door.

When he goes to bed and he knocks on the wall, two times, more tentative than usual, he doesn't get a response.

He sleeps badly.

The following morning, he gets up shortly after dawn and finds Justin in the kitchen.

"Hey," Rome says. "Have you seen Damien?"

Justin blinks at him. "He left yesterday."

"Left?" Rome repeats.

"He went home early. Or I assume he did. He was leaving the dorm when I got back from the airport, and he had his bags with him."

"I thought he wasn't heading out for another day or two?"

"I know. It's weird. He'd said he was going to wait until after everyone else left. But maybe his parents were able to come back after all."

Rome, head mostly in the freezer, hopeful for something vaguely edible, goes still.

He closes the door, turning to face Justin.

"What about his parents?"

"Oh. I don't know. I just caught the tail end of Damien and Chai talking the other day. It sounded like Damien was going to be alone for Christmas. Because his parents got caught up in, uh, the Maldives? I think. Since we only have five days off because of hockey, it wouldn't be worth the crazy long plane trip both ways to get him to them. And they couldn't cut the trip short for whatever reason. He seemed pretty bummed. Especially since they missed parents' week and Thanksgiving this year too."

"So," Rome says, crossing his arms and pressing his thumbs into his ribs because he deserves a little bit of pain. "So Damien is spending Christmas alone."

"Yeah. Unless his parents could come home after all. And maybe they could. I don't know why else he would leave early."

Rome does though.

Because he just keeps fucking things up.

"Do you know his address?"

Justin frowns a little at the urgency in Rome's voice. "The one in New York City?"

"Yeah."

"I think so."

"Justin," he says. "I need to borrow some money."

Justin abandons his coffee. "How much?"

"I don't know. I need to get a train ticket. Damien invited me to spend Christmas with him. And I thought it was a pity thing. And that I'd just be in the way while he was spending time with his family. I didn't realize..."

"Oh," Justin says, and then, with more understanding, "*Oh*. Yeah. Here." He pulls out his phone. "I'll get you a ticket right now; go pack. You want to leave today?"

"Yeah. Or first thing tomorrow if it's sold out today."

"No. Looks like there's one leaving in an hour and a half out of Boston that still has tickets available. I can drive you to the station if you can be ready in ten?"

"Yeah. Yes. Thank you."

He goes to pack.

He probably does a shit job, but it isn't like he has a wide range of clothes and toiletries to choose from. So he puts on his warmest clothes, throws the rest of his shit into his backpack, locks his room, and meets Justin downstairs.

"Is this stupid?" he asks, as they get into Justin's car. "I mean. Is this a stupid thing to do?"

"No," Justin says. "I don't know. Maybe. But it's probably the right thing."

So at least he has the blessing of his captain.

Rome makes the train with five minutes to spare, and it feels weirdly reminiscent of a moment months before: Looking out a bleary window. Bag in the seat beside him. Nose tucked into the collar of his leather jacket. An address in black sharpie on his wrist.

He texts Damien that he's on his way, curls toward the frosted window, and goes to sleep.

*

NEW YORK CITY is a lot bigger than Rome anticipated. Which is probably a dumb observation considering that, obviously, NYC is massive, but he just wasn't prepared. He feels like an idiot, trying to maneuver his way through snow-covered, pedestrian-crowded sidewalks, in and back out of the subway, without getting lost or gaping at buildings that are taller than anything he's ever seen before.

Damien still hasn't answered his text, and Rome is afraid he's going to arrive at some fancy-ass place in Manhattan with no way of getting inside.

It's a little after 3:00 p.m. when Siri tells him he's reached his destination.

Rome ends the route on maps, considers the soaring, regal face of the building, and calls Damien.

No answer.

He calls again.

No answer.

He calls again.

"—the fuck," Damien says. "*What*?"

"Answer your goddamn phone, maybe," Rome says. "I'm outside. Let me in."

"What?" Damien says.

"I'm outside your stupidly tall New York City building. And I'm freezing my ass off. How do I get inside?"

"What?"

"Damien, come on. It's fucking cold out here."

"I'm—hold on."

Rome hangs up and shoves his hands back in his pockets, hunching his shoulders.

A minute later, a man in a suit opens one of the front doors. "Rome?" he asks.

"Uh, yeah?"

"You can follow me."

The doorman—*that's what he is, right?*—lets Rome into a mirrored-chrome elevator, scans a fob, and presses the thirtieth-floor button.

"Mr. Bordeaux's apartment is the one on the left," he says.

And then Rome is alone.

His ears pop as the elevator ascends.

On the thirtieth floor, there's a polished atrium with two doors. One left. One right. He knocks on the left.

After a moment of fumbling from inside, Damien opens it.

He's wearing sweatpants and fuzzy socks—no shirt. His hair is a wreck. And he absolutely reeks of scotch.

Rome takes a step back without meaning to. Then very intentionally steps forward again.

"Are you drunk?"

Damien blinks at him. "A lot more drunk than I

thought if I'm hallucinating."

"Fuck you. What the hell are you doing, drinking alone at three in the afternoon?"

"I'm not alone," Damien says, voice cutting, gesturing expansively with the bottle in his hand. "I'm drinking champagne with my massive rich family. We'll get out all the different fancy forks soon."

And, okay, he maybe deserved that, but wow. Rome really does not like Damien when he's like this. "All right, asshole. I made a shitty assumption. Get over it. I'm here now. Move."

He pushes past Damien to get inside and locks the door behind him. He takes a moment to shed his jacket and boots before stepping onto the ridiculously plush rug demarcating the living area from the rest of the open-concept first floor. Everything is decorated in shades of gray: minimal but opulent. The ceilings are vaulted. The appliances in the kitchen on the opposite wall are sleek. The windows are clear. The counters are empty.

The room feels cold despite the gigantic electric fireplace in the middle of it. Like it should be in a magazine, but not lived in. Like he should be careful not to leave fingerprints when he opens the lacquered cabinets.

He has to try six different cabinets before he finds one full of heavy glasses in various sizes. He fills one up from the water dispenser in the behemoth stainless steel fridge and returns to Damien, who stands watching him in the living room.

"Give me that." Rome reaches for the bottle in Damien's hand. "Drink some water, and then we'll figure out what to do with you."

But Damien's hand goes tight around the neck of the scotch. "Stop it," he says, petulant. "It's mine."

Rome pulls harder, thinking, a little hysterically, that they're probably going to end up with several hundred dollars' worth of spilled liquor on several thousand dollars' worth of fancy rug. "I'm serious," he says. "Give it to me. You're not drinking anymore."

"Why not?"

"Because the smell of scotch is tied to every single memory I have of my dad beating the shit out of me. So give it to me and take the fucking water, or I'm going right back to the train station."

Damien lets go of the bottle. "What?" he says.

"Here." Rome pushes the glass into his hand, then holds on to the bottom for a minute, fingers overlapping Damien's, to make sure he won't drop it. "Okay, good. Drink that. I'm gonna go...do something with this."

He ends up shoving the scotch in the back of one of the cabinets in the kitchen and then stares hopelessly into the empty refrigerator. When he returns to the living room, Damien is glaring at the fireplace, the cup half empty.

"Hey," Rome says, dropping onto the couch next to him. "Finish it."

Damien tips the glass up. Four swallows. He sets it, empty, on the coffee table.

"Your dad hit you?" Damien asks, wiping his mouth on the back of his wrist.

Rome sighs. "Yeah."

Damien crowds into Rome's space, and the full

force of his attention is disconcerting.

His dark eyes. The upset crease between his brows.

Damien touches the scar on Rome's chin with a cautious finger. "He hit your face?"

"Pretty much wherever was available."

Damien's expression does something. Rome can't really parse it, this close. But it's certainly...something.

"Is that why—Elle—with the—um. Emancipation?" He says the word carefully.

"Yeah. Come on. Let's get you upstairs. You're going to take a nap, and I'm going to go get some groceries."

"No." Damien goes limp when Rome tries to pull him to his feet. Like a goddamn toddler.

"Oh my god. Why not?"

"Don't want you to leave."

"What the fuck, Damien."

"You should nap with me."

"Fine. Whatever. Let's go."

They make it up the stairs with only one near-death experience. Rome convinces Damien to shower and change into pajama pants by reminding him that he smells like scotch. And then Damien is damp and bedraggled and very sad-looking, sitting on his bed in an equally bland, magazine-pretty room. He looks betrayed as Rome tells him he's going to find a store, and he'll be back in a little bit.

"But you said you'd stay," Damien says.

"I'll be back in thirty minutes."

"Please," Damien says.

Dammit.

"Fine. Just until you go to sleep though."

Damien nods solemnly.

Except, the minute Rome sits down, Damien pulls at his shirt—pulls it up, tangling it around Rome's shoulders and head and—

"What the hell are you—"

Damien gleefully throws his shirt over the side of the bed, laughing into Rome's chest, looking incredibly proud of himself. "Better," he says. "Now we match. And you won't be hot."

"You're a mess," Rome says.

"Yeah," Damien agrees.

And then he sort of molds himself to Rome.

As close as friends are allowed to be when one of them is drunk.

Maybe closer?

Rome doesn't know.

"Tell me," Damien says, poking the tattoo under Rome's collarbone, "about this."

"It's a tattoo."

Damien pokes him harder.

"Ow, asshole. Fine. One of my cousins is a tattoo artist in Portland. She did the one on my arm too. Free. The rabbit on my foot was her, too, but back when she was fifteen and DIYed her own tattoo machine. I was twelve. Probably a miracle I didn't get gangrene or something."

Damien pokes the rose again.

"Would you stop. What? What do you want to know?"

"Why a rose?"

"Because I fucking like roses. Quit."

Damien trails two fingers down the center of Rome's chest and then to the right, over the landscape of his ribcage, so lightly Rome can barely feel it.

His skin pebbles in the wake of Damien's hand.

"What happened on February eleventh?" Damien's palm is flat against Rome's side now—thumb against the tattoo on the thin skin over his ribs—rubbing back and forth as if he expects to feel the numbers.

Rome closes his eyes. "I don't want to talk about that one."

"Okay."

The acquiescence is surprising.

Damien wraps his arm around Rome's waist, pushes his face into Rome's neck, and after what seems like a more-than-necessary amount of wiggling, he exhales, going lax and heavy.

"Hey," Damien says, suddenly urgent.

He knocks a fisted hand between Rome's shoulder blades.

Two times.

Gently.

Skin to skin.

Damien's knuckles against Rome's spine.

Rome laughs into Damien's wet hair without even really meaning to.

"Hey," he agrees.

He knocks back.

CHAPTER ELEVEN

DAMIEN GREW OUT his hair for the first time when he was thirteen years old.

As long as he can remember, every third Friday, his father would strip off his shirt and sit on the settee in the bathroom—or the wing-backed chair, or the vanity stool, or the edge of the tub, depending on where they were— with a towel around his neck and a wide grin on his face as Damien's mother touched up his crew cut.

Until his thirteenth birthday, Damien's mother would cut Damien's hair afterward.

It didn't really occur to him until middle school that other hairstyles were an option.

Except then, in eighth grade, he made a friend with locs, whose little brother had a small but impressive

Afro, and whose older sister had braids one month and then little pigtail puffs, and Damien realized his close-clipped curls had the potential to be a new form of self-expression. At very nearly thirteen, he was, of course, all about self-expression.

So on his birthday, his baffled mother took him to a barber shop where the man patiently walked them both through different style options and how to achieve them with Damien's particular hair texture, and it kicked off several years of experimentation.

Damien missed it a little now, though—his mother cutting his hair, the every-three-weeks necessity of time spent in the bathroom with one or both of his parents, talking about nothing over the soft buzz of clippers.

He knows his mom still cuts his father's hair each month.

It's an amusing anecdote that is often trotted out at parties over wine and a selection of cheeses, the elite laughing about Elric Gwain Bordeaux, who still has his wife cut his hair.

His dad usually says something bland about self-sufficiency, and his mother says something not so bland about perfectionism and ego and not trusting anyone but himself or her with his Very Important Head.

It wasn't until Damien was in high school that his father admitted he just liked it. The habit. The intimacy of it. Every three weeks. A buzzing razor. Soft hands. A kiss on his forehead at the end.

He also said he was allowed to enjoy the neck massage his wife gave him more than one by some stranger, and Damien said, *Ugh, do not*, and that was the end of the conversation.

He didn't really get it though.

Not really.

Not until now.

Damien wakes up to someone playing with his hair.

He's still a little drunk, but in an almost painfully lucid way—overly conscious of the mess he was in when Rome found him. How raw. How needy.

Despite that, though, Rome is in his bed. Holding him. One arm draped around his shoulders, one hand tucked up against his skull, palm fit to the curve of the back of his head. He intermittently twists a curl around his finger.

It is a shadowed moment of stillness, the blunt edges of Rome's fingernails moving gently over Damien's scalp, and he understands with startling clarity why his dad has always eschewed professional, potentially more flattering hairstyles for a crew cut and his mother's hands.

Because this is something entirely different than when a stylist, or even his mother, touches his hair.

This is something more.

"Hey," Rome says, whispers, despite the fact that they're alone. "You awake?"

Damien considers pretending he's not.

"Let me rephrase that," Rome says. "I know you're awake. Are you okay to get up?"

Damien grunts and pushes his face harder into Rome's bare neck because Rome isn't shoving him away and his fingers haven't stopped moving and Rome doesn't know exactly how lucid Damien is right now so he can get away with it.

"Let me rephrase again," Rome says a moment later. "Get the fuck up."

Damien sighs and gets up.

"Thought you were getting groceries," he says because it's the first thing that comes into his head, and he's maybe a little embarrassed and definitely not equipped to handle this situation.

"I was. But then I had two hundred pounds of drunken hockey player fall asleep on top of me."

"You are fully capable of moving me," Damien points out.

Rome doesn't deny it.

Damien isn't sure what that means.

"I should go get food now, though," Rome says. "Will you be okay by yourself for thirty minutes or so?"

"I'm coming with you," Damien says, despite wanting to do anything but.

"No, you're not."

"Then I'm giving you money."

"No, you're not."

"Then I'm coming with you."

"Damien."

Damien stands, stumbles a little to where his wallet is on the dresser, and then throws it at Rome.

It hits him in the chest, and he catches it, probably instinctively, before it can slide onto his lap.

"Those are your options," Damien says. "And I will literally fight you at the register if I go with you, so."

He can tell that Rome is getting ready for an argument, so he cuts him off. "You're here." Damien doesn't know how to say it better. "You're here. And because you're here, I'm not alone. That's worth a hell of a lot more than whatever the groceries for us are going to cost."

Rome doesn't say anything.

"Are you—" Damien stalls, not sure how to ask. Or even if he should ask. "Can you stay for the whole break?"

"No," Rome says.

And, okay, that hurts more than anticipated.

"I would," Rome continues. "But my hearing is the twenty-seventh. So I'll need to leave here the morning of the twenty-sixth. I think it'll take a couple different buses to get there."

"I'll drive you," Damien says. Because he's drunk and apparently in the mood to just say whatever he's thinking.

"What? No."

"It's not like I have anything better to do."

"No," Rome repeats. "It's a seven-hour drive from here. In snow."

"You would be doing me a favor," Damien says, suddenly viciously attached to the idea. "I like road trips. And you could show me around your hometown. And I could go to the hearing to support you. And it would distract me from being lonely and self-pitying."

Rome doesn't say anything. Which may mean he's about to give in or may mean nothing at all.

"I'll probably just spend the rest of break drinking if you leave me here," Damien adds, which isn't fair, or true, but—

"Okay, no," Rome says. "You can't fucking emotionally blackmail me with your well-being."

"Please," Damien says, putting as much supplication as he can into the word. He meets Rome's eyes. He holds them. "Please let me drive you."

"Fine," Rome says, his expression completely unreadable.

"Thank you."

They just look at each other for a moment, seemingly stuck now that they've made eye contact. Now that they've made a tentative but not insignificant commitment.

"I want KD for dinner," Damien says pointedly, belly flopping onto the bed. "You should probably get to the store."

"You're an asshole," Rome says. But it sounds like *thank you.*

*

ROME DOES MAKE them mac and cheese for dinner. He insists on a chicken salad as well, and Damien eats it. He doesn't want to do anything that might make Rome change his mind about letting him drive.

"So," Damien says, "can I ask about the hearing or—"

Rome looks cautious, but not angry. "What do you want to know?"

"What exactly is it for? How will it work?"

"My father was arrested in February. He's in prison for the next few years, and my stepmom decided to pick up and move to Phoenix in March. Neither of us were interested in me going with her. I couldn't just fly under the radar until I turned eighteen since family services and stuff were involved, so in April, I made a petition for emancipation. At first, it was because we didn't know if one of my uncles would be awarded temporary custody, and I didn't want to end up in foster care long-term. My uncle Bruce was, though, so none of this is necessary anymore. But I already paid the fees and did all this work, and...I'd rather be the only one in control of me."

That last sentence certainly seems to distill all of Rome's Rome-ness into one statement.

"Okay," Damien agrees.

"So I got Elle assigned to me. And we put together evidence that I'm self-sufficient. My father's parental rights have already been terminated. Elle tried her best, but she couldn't find my biological mother. So there's nothing actively standing in my way. No one to fight. It's up to the judge at this point. Elle is feeling positive."

Damien wants to hug him, but there's a very wide tabletop between them, and he's no longer drunk so he doesn't have an excuse for the action.

He nudges Rome's fork with his own.

"Can I come with you into the courtroom? Or is that not allowed?"

Rome turns the fork nudge into a minor battle.

He answers when the tines get locked, and they're both looking down at the entangled utensils.

"No. I mean, yeah. It'll be boring as hell, but you can be there. If you want."

"I'll be there, then."

"Okay."

They keep eating.

They don't talk about sleeping arrangements for the night.

There are three bedrooms. Damien knows he should show Rome the guest room. It's made up and ready. But he doesn't want to. He wants Rome with him. Close enough to touch even if he's not allowed to actually touch anymore.

So he casually asks after dinner if Rome wants to watch TV, and then, after Rome has agreed, he leads them straight past the fully appointed entertainment center in the living room and back to his bedroom with its smaller but still perfectly acceptable TV. Damien pulls up the Netflix menu and then tosses Rome the remote so he can choose. He hopes if he doesn't say anything maybe Rome won't say anything either, and they can just watch TV on the bed together. And then maybe fall asleep, and then—well, then they don't have to talk about sleeping arrangements.

Rome catches the remote. He considers Damien, furiously casual at the foot of the bed, and then the TV, and then the remote in his hand.

He tosses it back. "You pick. I need a shower."

Damien exhales. "Okay."

Rome goes to shower.

When Rome emerges from the bathroom twenty minutes later, he's wearing the green sweater, and the flush on his neck could be due to the humid heat that follows him, or it could be because they are both very aware he's wearing the green sweater.

That was a choice he made, Damien thinks. He had other clothes. A backpack full of them.

It might mean something. What, Damien isn't sure.

Rome sits on the bed next to him, closer than expected, and crosses his legs so his knee rests on Damien's thigh.

"If you come," he says, slow and careful, attention on the wide knit cuffs of the green sweater, "you'll have to meet the rest of my family. And there's not a hotel or anything in town. And no extra bedrooms at my aunts' and uncles' places. I usually sleep on the couch or at the boathouse. But it's not—"

He gestures a little, maybe at Damien, maybe at the room in general. His voice goes a little harder. "It won't be five-star accommodations."

"Good thing I don't need those, then. Tell me about the boathouse; that sounds cool."

Rome coughs out a disbelieving laugh. "It's basically a futon and an electric heater crammed into a cinder block hut full of old equipment. No bathroom. How do you feel about shitting in the woods?"

"Will you be there?"

Rome grins. "Fuck no. What kind of kinky stuff are you into?"

Damien shoves his elbow into Rome's side. "I didn't mean *while* I was— Shut up. I was trying to be nice. I was trying to say that I don't mind giving up plumbing if it means spending time with you."

"Well, stop. That's gross."

"No. Shitting in the woods is gross. The feelings I have for you are not gross."

And that—is a lot more than he meant to say.

Shit. Shit. *Shit.*

Rome is startled enough to look up at him. "All feelings are gross," he says.

It sounds more like an instinctual response than anything else, but now that it's out there, Damien can say "Whatever," and they can move on without addressing the fact that Damien has a very inadvisable crush.

Rome clears his throat. "Did you pick something to watch?"

Damien did not. He's about to hand the remote to Rome when there's a spattering succession of pops, a shrill whine, and then more pops from outside.

Rome stands and moves toward the window. "What's that?"

"Fireworks. Someone is probably having a Christmas party."

"People set off fireworks at Christmas parties?"

"Some people do."

"I can't see them."

They can still hear them, though: more shrieking, a deeper boom, rapid machine-gun-fire explosions.

"Might be the other side," Damien says. "You want to go look?"

"Yeah."

Damien takes them through the hall and into his parents' bedroom, which hosts a balcony. It isn't a very wide balcony, but it's long, hugging the entire glassed wall. They can see the fireworks before they even step outside, but they go out anyway, leaning into the cold wind.

Rome isn't cautious so much as awed as he walks, still barefoot, up to the railing, eyes wide and bright in the darkness.

The explosion of color is off the left-hand side, coming from the rooftop of another high-rise—eye-searing, wheeling smears of yellow and white that end in blues and reds and purples and greens.

Damien rests his elbows on the railing next to Rome, and Rome leans into him. Like it's natural. Like they do this, together, all the time. Maybe it's because Rome is cold. Maybe it's because he wants to thank Damien for coming with him to the hearing, and the contact between them is the only way he knows to express appreciation.

Maybe it's because he wants to.

Considering Damien's earlier admission, it feels significant regardless.

Damien turns his attention from the night sky to Rome. His profile. His parted lips. The little bump in his nose and his shaved head. His stupidly long eyelashes.

Rome is built out of a sepia palette, a golden out-of-doors creature made for fall forest foliage and cool winds. Against the snowy backdrop of a lit-up winter-clad city, he is something else entirely. An anachronism. A living midnight sunset. Something timeless and untouchable.

But Damien does get to touch him.

He's allowed, now, he thinks. He's pretty sure that means something.

CHAPTER TWELVE

ROME WAKES UP next to a still-sleeping Damien Raphael Bordeaux, and it feels disconcertingly normal. His ability to sleep at all with someone beside him is surprising enough, but waking up after a full night's sleep, syrup-slow and utterly content next to the warm bulk of Damien is—

A problem, maybe.

Definitely.

He gets up, steals Damien's headphones, and goes for a run. He needs the smack of cold air in his face, the burn in his lungs, to clear the slightly frantic static in his head. Afterward, Rome makes himself breakfast without going upstairs to take a shower because if Damien is still in bed, he doesn't know if he can resist crawling back in with him.

Damien comes slouching down the stairs, bleary and soft-looking, as Rome washes dishes.

"Hey," Damien says, leaning against the counter next to him.

"Hey," Rome agrees.

"So, I was reading earlier."

Rome pushes the headphones down to his neck. "Shocking."

"Stop it. I'm trying to tell you a thing."

Rome gestures obligingly with a sudsy fork.

"I was reading," Damien says. "About emancipation."

"Okay."

"About options. For if they decide not to grant you the emancipation for whatever reason."

Rome runs his tongue over his bottom lip. "There aren't any options at that point. Other than to wait until I'm eighteen. Which isn't a huge deal now." He shrugs.

"Well," Damien says. "If you still wanted to. There's marriage."

"Marriage," Rome repeats flatly.

"Yeah. If you're seventeen, you can get married as long as you have a parent's or guardian's permission. So if your uncle was cool with it. And anyone who's married gets automatic emancipation. I checked."

"You checked."

"Yeah."

"And who the hell am I supposed to marry?" Rome says. "You?"

Except Damien is looking at him like he's expecting

Rome to punch him.

Oh no.

Oh hell no.

"What the fuck, Damien."

"I mean, I'm already eighteen. And it's not like it would be for long? Just until you're eighteen."

"No."

"It wouldn't have to mean anything."

Of course it fucking would.

"No," he repeats.

"But it's an easy fix! And you wouldn't be stressed about it anymore."

"You think it wouldn't stress me out to be fucking *married* to you?"

Now Damien looks hurt. "Right. You're right. It was a stupid idea. I'm still mostly asleep, so—" He turns back toward the stairs.

"Wait."

Damien waits.

Rome rinses his hands. The bottom of his T-shirt is wet where he's been leaning against the counter. He looks at that wet line and not Damien.

"I appreciate you'd be willing to do that," Rome says. "It's stupid as shit and completely unnecessary, but it's...nice."

Damien grins. "That looked like it hurt."

"It did."

"Well, put the idea on the back burner. Just in case something changes. Because I'm down. A marriage before I'm out of high school would be a great cry for attention. My parents might actually show up for a wedding."

The words are a little too brittle to be entirely a joke, but Rome isn't sure what to do with them. "Fine," he says. "Now fuck off."

"This is my kitchen," Damien points out. "And I'm hungry."

"Then sit down and shut up. I'll make you an omelet."

He doesn't know why he has decided Damien needs an omelet, but he's suddenly certain of the necessity.

"Okay," Damien says, and he's smiling at Rome in a way that makes Rome feel squirmy and warm.

He dries off the pan he just finished washing and puts it back on the stove.

"You want spinach?"

"Nah," Damien says.

"You should have spinach."

Damien squints at him. "...Yes?"

"Good."

Rome gets out the spinach.

Damien continues to smile at him.

He puts the headphones back on.

*

DAMIEN NAVIGATES THE city like it's an extension of himself.

They spend the rest of the day, Christmas Eve, hitting tourist destinations, ostensibly for Rome, but more likely because Damien just likes showing off his knowledge. As day turns to afternoon, Damien shows him the not-tourist-destinations. His favorite hole-in-the-wall Chinese place. His favorite tiny cafe. His favorite tucked away scraps of greenery—desperate plots of earth wedged between concrete and metal, frozen and stark but still vibrant, somehow, in their tenacity.

They go to the Met as the sun sets, taking advantage of extended holiday hours. Damien pulls him from exhibit to exhibit, with a low, constant commentary that evolves as they progress from Picasso to Klimt, to ceramics from the Qin and Han dynasties, from charcoal to oil to photography to sculpture.

Fifteen minutes before close, Damien grabs the cuff of Rome's sleeve and tugs him into a new room to stand in front of a painting that Rome knows intimately.

It's brighter in person, the colors more vivid than those on the bulbous blue-tinged library computer monitor.

War.

"This is one of my favorites," Damien says. "Do you like Jackson Pollock?"

Rome laughs helplessly. "Yeah," he says. "I do."

He knows most of the paintings in the room, each lit by a spotlight. *Autumn Rhythm* is to their left. *Pasiphaë* is to their right. A string of numbered works—enamel, acrylic, wax—hang on the wall behind them.

"Yeah?" Damien says, maybe a little disbelievingly.

"Yeah."

Rome points to each in turn. He names them. He likes the way Damien looks at him as he does.

"What's your favorite?" Damien asks. There's a sharpness, a challenge to his voice that makes Rome stand up straighter.

"Here? Or out of all of his works."

"Both."

Rome steps to the left, and Damien moves with him.

"Here, *Autumn Rhythm*," he says. "Out of everything? Probably *Convergence*. Or *Reflection of the Big Dipper*. Or maybe *No. 5, 1948*. It's not actually the 1948 painting though."

"No," Damien agrees. "Because when it was damaged in 1949, Pollock completely painted over the original instead of just fixing the one spot that was messed up."

"Yeah."

Neither of them is looking at the art anymore.

"Why do you like it?" Damien asks, and it feels urgent. Important.

Rome doesn't know how to put it into words, but it also seems necessary that he try.

"It makes me feel things," he says, and that's...not enough. "It's so full. Overwhelming. Like I don't want to look at it too long but also don't want to stop looking at it once I start. And I like that when the original buyer, Alfonso Ossorio—when he saw that Pollock had repainted it, he wasn't mad because he said it was an example of a second chance. I like the idea of that. That things can be damaged and remade—maybe not the same as they were before the damage, but still beautiful afterward."

Damien doesn't say anything, just looks at him.

Rome thinks maybe he's ruined whatever the moment was. Because surely his badly phrased analysis is an affront to whatever the real artistic merit of the painting is.

But maybe not.

"I really like that one too," Damien says finally.

"Supposedly, it's in a private collection here in New York somewhere," Rome says, dragging his eyes away from Damien's. "No one knows who the current owner is though."

"Yeah," Damien says. He steps back, shoving his hands into his pockets, bottom lip tucked between his teeth.

He laughs, more exhalation than sound.

"Yeah," he repeats. "You want to see it?"

*

THERE'S A JACKSON Pollock painting hanging on the wall in Damien's house.

That feels like it means something.

Thirty-two square feet. Millions of dollars' worth of fiberboard and synthetic resin. A barrage of color.

And it's just.

There.

On the wall.

In the *closet*.

Admittedly, the master closet in the Bordeaux house is bigger than some people's living rooms, but still.

A closet.

And it's behind a fancy-ass glass case that monitors the conditions inside, apparently, and protects it from all the whatever in the air, and it has a billion different security measures, but it's—it's just there.

Lit up between a wall of shoes and a line of nearly identical black suits.

There.

Right in front of him.

Rome might be having a slight crisis.

Damien stands next to him, has been standing next to him for some time, looking unsure.

"Are you okay?" he asks.

"I have no idea," Rome says.

They eat dinner in the closet because he doesn't want to leave. Because if they do, then the painting will just be sitting there in the dark not being appreciated, and that seems wrong.

Eventually, Damien coerces him away with a promise that they can visit again first thing in the morning, and Rome gets ready for bed on autopilot, still trying to wrap his head around the fact that *No. 5, 1948* is in the goddamn closet.

"I feel like I maybe shouldn't have showed you," Damien says, sitting on the bed, watching him brush his teeth through the open bathroom door. "You're being weird."

Rome shrugs. He is being weird. He knows.

"It's my dad's favorite painting. He got it in 2006. One part investment. One part gift to himself. My mom was pissed because it was a pretty big chunk of their savings, I guess."

Rome feels a little hysterical about that sentence.

"You can't tell anyone," Damien adds. "Uh. Please."

"Yeah," Rome agrees. "No problem."

"Should I not have shown you?"

And the soft uncertainty there breaks Rome out of whatever reverie he's been in. Because Damien should never sound like that. "No," he says. "I'm glad you did. I'm just..."

And he realizes he's going to have to explain. He's not sure if he can though.

He spits in the sink, rinses his mouth, and moves to sit on the bed.

"When I was a kid, one of my cousins used to make fun of my freckles. She said I looked like a Jackson Pollock painting."

"That doesn't seem like an insult," Damien says.

Rome shrugs. "So I looked up who he was at the library. Got a little obsessed, maybe. The paintings, though, they didn't seem real on the computer screen. Or even at the Met earlier. Like, there's art that's real, and there's art that's bigger than real. You know? Art that you can touch and own, and art that exists more as an idea than a thing. And I was just used to how, in my lifetime, the art that would be accessible to me would be...crayon drawings on the refrigerator or whatever. And then there's you. With a Jackson Pollock in your closet."

"My dad's closet," Damien corrects quietly.

"The point is, it's suddenly tangible. Almost touchable. But still not."

"Touching it is a bad idea," Damien says.

"Okay, asshole. That's not— I'm just trying to wrap my head around the beauty of it. But also, the circumstances? What it means? If that makes sense."

Rome gestures between them, not at all sure if Damien is following him because he's not entirely sure where he's going with this himself. "You have a multi-million-dollar painting in your closet."

"My dad's closet," Damien repeats, even quieter.

"And Justin had to buy my ticket so I could take the train here."

"Oh-kay," Damien says.

He doesn't get it.

"We are," Rome says, "from two really fucking different worlds. And I was sort of getting comfortable in yours. A little. But now..." He gestures vaguely toward the master suite.

"So," Damien says slowly, "you're saying you're having some sort of crisis because you're the crayon drawing on the refrigerator in this analogy. And I'm the Jackson Pollock?"

"No. Maybe. I don't know."

Damien reaches out. Slowly. Giving Rome plenty of time to stop him.

Rome doesn't stop him.

He tucks two curled fingers under Rome's chin and rubs his thumb over the crest of Rome's cheekbone, where Rome knows his freckles are most dense.

"I thought we'd already established that you were the Jackson Pollock."

"Shut up," Rome says. The words are thin. "You know what I mean."

"I do. And I think you're wrong." He doesn't give Rome a chance to respond. "When Alfonso Ossorio bought the painting in 1949, he paid one thousand five hundred dollars for it. And his partner, Ted Dragon, reportedly responded when he brought it home, 'You spent money on that?'"

"Ted Dragon was an idiot," Rome says. The words are heavy in his mouth. "What's your point?"

"The point is that some art critics were calling Pollock a prodigy, but others looked at his work and just saw ugly chaos. The only reason that painting costs millions of dollars is because *someone thought it was worth* millions of dollars."

Rome is hyperaware of Damien's fingers pressed up under his jaw, his thumb now rubbing at the hinge where he's clenching his teeth. "You saying you think I'm worth millions of dollars?"

It's meant to come out derisively. It doesn't.

"More, probably," Damien says, utterly without artifice.

And Rome.

He wants to—

He *wants*.

But he can't. He leans back.

Damien's hand falls to the duvet in the space between them. "Sorry," he says as if that even makes sense. As if he's done something that requires an apology. "Do you want to watch *Deadliest Catch*?"

Rome feels like he may be suffering from conversational whiplash.

"Sure," he says faintly.

CHAPTER THIRTEEN

DAMIEN WAKES UP next to a still-sleeping Patrick Roman. Looking at him—mouth parted, freckles spilling over the edges of his lips and crowding across the bridge of his nose, eyelashes resting dark and spiky on pigment-spangled cheeks—makes his stomach clench.

He slips his journal off the nightstand, pads on socked feet to the living room, and stands in the window, watching the city move with sluggish midnight familiarity.

Eventually, he starts writing.

When he finishes, eyes gritty, it's near sunrise.

When he returns to bed, he leaves the journal and its most recent, damning poem buried in his backpack. Just in case.

sometimes i feel like i am out of season
a pale and tasteless imitation of myself
i am too much
i am not enough
i am tired

but in the gray post-night
when I am sleepless
and left only with
my thoughts
my thoughts
my thoughts

at least sometimes now
they are of you.

The feelings situation isn't getting any better.

And now, running on three hours of sleep and the beginnings of an existential crisis, he's struggling to watch Rome sleep without doing something drastic.

If it were anyone else, Damien would just lean over and kiss him awake, consequences be damned.

But it's Rome.

Rome, who is...difficult. Complicated.

As much as Rome has changed in the last couple of months, Damien also remembers the boy who was needlessly cruel. Who hated him, maybe. Who, more often than not, made Damien feel terrible and hollow.

But Rome has changed. And where he hasn't changed, he's trying. He instigates physical touch. He's trusted Damien with parts of his past that it's unlikely he's shared with anyone else. The scar on his chin seems a lot more ominous now.

He's here, is the point. In Damien's bed. Vulnerable and soft and infuriatingly pretty.

But Damien also doesn't want to ruin whatever this is. And kissing him probably would. Rome has never shown any interest in girls. But he's never shown any interest in boys either.

Rome opens his eyes, meets Damien's, and Damien starts to deny he was watching Rome sleep, except he can't. That's exactly what he was doing, and it's obvious. Rome just blinks at him.

It's snowing, the light from the windows gray and muted behind the partially closed curtains.

"Morning," Rome says roughly.

"Morning," Damien agrees.

They go for a run together, navigating traffic and snowy sidewalks and slick ice patches.

They take turns showering.

They make breakfast, sharing quiet morning space, talking with their bodies: hip checks and elbow nudges.

They eat in the closet with the painting.

Neither of them brings up their conversation from the night before.

Neither of them mentions it's Christmas.

They spend most of the day out in the city again. Damien takes Rome to Coney Island, and they nearly freeze to death in the harsh icy wind on the pier.

They huddle together on the train, laughing about nothing, bicker happily through another Chinese dinner, tucked in a booth by the window, watching the snow through frosted glass and then—

Then they go skating in Central Park.

Damien knows most New Yorkers avoid the tourist mayhem of it, especially on Christmas Day, but some of his best childhood memories were made skating at this rink because his parents loved New York City at Christmas. It's the kind of idyllic shit Damien lives for: Light snow and hot chocolate and the jut of skyscrapers backgrounding trees backgrounding lights reflected on ice. It's Christmas music and wobbly kids in puffy down parkas and people holding hands. It's Rome's shoulder, pressed warm and firm against his as they stand in line at the rental counter.

"I'm getting your skates," Damien says.

"No, you're not," Rome says.

"You had to take care of my drunk ass. Consider it an apology."

"I may not be able to afford a Jackson Pollock," Rome snaps, "but I can manage five-dollar rental skates."

Damien exhales, long and slow. He doesn't say what he wants to say. Instead, he pulls Rome out of line and out of earshot of other people.

"The fuck are you doing?" Rome says once they're at the scrubby edge of the trees. "We just lost our spot."

"My father," Damien says slowly, "bought that Jackson Pollock. Just like he bought the rest of my parents' art and jewelry and various houses and cars. But none of it is *mine*. And I'd really appreciate it if you'd stop conflating the two."

Rome blinks at him. "Uh. Okay?"

"It bothers me. When you act like it's mine. I'm not joining the family business or getting into the NHL. I'm just a glorified mooch. And eventually, when I've figured out what I want to do with my life, I won't even be that anymore."

Rome looks like he cycles through several responses before settling on: "But you're their kid. Their only kid. And they sent you to private school for the best education. Paid for your car and all your gear, and your mom sends you shit all the time. You don't think they're going to want to keep taking care of you for as long as you need? Probably longer? Isn't all of their stuff going to be yours someday anyway?"

Damien crosses his arms. "I don't know. Maybe."

Rome crosses his arms too. "I feel like we're talking about two different things here. You wanna tell me why your face looks like that?"

Damien doesn't know what his face looks like, but he can imagine.

He doesn't want to talk about it though.

He hasn't talked about it with anyone except, very briefly, Kaner, and even then, it was more of a "hey, so I'm not sure my parents love me anymore, and it kinda sucks; did you know the cafeteria has fudge? We should go get some and never speak of this again" sort of thing.

"Damien," Rome says.

"It's nothing. Parent stuff. Whatever."

"Parent stuff," Rome repeats. "Should I call Kaner? Or Brass? Because this is really not my wheelhouse."

"I think they got tired of me," he says. Mostly because Rome probably *would* call Brass if he doesn't say something. "I mean, they haven't cut me off or anything. And, yeah, my mom still checks in with me and sends me stuff. But I think maybe now that I'm an adult, I'm...not interesting anymore."

Rome is frowning at him.

Damien tries again. "I turned seventeen, and they just...started pulling back. They've always traveled, but they've also always come back. For big things, anyway. Thanksgiving. Christmas. My birthday. Except they missed one or two for the last couple years and all three this year. I haven't seen them in person since the beginning of summer, and even then, it was for a week."

"Have you, uh, asked them about it?"

"No."

"You think maybe you should?"

"Probably."

Neither of them says anything for several seconds, hands in pockets, not looking at each other.

"I'm really not the person to talk to about parent shit," Rome says lowly.

"Then maybe you should stop making me talk about parent shit."

Rome sucks his bottom lip between his teeth.

It shouldn't be cute. It is.

"You think maybe they assume you don't want them around as much? Because you're getting older and becoming your own person? Maybe they don't realize how important it is to you to stay as close as you used to be?"

Damien shrugs.

"Your mom is clearly thinking about you all the time from the cards and weird stationary and little gifts she sends you from all over the world. I find it hard to believe she's gotten bored of you if she's putting in that effort."

Damien shrugs again. Maybe he's being ridiculous. Probably, he is.

Rome makes a harried noise. "Have you thought about just fucking saying you miss them? In a text or something?"

"Look," Damien says. "We really don't need to do this. Are you going to let me rent you skates or not? It's not charity or pity or whatever the hell you think it is. I just have an unlimited credit card in my wallet, and you don't."

Rome sighs. "I'll let you rent us both skates."

"Thank you."

"But only if you get us figure skates." He looks pleased with himself.

It's bold of Rome to assume this will win him the argument.

"Fine," Damien says. "Figure skates it is."

"Wait," Rome says, "what?"

"Come on," Damien says, grabbing his wrist and towing him back toward the ice. "Let's see if the nice people who were behind us in line before will let us cut back in front of them. Try to look a little less like you're planning a murder, maybe."

Ten minutes later, Damien is beginning to suspect he's made a mistake.

"I think," he says, "this might be a mistake."

"What gave you that idea?" Rome says, grinning down at him.

Damien, sprawled on the ice, takes a moment to

catch his breath. His tailbone hurts. "How do people use these damn things?" he asks.

Rome helps haul him to his feet, still laughing, and then promptly trips over his own toe pick, and it's only through a combination of Damien's steading hands and a relatively impressive flail that Rome doesn't end up on the ice himself.

"Okay, yeah," Rome says. "This was fucking stupid."

"Maybe we should go exchange them." Damien doesn't let go of Rome's arm. "I mean, me getting injured is one thing, but I'd rather not be responsible for breaking a future NHL player months before the draft."

"We'll just go slow," Rome says. "And we don't know if anyone is going to draft me."

He hasn't tried to shake off Damien's hand.

"My money is on you going top of the second round. Justin thinks you might go end of the first round though. Just FYI."

Rome stops.

"Really?"

"Really."

"Huh."

It's Damien's turn to stumble again, losing the edge of his outside skate, and once Rome hauls him upright, laughing, Damien links their arms.

He doesn't think about it. Which is probably why he does it.

Rome looks sideways at him but doesn't say anything, and silence grows between them as they make a slow lap around the rink, elbow hooked around elbow, hands in the pockets of their coats.

It isn't anything so obvious or declarative as holding hands, but it's something.

And Rome has to know it's something.

Right?

Rome's cheeks and nose are pink under the dark pigment of his freckles. His eyes are so blue they look fake in the shadowed light from white bulb-wrapped trees.

After three circuits without either of them falling, Rome says quietly, "About the hearing."

Damien waits.

"I don't think it's a good idea for you to drive me."

"Rome," he says.

"Your car won't be able to handle the roads in my hometown. Not in the snow. And the driveway at my uncle's place isn't even paved."

"I won't drive us in the Porsche," Damien interrupts. "I was going to swap before I went back to school anyway."

"Swap," Rome repeats. "Swap what?"

"My dad keeps a Range Rover here in the city. When my parents got me the Porsche last year, the deal was that I had to swap it for the Rover during the worst of winter. So I have four-wheel drive in the ice and snow."

"Oh," Rome says.

Damien is thinking he should have found a better way of divulging that information. A way that didn't point out the fact that his parents have so much money they just leave cars scattered at various residences across the world. But Rome isn't pulling away from him. If anything, he's moving closer.

"They must care about you a lot," he says finally, "about your safety, I mean. To make that part of the deal."

It's quiet, but pointed.

"I guess," Damien agrees.

"Do you have chains for the tires? We probably won't need them on the drive until we get past Brunswick, but we will after that."

The way Rome says "after that" is full of apprehension.

The way Rome says "we" is a lot a nicer.

"I do have chains," Damien says.

Rome grins at him, no doubt knowing the exact follow-up sentence he neglected to say aloud. "Do you know how to put them on?"

"In theory. Do you?"

"In both theory and practice."

"Well," Damien says, "that's convenient."

Rome tucks his hands further into his pockets, forcing Damien's arm closer to his side. They lean into each other, warmth between them and cold air on the backs of their necks.

"I don't know how I'm going to be," Rome says lowly.

He's looking down at their rental skates, scuffed and snow-flecked and stark against the bright white of the ice.

"Even without him there"—the *him* feels weighty and terrible—"I don't know. I might not handle it well. I might be a dick."

"And that'll be different from usual, how?"

"Damien."

Damien swallows. "Sorry."

They're already pretty much pressed entirely together where their arms are linked. Damien is used to communicating with Rome through elbow nudges and hip checks and brief hands-on-shoulders, but right now, none of those are options.

He's supposed to be good with words. They're failing him, here.

"It's fine," Damien says after a too-long pause. "I'll give you a weekend pass or something. We'll figure it out."

"It's Tuesday," Rome says, sort of choked, and it takes Damien a minute.

"Okay, asshole. I'll give you a midweek pass. What the hell ever."

"Okay," Rome agrees.

And oh.

Apparently, they *can* get closer.

Rome abruptly takes his hands out of his pockets a moment later, pulls his arm out of Damien's, and points to the rink exit.

"I'm going to go get some hot chocolate. You want one?"

Hot chocolate is $2.50.

Damien considers and then immediately decides against fishing a five-dollar bill from his wallet.

"Your treat?" he asks.

"Obviously."

"Sure. I'll take one. Extra marshmallows."

Rome nods decisively and then, careful without Damien beside him, skates out.

Damien watches him go—freckled neck pink between the collar of his jacket and the gray knit of his hat.

Rome glances over his shoulder, notices Damien is watching, and grins a little before stumbling and apologizing to the couple he nearly ran into. He throws a glare over his shoulder a moment later as if it's Damien's fault.

Damien laughs and then has to reach for the boards to avoid falling.

Rome is...something.

Something important.

The potential there—in linked arms and over-the-shoulder glances—is both exhilarating and a little terrifying: necessary of caution.

He's like a poem in a language Damien doesn't know.

But he wants to.

CHAPTER FOURTEEN

THE RANGE ROVER that pulls up to valet the following day is freshly washed, which seems counter-intuitive considering the mire of slushy snow they're about to drive into.

Rome might have said something about it if he didn't feel like someone has a hand around his stomach and is just...slowly tightening their grip.

Damien has been looking at him all morning as if he's an animal that warrants slow movements.

He hates it.

Damien puts their bags in the back, and Rome moves to sit in the stupidly comfortable, heated passenger seat.

He texts his uncle that they're on the way and then

closes his eyes.

He didn't sleep well the night before. He should have been able to. He was tired and distressingly comfortable, and Damien was breathing, soft and reassuring, beside him.

But he couldn't.

Eventually, he gave up. He went down to the kitchen and packed food for the trip the next day, cleaned all the fingerprints off the lacquered cabinets, fixed the one drawer by the sink that wasn't rolling correctly, and then he went and sat in the closet with the painting.

Damien found him there shortly after dawn, chin tucked in the valley between his bent knees, shadows under his eyes. Damien didn't say anything about it.

And now they're in New York City traffic—horns and sharp movements and a communal blatant disregard for lane distinctions. Damien has one careless hand on the steering wheel, drinking tea from a thermal cup in his other hand, humming to himself, and there's no way Rome is even going to pretend to try to sleep until they get out of the city.

It's insane.

Which fits the theme of the trip, maybe.

He still can't believe he's agreed to this. Within eight hours, they're going to drive Damien's Range Rover down the pitted dirt driveway to his uncle's one-hundred-year-old, wood-shingled, wood-stove relic of a home, and then he's going to introduce Damien to his family.

Damien. With his Coach sunglasses and his three-piece matching set of Tumi luggage and his floral fucking Doc Martens.

Rome isn't embarrassed by Damien though. If anything, he's already feeling defensive of him. Because his family might make the same assumptions about Damien that Rome did initially, and he doesn't want that.

Yes, Damien is rich and beautiful, but Rome knows now that those are the least noteworthy things about him.

Rome blinks at his own reflection in the window.

Fuck.

He balls up the coat Damien had lent him and is clearly hoping he'll keep, shoves it between the headrest and the window and aggressively tries to fall asleep.

Surprisingly, it works.

He wakes up hours later at a gas station when the automatic pump shutoff thunks outside. He jumps a little, then gets out to clean the windshield.

Damien returns to the car with bananas and coffees for each of them less than a minute later, and before Rome can offer to pay for his, Damien is opening the passenger door and throwing himself inside, telling Rome it's his turn to drive.

Sleep-muddled and cold and honestly a little surprised that Damien is willing to *let* him drive, Rome forgets to argue about the money until he finishes his coffee twenty minutes later and reaches for the remaining banana in the cupholder. By then, Damien is either asleep or pretending to be, so Rome drops it.

He knows with the ice and snow it might be faster to stay inland and cut back east after going through Bangor, which is possibly why he decides to take HW 1 all the way up the coast.

When Damien wakes up, he notices Rome has

turned off the car's navigation system. He doesn't mention it.

They stop at the Narrows Observatory to eat a late lunch—chicken salads and leftover KD that Rome packed at 2:00 a.m. Damien coerces Rome into exploring the fort to "stretch their legs" despite the fucking snow. But Rome is plenty warm in his borrowed coat, and Damien's smile is bright against the grayness of the day, so he doesn't really mind.

Back at the car, Damien says it's his turn to drive again, and the clenching feeling in Rome's gut is just getting worse, so Rome doesn't argue.

As they're crossing the bridge, Damien turns on the radio.

Fifteen minutes later, he still hasn't settled on a channel, and Rome would usually be ready to strangle him, but he just doesn't care.

He's too—he doesn't even know. Too something.

He realizes his knee has been bouncing anxiously since they got back in the car, and he stops himself with a grimace, hooking his ankles together, wrapping his arms around his middle, pushing down, wondering why it's getting progressively harder to swallow.

And then the first guitar chords of "Iris," clear and loud and too perfect for the radio, come out of the Range Rover's speakers.

Rome straightens, looking at Damien. He looks at the aux cable connected to the phone in Damien's hand.

"Are you seriously playing the Goo Goo Dolls right now?" Rome asks.

Damien's attention is on the road. "It was the least

objectionable band on your phone," he mutters.

"Sure," Rome says. "Except that's not my phone. It's your phone."

Which means that either Damien specifically down-loaded the song for Rome, or he already had it.

Rome isn't sure which one he wants it to be.

Well. That's a lie.

It turns out Damien has the entirety of *Dizzy Up the Girl*, and they listen to the rest of the album before Damien switches to Matchbox Twenty. Green Day is followed by Blink-182 before they settle in for several My Chemical Romance songs in a row.

Somewhere around "American Idiot," Damien starts singing along, and by "Sugar, We're Going Down," he's goaded Rome into joining him.

They're more or less screaming "Teenagers" together when they hit the Port Marta city limit.

Rome turns down the music a few minutes later. "It's, uh—the directions are kinda complicated from here," he says, pointing out an upcoming turn.

Damien slows as they leave the main road, and the asphalt turns pocked and crunchy with half-frozen slush. A mile later, they stop and put the chains on the tires.

Afterward, without the distraction of cold and a task to accomplish, the anxiety from before comes crowding right back into Rome's chest.

Damien doesn't turn the music back up, but he does keep singing along, albeit much quieter.

Rome does not.

Rome is trying to breathe and not having much

success.

He thinks about the past two days.

He thinks about sleeping so close to Damien he can feel him breathing, about walking shoulder-to-shoulder with him down crowded sidewalks and tucking himself into Damien's space in cramped restaurant booths and subway cars. He thinks about the comfort of knocked elbows and grabbed wrists and linked arms.

Except Damien's massive car is too big and too luxurious, and there's too much space between them now to recreate any of those things.

Rome looks at the space between them and considers.

The Range Rover is an automatic, but Damien's hand rests on the ball of the gear shift out of habit: Perfect half-moon nails. A subtle map of tendons and veins on his forearm.

Rome thinks about how Damien volunteered to drive him home. About how Damien is planning to go to his hearing. Rome thinks about how Damien apparently has all of Rome's favorite music on his phone and has just spent the last hour distracting him. And that Damien has given him nearly every article of clothing he's currently wearing.

Rome grabs Damien's hand.

It isn't elegant.

It isn't slow or subtle or cautious because if he'd thought it through enough to attempt any of those things, he wouldn't have done it at all; *what the fuck, why did he do it?* Except now he *has*, and now he's sliding his fingers into the divots between Damien's fingers, lacing them together, palm to palm, pulling their joined hands to rest on his thigh.

Rome looks out the window.

He knows his face is red. He can feel the heat of it.

"What are you doing?" Damien asks.

He seems to realize what a stupid question that is as soon as it leaves his mouth, but it's already out there in the air between them, and now Rome has to answer it.

"Holding your fucking hand," Rome says. "You got a problem with that?"

"...No."

"Good. Slow down. You need to turn up here."

Damien turns.

He squeezes Rome's hand.

Rome presses his hot face against the window.

It isn't a big deal, he thinks (it is).

It doesn't have to mean anything, he thinks (it does).

*

WHEN THEY PARK in front of the house, the sun is nearly set—below the tree line but not yet the horizon. There's smoke coming out of the chimney.

The house looks the same as it always has, small and tilted and ramshackle, well-kept but wearing every one of its 103 years. It is a charming spot of warmth in the desolate winter landscape, yellow-orange light spilling out the windows to reflect on the icy porch.

The assortment of cars scattered across the yard, if it can be called a yard, are much in keeping with the house: old, functional, and loved, though not particularly pretty.

They park between his uncle's rust-spotted 1991 Chevy and his cousin's 1988 Jeep Wagoneer, which had once been his aunt's 1988 Jeep Wagoneer. The wood paneling is shiny in the fading sunlight. It's just as hideous as he remembers.

What makes Rome go still, however, is the car he didn't notice until Damien turns off the engine.

It's tucked around the corner of the house, nearly out of sight in the growing shadows under the trees.

A 1995 Subaru Forester. Silver, with bubbled tint on the windows and a blue front bumper that he installed himself at fifteen.

His father's car.

"Hey," Damien says. "We getting out?"

Damien manages to phrase the question entirely without judgment, as if there isn't an obvious answer.

Rome is reasonably sure that if he tells Damien no, and to turn around and take them back into town, Damien will do it without a second thought.

Rome swallows. "Yeah. Sorry." He nods to the Subaru. "That's my dad's car. It makes sense my uncle would have it now. I just—wasn't expecting to see it here."

"Oh. Shit."

Damien rubs his thumb against the back of Rome's hand. "You need a minute?"

"No. I can see Piper staring at us from the window. Let's go."

Damien doesn't ask him if he's okay, which he appreciates.

He's not okay. But he's working on it.

"Any last advice?" Damien asks.

"What?"

He nods toward the house. "To make them like me."

He probably means the words to come out joking, but Rome knows Damien.

It's a sudden and weighty thing to realize—the two of them draped in the faded colors of sunset, holding hands, car engine silent but the speakers still whispering the quiet chorus of "Set Fire to the Third Bar."

He knows Damien.

And Damien is nervous.

Rome just hadn't noticed until now because he was so wrapped up in his own anxiety.

"They'll love you," Rome says roughly, and everything about this moment feels illusory.

He doesn't understand how anyone couldn't love Damien. How he didn't, initially.

"If they don't," he adds, "they're fucking idiots. Come on."

He lets his fingers slide from between Damien's as he leans to open the door.

The breathtaking chill of icy, ocean-salted wind is a welcome sting against his hot face; the solidness of frozen ground under the tread of his boots is a comfort.

He flexes his empty hand before shoving it in his pocket.

He slings his backpack onto his shoulder.

He blinks snow out of his eyes and starts up the front steps.

CHAPTER FIFTEEN

ROME'S FAMILY DOESN'T hug.

They aren't unkind or anything, they're plenty welcoming, and there are plenty of them to welcome them. The house is crowded with people and the furniture that contains them. Couches and mismatched recliners fit like puzzle pieces around a TV that is probably the same age as Damien. The dining room has two tables in it. One round and painted yellow, the other a thick rectangular block of wood. They're pushed together with just enough room between table-edges and walls for people to squeeze into seats. Only three of the dozen chairs in the room match. The walls are painted a pale blue-green, and there's art all over them. Crayon drawings and splattered, slightly crumpled, watercolor paintings. Paper plate snakes and a model of the solar system hang from the ceiling.

A collection of women yell hello from the kitchen, and the men, scattered around the various couches, take turns doling out friendly backslaps and handshakes. Actually, there are several women in the living room, too, dressed in the same palettes and styles as the men: Carhartts and flannel and baseball caps. They hold beers and compliment Rome on his obvious muscle gain and ask if it's true he might get drafted. Wouldn't that be something.

Damien gets much the same treatment, except after the initial introductions and confirmation that, yes, he plays hockey with Patrick—that's going to take some getting used to—they don't seem to know what to do with him.

He took off his Doc Martens at the door when Rome removed his boots, and he occasionally glances over at the pile of shoes, where the largely untouched floral leather stands out, vibrant, against the battered browns and blacks of the others. Usually, it's a contrast he'd take pleasure in, but it makes him self-conscious here.

"Are those your shoes?" someone asks, and he turns to find a small, pink-cheeked girl looking up at him.

"Yes?"

"I like them. They're going to get dirty though. You probably shouldn't wear them in the snow or your mom will get mad."

"I'll take that under advisement."

"Hi," she says, extending one hand. "I'm Piper Eloise Roman."

She's wearing double-cuffed corduroy overalls over a double-cuffed thermal sweater. Her pigtail fishtail braids are thick and gold and nearly to her waist.

He's surprised by the firmness, or at least the attempted firmness, of the handshake.

"I'm Damien Raphael Bordeaux," he says.

"Is that a name from a special place?" she asks.

"Uh." He glances at Rome for assistance, except Rome is talking with one of his uncles about hockey, arms crossed, their heads ducked together, not paying any attention to Damien and his small inquisitor. "I don't know what you mean."

"Well, some people have names from special places," she informs him patiently. "So, they don't sound like regular names. Like my cousins Siobhan and Saoirse. Their names come from Irishland."

"You mean Ireland?"

She considers this, rocking back and forth on her heels. "Maybe."

"That's cool. Ireland is nice."

Her eyes widen. "Have you been there?"

"I have."

"Is that where your name is from too?"

"Oh. No. My father is French. Um. From France."

He hopes this is an acceptable explanation, but he's terrible at judging kids' ages. Does Piper even know what France is?

"Oh," she says after a moment of contemplation. "Cool," she says. "Do you want to see my room?"

"That would bring me the utmost happiness," he says.

"You're kind of weird," she says, offering him her hand.

He accepts it. "I know."

He learns a few important things from Piper in the next fifteen minutes. Her favorite color is yellow but sometimes blue. She hardly ever got to see her cousin Patrick when she was "little." And then she saw him all the time for a while because he lived with them and it was great because he would play with her but now he's gone at school and she misses him a lot. He learns that she has two favorite stuffed animals: a dog and a lobster. The dog's name is Brownie despite the fact that he's black. The lobster's name is Nicolaus Copernicus. He learns that she really likes the stars and maybe wants to be an astronaut one day and that she asked for a telescope for Christmas this year except telescopes are a lot of money so she'll have to wait until she's older.

He learns that she doesn't like her uncle Patrick—Patrick Senior—because he was mean to Aunt Maura, and he gave her cousin Patrick—Rome— nightmares, and dads shouldn't ever give their kids nightmares.

He learns that, sometimes, if Piper woke up because Patrick was having a nightmare on the couch, she'd bring him Nicolaus Copernicus and let Patrick sleep with him so he wouldn't be afraid.

Damien thanks her. And then, just as seriously, he thanks Nicolaus Copernicus.

"No problem," says Nicolaus Copernicus.

Nicolaus Copernicus has a very squeaky voice.

*

DINNER IS A cacophony of happy noise.

There isn't an overabundance of food, but everyone has fish and potatoes and greens on their plates, and none of the kids complain, though Piper does make some relatively impressive faces while finishing her broccoli. Damien serves himself less than he would normally, and Rome probably notices, but it's nice. Everyone is smiling, even when they're arguing. And Rome isn't *talkative*, but he's said more in the last hour than he usually does in a day.

Damien is just starting to relax when Rome's uncle Joe moves the conversation to hockey and Rome's draft prospects. One of the cousins—maybe a year or two older than them—says that if Patrick makes it to the NHL, he might finally get a girlfriend.

And maybe the comment would have been overlooked, except Rome flushes, glancing down at his plate.

"Oh," one of the women says. "Patrick, honey, do you have a girlfriend now?"

"No," Rome says.

"Not from lack of interest," Damien says loyally. "He's just always practicing or doing school stuff or working. He hardly ever has extra time and never breaks curfew. The coaches love him."

Everyone over the age of thirty in the room nods approvingly.

Everyone under the age of thirty rolls their eyes.

"What about you, Damien?" one of the aunts asks. "Do you have a girlfriend?"

"I bet," Piper's teenage sister murmurs.

It's the uncles' turn to communally roll their eyes.

"No," Damien says. "No girlfriend."

"Why not?" Piper asks.

And Damien doesn't know how to respond.

This isn't something he's prepared for. He doesn't know if the rules here are different. If he needs to lie by omission or risk being kicked out—risk having to leave Rome to handle the hearing alone. Potentially risk his own safety.

He looks sideways, hoping for assistance, and Rome has stilled, but he meets Damien's eyes calmly.

He lifts one shoulder subtly, not a warning, just an indication to proceed as he wants.

"Because," Damien says. "Girls aren't really my thing."

The table goes briefly silent.

A woman in a Habs hat on the opposite side of the room grins widely at him.

"What *is* your thing?" Piper asks around a mouthful of potatoes.

"Boys," Damien says.

Piper looks crestfallen. "Does that mean you don't like to be friends with girls then?" she asks.

"Oh, no. I totally do. It just means I don't want to kiss girls."

"Well, that's fine," Piper says, like he's being stupid. "Kissing is gross anyways. So you're going to marry a boy some day? Like Aunt Maura is going to marry a girl some day?"

"Maura?" Damien says.

"Hi," Habs hat says. "I'm Maura. Resident Lesbian. Congratulations. You've upped Port Marta's current out queer population to three. Charles at the general store would be delighted to meet you, just FYI."

The relief is like a punch to the chest.

Damien grins back at her.

"Guess we should have known, considering those flowery boots," one of the men at the table says. It's clearly not malicious, meant to be a joke, but Rome shoots him a glare with such vitriol that Damien feels oddly warmed.

"Don't be ignorant, Joe," one of the women says—Piper's mom, maybe? "Just because I grew up wearing your hand-me-down clothes with trucks and boats on them doesn't mean I ever wanted to steal your girl-friends. Though I probably could have. If I wanted."

"And god knows all the bows Mama tried to perma-nently affix to my head didn't make any difference in me *trying* to steal your girlfriends," Maura adds.

The gray-haired woman at the end of the rectangle table, who Damien guesses is their mother, sighs.

"Speaking of," Maura says. "When was the last time you had a girlfriend, Joe? Longer than it's been for me, I think."

Rome's uncle—Bruce? Piper's dad, Damien thinks—brings the conversation back around to school and asks about Rome's grades, and Damien exhales.

Shortly after dinner, the house empties because everyone over the age of sixteen has to work the next day.

The house feels strangely silent after the last car has left, even though it's still full of people. Bruce and Elaine, Rome's aunt and uncle, owners of the property, are washing dishes together in the kitchen, their movements habitual and sweet. Their kids take turns getting ready for bed in the house's single bathroom.

Damien and Rome set the living room to rights, straightening recliners and folding blankets and tossing communal toys into a basket under the TV. Then Rome goes to bring some firewood in from the porch while Damien gets coerced into reading Piper her bedtime story.

Later, Damien lies on his back on one of the couches, a handmade quilt tucked around him, and stares at the shadowed ceiling.

"Hey," Rome says from the other full-sized couch, head only a foot or so away from Damien's, feet hanging off the opposite end. "I should have told you about Maura. I didn't think to."

"It's okay. I should have asked, but I didn't think it'd come up, and then I didn't want to lie, but I also didn't want to get kicked out."

"Yeah," Rome says wryly. "Because driving a half hour to the nearest hotel would have really sucked in comparison to this."

He can't see Rome very well in the dark, but Damien can tell he's gesturing to their current accommodations.

"Well," Damien says. "I would have been alone. And I wouldn't have been able to go to your hearing. So. Yeah. That would have sucked."

Rome doesn't say anything for several seconds. "Anyway," he mutters roughly. "Sorry."

"It's fine. When did Maura come out?"

Rome makes an uncertain noise. "When I was pretty young, I guess. My dad wouldn't let me spend much time with her growing up because of it. She's cool though. I took her place as a sternman on Uncle Bruce's boat when she got her own boat a few years back. She has an all-female crew, and they consistently have some of the highest numbers in the harbor. She's kind of a legend. Her call name is Anne Bonny."

Damien knew he liked Maura.

He thinks about her sharp smile.

He thinks about the critical way she'd watched Damien and Rome.

He thinks about what she said—that Damien upped Port Marta's out queer population to three.

He thinks about that number: three.

One: Maura. Two: Charles from the general store. Three: Damien.

He wonders if the way she'd said *out* was pointed.

He thinks about Rome holding his hand in the car.

He wants to ask, but he doesn't.

"How are you feeling about tomorrow?" he says instead. "Nervous?"

"As fuck," Rome agrees. "Probably won't be able to sleep."

"You need me to go get Nicolaus Copernicus?" Damien asks.

Rome says nothing for several seconds and then: "I'm going to kill Piper."

"She's my favorite."

"Of course, she is. Fucking assholes, the both of you."

He can tell Rome says it with a smile though.

It's quiet for several minutes, a quiet full of wind

and creaking old-house noises and the gentle crackle of shifting logs in the fireplace.

He rolls a little so he can consider the shadowed shape of Rome's body: his head tipped back against a crocheted throw pillow. The position exposes the long column of his throat, the sharp jut of his nose, the lax curl of his fingers on the hand resting beside his face.

He's beautiful.

There's no point in denying it.

Damien can't decide if his attraction to Rome was easier to manage when he hated him. He thinks maybe it was.

Because now he wants—

He wants.

But he's not sure he can do anything about it.

Love is supposed to be a reckless thing. But all I'm made of is caution.

Damien is starting to fall asleep when he hears the cadence of Rome's breath change. It's subtle. But it's there.

Damien untucks one of his arms from the blanket and reaches blindly toward Rome's couch.

He ends up slapping Rome in the face.

"*Ow*," Rome says. "What are you doing?"

"Give me your hand," Damien says with more confidence than he feels.

"Why?"

"Why do you think, asshole?"

Rome gives him his hand.

It's awkward, their joined fingers hanging in the triangle of empty space between them.

"I know I'm not a stuffed lobster," Damien starts, "but—"

"You'll do," Rome interrupts him.

CHAPTER SIXTEEN

THE HEARING IS utterly unremarkable.

Short.

Practically casual.

Damien volunteers to drive, and Rome offers his uncle the front seat. Rome sits in the back and plays with the cuffs of the green sweater and watches the snow fall outside. They have to drive forty-five minutes to Chissa-pee Falls because Port Marta doesn't have a courthouse, and even there, the courthouse is a small brick building next to an even smaller building that claims to be the post office, next to a bait and tackle store.

Elle meets them there with a hug for both him and Damien and a handshake for Uncle Bruce.

She greets the judge by name, asks about his

daughter's gymnastic aspirations, and then spends ten minutes looking at pictures on his phone from said daughter's most recent competition. The actual hearing takes about the same amount of time as looking at the pictures.

Rome, originally afraid he'd be underdressed in khakis and the green sweater, considers the judge's scuffed waterproof boots—the same pair, incidentally, that his uncle is wearing—and the camouflage paracord bracelet on his wrist, and feels like the whole thing is bizarrely anticlimactic.

Twenty minutes later, he pays $25 at the clerk's office for a certified copy of his Declaration of Emancipation.

An hour after that, they're farther inland at yet another larger, town, and he's at a DMV office, waiting to file his MC-315 form and get a new ID that says he's—

Emancipated.

He doesn't know what his feelings are doing. He's not going to try to figure it out until he is far, far away from other people.

When they get back to the house, his uncle doesn't seem to know what to do.

"I told Joe I'd be in as soon as we finished," he says, arms crossed, leaning against the Formica countertop. "But he'd understand if—"

"No," Rome says. "I'm fine. I was going to take Damien to eat at Luella's anyway and check the boat. Maybe take him down to the lighthouse after. So. We've got a full day planned."

"Well," he says, sounding relieved. "All right. You be

careful if you go out on the water."

Rome gets a soft pat on the shoulder which is the Uncle Bruce equivalent of a sobbing, full-body hug from Kaner, and then he more or less runs out the door.

"So," Damien says, tossing his keys. "Luella's?"

"Actually," Rome says. "I want to check on the boat first. Can you drop me off there and then go explore the docks on your own for a few minutes while I take care of things?"

Damien catches his keys and doesn't throw them again. "Uh, sure? What stuff do you need to do though? I could help."

"You can't," Rome says. "Just wander around and take pictures for your Insta. The aesthetics at the cove are right up your stupid hipster alley."

"Rome," Damien says.

"Look," he snaps. "I just want to be alone for, like, five minutes, okay? Take a fucking hint."

"Okay," Damien agrees placidly. "Do you actually want to be alone though? Or do you feel like you have to be?"

"The hell does that even—"

"Hey," Damien says. "If you need to be a dick to me right now, that's okay. If you need me to leave you alone, I will. But don't make me leave because you feel like you're not allowed to have feelings in front of other people."

Rome wants to hit him. And is then immediately, viscerally horrified with himself.

He wouldn't.

He *wouldn't*.

And it isn't like Damien is wrong.

"Fine," Rome says, "but we're not talking about it."

"Okay."

"At all."

"Okay."

Damien hands Rome the keys.

Rome drives them to the docks.

The boathouse is at the far side of the cove at the end of a rocky, desolate road that necessitates four-wheel drive. The cinder block cube of a structure is perched on a little spike of land that juts out into suddenly deep, dark water.

Rome maybe stomps around a little more than necessary as he turns on the generator and then the space heater, then heads down the dock to see to the boat while they're waiting for it to warm up inside. He checks all the moorings, coaxes the engine to life, then circles the deck while it runs, more out of habit than necessity, making sure everything is okay. Damien trails quietly after him.

"I feel like this is probably a stupid question," Damien says after they've locked her back up again. "But what happens when the water freezes?"

"It won't. Not here in the harbor. Some people will dry-dock for the winter just to be safe, especially if they've got smaller, older boats, but they're all right through the winter as long as you check on them and make sure none of the fuel lines freeze up."

They leave the boat and return to the boathouse, ducking through a door several inches shorter than either of them. The small space has warmed up quickly in their absence, and they strip out of their boots and coats.

There are piles of nets and gear, rolled up maps, lightbulbs, radios, replacement parts for the trap hauler, and an assortment of toolboxes varying in age and size.

Rome turns on one of the solar lanterns and sets it on the tiny table under the single window.

"Well," he says. "Here's the boathouse."

Damien stands in the center of the room, considering the deluge of machinery and tools sharing space with a futon piled with blankets. Rome watches his eyes track from the old hockey sticks, slowly increasing in size, mounted on the wall, to the milk crate full of medals beside the futon, to the curling posters on the back of the door, to an old spiral-bound notebook of now-useless English notes on the table.

Everything is crusted with salt and smells like fish.

He doesn't want to look at Damien's face because this is the closest he still has to a childhood bedroom, a space that belonged to his previous self. And if Damien finds it lacking—how could he not?—Rome doesn't know if he can handle that.

Rome sits on the edge of the futon and pulls his wallet out of his back pocket.

At the DMV, they'd said he could keep his old license picture, but he'd asked to retake it anyway, even though that meant spending an extra five dollars.

He sets the two IDs, old and new, side by side, one on either of his thighs.

In his old picture, he's wearing one of his uncle's T-shirts and the yellow-green remnants of a week-old bruise on his temple. The stitches in his chin are fresh, and his expression dares anyone to ask how he got them.

At the time, his uncle Bruce had said Rome needed a license so he could pull his weight and help drive the younger kids to school if he was going to be living with them. He knows now it was just his uncle's way of giving him some measure of independence in a world where he felt he'd lost all control. He doesn't hate it, the picture. It reminds him of his uncle's kindness. But he doesn't like it either.

In the new picture, his shoulders are broader, his cheeks less hollow, and the most noticeable things about his face are his eyes—confident—and his freckles—everywhere. He can't even see the scar on his chin. It's a good picture. He thinks he likes it.

But.

He touches a finger to the moose head lurking in the background of the new ID, then drags the same finger to blot out his small, pixelated face.

He looks so young.

He *is* so young, even if he forgets sometimes.

And he's now entirely responsible for himself. Officially, legally, he has no family.

It doesn't mean anything, really.

Nothing is going to change.

He'll still be welcome in his aunts' and uncles' houses.

He'll go back to school and live the same exact life he's had for the last six months until graduation. And then he'll find a shitty apartment and a second job and make ends meet for a month before the draft and then...then, he'll turn eighteen, and he'll hopefully be signed somewhere or at least headed to college to start a life where it doesn't matter that neither of his parents wanted him. And he can make sure, at least, to not repeat their mistakes with his own children. He will never be so cruel, so selfish as to create something that needs love and then abandon it.

Suddenly, the minor peace he'd found in the habitual movements of checking the boat is gone.

He takes a breath, chokes on it, and then takes an angrier one.

He folds the cuff of the green sweater over his knuckles and drags it viciously across his face.

"Hey," Damien says. "What can I do?"

"Shut up," Rome says.

Damien shuts up. He moves to stand next to Rome, arms crossed, but not impatient, and waits.

"You're going to sit there," Rome says, pointing to the far side of the futon, "against the wall."

"Okay."

"And I'm—"

Damien keeps waiting.

"I'm going to sit in front of you and lean back against you. And you're going to hold on to me. Really—" He swallows. "Really fucking tight. And you aren't going to say *anything*."

"Okay."

Damien listens. He doesn't say anything as he follows Rome's instructions. He doesn't say anything about how Rome is maybe, definitely, crying, or how he's stretching out the cuffs of the sweater Damien gave him because Rome has balled the sleeves into his fists and is pressing them into his eyes.

Damien wraps his arms around Rome and pulls Rome back solidly against his chest. He hooks his chin over Rome's shoulder. He brackets his hips, tight, with his thighs.

It helps. Maybe.

But it isn't enough to stop whatever is happening in his chest.

Rome knows how to deal with sadness. He knows how to deal with pain and disappointment and regret. But this is a different sort of beast than mourning. This is grief mixed with anger mixed with triumph. And it sits like a fiery, screaming thing inside him that he doesn't know how to let out or even if he should.

"Hey," Damien says, and Rome realizes, absently, that he's shaking.

Damien shifts him, shoves him, so his knees end up hooked over one of Damien's thighs and his face is pushed into Damien's throat. One of Damien's arms wraps around his rib cage, crushing them even tighter together, and his other hand cups the back of Rome's neck, thumb pressed to his pulse.

"Hey," Damien says, more urgently. "Hey, you gotta breathe, Rome."

Rome tries to respond. He tries to say *shut the fuck up, I said no talking.*

Except it doesn't work.

His mouth is open, but he doesn't think he's making any noise, or at least not words. It's just hitching, wet breaths that shudder in and out of him, horrible and unwieldy and entirely without his permission.

Rome pushes his fists harder into his eyes.

"Hey," Damien says again. "Hey, no, it's okay."

His mouth presses against Rome's temple—maybe a kiss, maybe just an accident.

His arms around him tighten.

"Just breathe," he says. "I've got you."

And he does.

*

ROME WAKES UP with a headache, a dry mouth, and a strange cathartic emptiness in his chest.

His eyes feel gritty and swollen.

"Hey," Damien says, inches away, when he opens his eyes.

Rome closes them again when he remembers.

"No," Damien says, "come on."

"I'm sorry," he says.

"Don't you fucking dare."

Rome opens his eyes.

They've sort of managed to slump horizontally on the futon, but Damien is still partially propped on the wall, and it can't be comfortable.

"How long was I asleep?" Rome asks, straightening.

His face is a mess of dried snot and tears, but he doesn't want to wipe it on the green sweater. He's already stretched out the sleeves; he doesn't need to completely ruin it.

"Not long. Maybe fifteen minutes. Seems like you needed it."

Damien stretches, leaning over the side to pull a water bottle out of his backpack, then shifts so he's sprawled in the space Rome has left. "Hey, come here."

Rome looks down at him. "What?"

"Come here."

It takes a series of halting movements, but he obeys.

Rome accepts a drink out of the proffered water bottle, belly down. He's propped up on his elbows, then tips a little into one hand and drags a wet palm over his face. Except then, he has a wet face and still nothing to dry it with. He elects to use the quilt on the futon. It's seen worse.

Damien laughs and smooths Rome's eyebrows flat again with his thumbs. "You feeling better?" he asks.

"Yeah." He considers apologizing again but doesn't. "Thank you," he says. It takes effort.

Damien grins because he knows. "So you said something about a lighthouse earlier?"

"Yeah. We can go if you want. We'll need to stop for food first though. It's way past lunch."

"Are we going to argue about money?"

"Probably."

"How about..." Damien pauses, sitting up. "First one back to the car pays?"

"Deal," Rome says, already diving for his shoes.

Except Damien doesn't stop to put on his shoes. He just scoops them up with his coat on his way out the door and runs in his socks, shrieking like a loon, to the Range Rover.

By the time Rome has laced his boots, locked up, and joined him, Damien is sitting in the driver's seat, laughing uproariously, pulling off his damp, snow-covered socks and shaking them out the open window.

"I hate you," Rome says, slamming the passenger door.

"Don't play," Damien says. "You love me."

He might.

It's sort of becoming a problem.

*

ROME TAKES DAMIEN to the most beautiful spots he can think of. They're all pretty bleak, considering the heavy blanket of winter and intermittent snowfall, but Damien seems excited about every new location. Between making Rome take pictures of him, backgrounded by steep cliffs and giant rocks and crashing surf, and making Rome take pictures *with* him, he runs out of phone battery.

They hold hands again, without either of them discussing it, while they drive back to the house. And when they get there, Rome slips his hand back in Damien's as they walk across the yard, and up the steps, and onto the porch, just because he isn't quite ready to stop yet.

Because Damien will let him.

Because he wants to.

Because it makes him happy, and he's decided he deserves happiness.

They separate before he opens the door, and he's afraid Damien might try to make him talk about it. Except, once inside, they're almost immediately accosted by Piper, who commandeers Damien for an "important mission."

Nearly simultaneously, Uncle Bruce asks Rome to

help him bring wood from the wood pile up to the porch.

"So," his uncle says as they descend the steps.

Rome braces himself because a "so" in that tone from anyone in his family means nothing good.

"Henry said he saw you two at the docks earlier."

Rome briefly considers going and locking himself in the Range Rover. He still has the key in his pocket. It's an option.

"He said you got there looking real upset and came out of the boathouse an hour later looking a whole lot better."

Rome shrugs.

"You said you don't have a girlfriend," his uncle says. "Should I be asking if you have a boyfriend?"

Rome throws another plaintive look toward the Range Rover. "No."

"No," Uncle Bruce repeats. It's a very judgmental no.

"We're not together. I mean, I do...I would. But we're not. So."

Jesus. He's a train wreck.

"Not together," Uncle Bruce repeats. Uncle Bruce likes repeating things. "You telling me you hold hands with all of the boys on your hockey team?"

"What? *No.* What do you mean?"

"The house has windows, son."

Right.

His uncle also manages to make silence judgmental.

"So, what," Uncle Bruce says. "You're hoping the two of you might just accidentally fall into a relationship without ever having to talk about it?"

Rome winces.

"Kid. Your grades tell me that you're not stupid. But that? Is pretty damn stupid."

"I was really fucking terrible to him," Rome admits. "I treated him like shit for the first solid month that I knew him."

"Did you apologize?"

"Yeah."

"With words?'

"Yes."

"Have you quit treating him like shit?"

"I mean. Obviously."

"I don't see the problem, then."

Rome sighs. "It's complicated."

"That boy looks at you like the sun shines out your ass," Uncle Bruce says. "I don't think he's holding any grudges."

Rome would really like to not be having this conversation anymore. "His family is— He has a lot of money."

"No shit?" Uncle Bruce glances at the now-mud-splattered Range Rover. "I never would have figured."

"Oh my god, would you stop?"

"Still don't see the problem."

"I thought we were getting wood," Rome says, maybe a little desperately.

His uncle shakes his head and looks at the porch, already fully stacked with split logs. He throws his hands up and walks back toward the house. "Maybe the boy really is stupid," he mutters to himself.

Rome can't argue with him.

CHAPTER SEVENTEEN

THEY DRIVE BACK the next day.

They wait until midday to leave, but the roads are still icy and the sky gray. Intermittent snowfall shadows them from slushy, one-lane back roads to the slick, salted highway.

Damien drives while Rome sleeps. They stop for gas, swap places, and Damien tries unsuccessfully to nap for another hour or so.

They're passing through Portland when he gives up, and Rome says, suspiciously casual, "You want to play some music?"

Damien raises an eyebrow at him. "Only if you're going to sing with me."

Rome grins.

By the time they hit the Maine/New Hampshire line they're both hoarse and hungry. They stop for food just past the bridge and switch drivers again.

Rome, holding Damien's phone, aux cable tangled distractedly around his wrist and between his fingers says, "Do you want me to play some of your music?"

"My music," Damien repeats.

"Yeah. Like, you don't need to distract me anymore or whatever. I'm okay."

That seems fair.

Damien requests some Ibeyi first, then Childish Gambino, then FKA Twigs. He mixes it up with some Joanne Cash, Michael Burks, and Nina Simone before switching gears entirely to The National.

He requests "Slow Show" specifically, immediately regrets his life choices, and then stares studiously out the front window, refusing to look at Rome, for the following three minutes and fifty seconds of damning lyrics.

When he does hazard a glance at Rome, his face is turned away, looking out the passenger window, and Damien can't tell if the back of his neck is slightly pinker than normal or not.

Damien decides he's done with potentially damning lyrics for the day. He asks Rome to find Explosions in the Sky and selects the entire *The Earth is Not a Cold Dead Place* album to play.

He waits several minutes to say, "So I might have done something stupid."

Rome shifts his whole body when he turns to look at him.

"What?"

Damien opens his mouth and then closes it again. He wonders if maybe Rome will forget he said something if he just...stays silent.

"Damien," Rome says.

"It's nothing bad. Nothing that will affect the team."

"Okay," Rome says. "But will it affect you?"

Damien swallows. "We don't actually have to talk about it. I don't know why I said anything. It's personal shit."

"I fucking cried on you yesterday," Rome says. "I think we're at the point where you can tell me personal shit."

It sounds like maybe Rome is saying *I want to hear your personal shit.*

Wouldn't that be something.

"My adoption was closed," Damien says. "Which means my birth parents didn't have any contact with me. In a closed adoption, once a kid turns eighteen, they can contact the agency and request information, and there's this reunion registry so biological family members can find one another."

He hasn't told anyone this.

Rome's fingers, worrying absently at the aux cable, go still. "Okay."

"So when I turned eighteen, I did all that shit. Except after a few weeks, nothing turned up. So I ordered the 23andMe thing. Where you spit in the tube and send it off, and they tell you all about your genetics but also have this massive database that can connect you with people who are related to you."

"Okay," Rome says again. He turns the volume down.

"But I just kept the box. Without opening it. For a month. Except then, four days ago, the day you showed up, I woke up that morning and just did it. I walked the test down to the post office and sent it. And then freaked out and got drunk."

"Okay."

Damien lapses into silence.

He turns on the windshield wipers because it's started snowing again.

"How is that stupid?" Rome asks. It's tentative, which is strange. Damien can't remember a time when Rome has ever been tentative.

"Because I think I waited so long for a reason. And now I'm afraid to get the results back."

"Why?"

"I don't know. Never mind."

"Why did you want to contact your birth family anyway?" Rome asks.

Damien knows what Rome is doing.

"My therapist would probably say I'm looking for validation I'm not receiving from my parents."

"I didn't ask for your therapist's opinion."

"Fuck you."

He says it so quietly, so self-consciously, that Rome doesn't respond.

Damien sighs. "I'm probably just setting myself up for an even bigger letdown," he admits. "Whoever my biological parents are, they haven't updated their contact information. They haven't registered online. Clearly, they don't want me to find them, and they never wanted me in the first place, so..."

Rome's hand circles Damien's right wrist, tugging until he lets go of the steering wheel.

"I don't know much about adoption," Rome says, forcing his fingers between Damien's. "But I'm pretty sure that's a huge oversimplification. And this shit probably takes time. It's only been a couple months."

"What if I do find them, and they don't care though? What if they're awful? What if they want nothing to do with me?"

And that's the crux of it.

That's why he waited so long to spit in the stupid tube.

What if knowing is worse than not knowing.

"Then fuck 'em," Rome says easily. "There are a shit ton of other people who do care. That want you. That love you."

He stumbles a little over the last sentence, fingers curling a little, nails scratching a little, against the back of Damien's hand. "You're worth that. Being wanted. Loved. And if they've got shit for brains and can't see it, or aren't willing to take the time and figure it out, then— fuck 'em."

The speakers take over the following silence, the last bars of "Memorial" fading into the first isolated chords of "Your Hand in Mine."

He laughs, maybe a little hysterically.

"So," Damien says because it's more than time for a subject change. "I've noticed we've started holding hands."

"No," Rome says.

Damien glances at their fingers, linked together and resting on the center console.

"What do you mean, 'no'?"

"We're not talking about it," Rome says.

"I mean. We are. Kind of. Right now. And we probably should."

"No talking," Rome says. "If you're holding my hand, you're not allowed to talk about holding my hand."

That's an easy choice to make.

They lapse into silence for the rest of the drive. It's a quiet filled with the lull of windshield wipers and the soft acoustic ebb and flow of *The Wilderness*.

Rome doesn't let go of his hand until they park in the student garage.

*

THINGS GO TO shit the next day.

They're fine that night, through defrosted TV dinners and two episodes of *Deadliest Catch*, and then Rome goes to bed early. But Rome still initiates their knock-through-the-wall routine, so that's okay.

The following morning, though, Damien can't find Rome.

There's no answer when he taps on Rome's door at 9:00 a.m., so Damien runs alone, eats breakfast alone, and then, after waiting an awkward amount of time in the common room, decides to go into town for groceries. It will be another day before the dining hall opens for spring semester and the options in the dorm kitchen are pretty much down to peanut butter and protein powder.

He picks up KD and chicken salad fixings, feeling a little nostalgic.

Except then he goes home and fills up the refrigerator and...there's still no Rome. And his phone stays silent. And he's lost.

Because he basically bared his soul the day before. Told Rome how messed up he was over feeling abandoned and then Rome—

Whatever.

He makes dinner by himself.

At 7:00 p.m., he decides the day is a wash and goes upstairs to lay on his bed and listen to too-loud music. Except when he hears Rome's door open in the hall, he forgets for a minute that he's angry.

He remembers by the time he's standing in Rome's room, but by then it's too late.

"Hey," he says, feeling a little off-balance. "Can you talk?"

"Since I was two." Rome is mussed and breathless, T-shirt dirty, cheeks pink, hands tucked under his arms. He smells like sweat and gasoline and outside. He's looking in his closet, not at Damien.

"Okay, asshole," Damien says. "I meant can you talk right now?"

"Do you hear the words coming out of my mouth?"

"Unfortunately," he grits out.

Rome still doesn't look at him.

"You know what? Never mind."

"*What*?" Rome says, exasperated, shutting his closet door.

"Nothing," Damien says again.

"Well, obviously it's something, or you wouldn't have decided to grace me with your presence."

Damien opens his mouth to argue because, what the fuck, Rome is the one who's been avoiding *him*.

He exhales. "No. I can't do this with you tonight. So I'm just—I'm going to go."

Rome's obstinate expression wavers. "What? You can't do what?"

"Pretend I hate you. Or whatever it is that we do. Pretend we don't care. Because I do. Even if you don't. And I'm just so tired of—"

Rome kisses him.

Well.

There are things that happened leading up to it.

Like Rome closing the space between them and pushing him up against the door and wrapping one of his big, callused hands around Damien's jaw.

But the point is: Rome kisses him.

It's quick and rough and more of an argument than a gesture of affection.

It's still a kiss.

"I fucking care," Rome snaps.

"Oh," Damien says. "Well. Okay. Good."

He doesn't know where to go from here.

Luckily, Rome does.

The second kiss is better.

The second kiss is: Soft. Hesitant. Chaste.

It is: Gentle. Cautious. Achingly sweet.

The kiss is full of adjectives that do not apply to Rome. Full of adjectives that are, in fact, the opposite of

Rome.

And yet.

The kiss is very, very Rome.

The third and fourth and fifth kiss sort of merge together, and then Rome is dropping his forehead to Damien's shoulder, breathing hard.

"Sorry," he says. "I'm sorry. I shouldn't have..."

"If you're apologizing for kissing me—"

"I'm not. I'm apologizing for being a dick before kissing you."

"Oh. Well, carry on then."

"Sorry," he repeats.

"Wow. Solid apology, Roman. A-plus work."

"Now who's being a dick?"

Damien grins. "Why have you been avoiding me all day?"

Rome straightens. "I haven't. I was working. And then I came home and all the lights were off and *you* were in your room avoiding *me*."

"Oh."

It occurs to Damien that they're both idiots.

"Why didn't you tell me you had to work? I was wondering where you were all day."

"I...didn't know you would care? And I didn't want to be clingy or whatever. I figured you'd want some space."

"Why would I need space?"

"Because you just spent the last four straight days with me."

"Yeah, it was great."

"Damien."

"Rome."

"I don't want you to get tired of me," Rome says quietly.

"Not going to happen. And if I need space, I'll tell you. So maybe don't assume what I want next time. Because I would have rather spent my afternoon with you."

Rome rolls his eyes, but he sways forward a little, leaving them chest to chest. "I spent my afternoon at the garage."

"I like the garage. I could have hung out there. Watched you work." The last sentence comes out a little more suggestive than he intended. He clears his throat before Rome can comment on it. "I mean. Are you tired of me?"

"No."

"Right. Good."

They just stand there, braced against each other, breathing in each other's secondhand air for a moment.

"So," Damien says lowly. "I can't help but notice that we're kissing now. Are we allowed to talk about that?"

"No."

"Same rules as hand-holding apply? If we're kissing, we're not talking about the kissing?"

"Yes," Rome grits out.

"Well, technically, we're not currently ki—"

Ah. But apparently, they are.

He lets it happen.

And he lets it keep happening until Rome has him pushed against the door again, mouth hot and wet, hands uncertain but charmingly desperate as they pull at his shirt.

Damien grins into the kiss, leaning away so they can both take a breath. "You have no idea what you're doing, huh?"

Rome jerks back, the flush on his neck creeping quickly into his cheeks. "Fuck you."

"No, I mean— That came out wrong. You haven't done this before, though, have you?"

It's less of a shock than it should be, probably, considering the way Rome looks. Yes, he's attractive, but it's hard to imagine him being vulnerable enough, gentle enough, to kiss someone.

Well.

Someone other than Damien.

And isn't that thrilling.

"No," Rome confirms grudgingly and then: "Try not to look so happy about it, asshole."

"Sorry," Damien says.

He's not sorry.

"I wasn't trying to make fun of you," Damien says. "It's not like you're bad at it or anything."

"Oh, thanks."

"Just, slow down. We've got time."

Rome looks like he doesn't believe him.

"Also, as hot as you manhandling me is, I have a doorknob in my back right now, which isn't the most comfortable."

"Well, I've got a bed," Rome says. Like it's Damien's fault they aren't there already.

Rome is so infuriating.

Damien pulls him over to it and then has to stop

Rome from climbing directly into his lap.

"We can go slow."

"No," Rome says and then bites his lip. "I want—" He stalls out, shifting, his knees butting against Damien's thigh, fingers still curled in the hem of Damien's shirt. "I want you."

"Okay," Damien says, and he has to close his eyes for a minute because he doesn't know if he can get the next few sentences out with Rome looking at him like that.

"Okay," Damien says again. "But I think this is something we should talk about. Even if it's just in terms of what we want. And if we can't talk about it, we probably shouldn't do it."

Rome doesn't move. But he doesn't say anything either.

Damien opens his eyes.

Rome's head is ducked, eyes on his hands—the black edges around his nails. Damien can see Rome's pulse jumping in his throat. He wants to put his mouth over it, but that would sort of negate everything he just said.

"I don't know," Rome says finally. "But I fucking—I want to touch you *all the time*. Have been wanting. So. There's that."

"Well," Damien says. "Okay."

And he can see exactly how this might go. He'd lean over and press Rome back against the pillows, pull his shirt up and his jeans down, and lick the dried sweat off his skin.

Rome would let him.

Rome would probably let him do just about anything right now.

But he also knows that's a very, very bad idea.

"Full disclosure," Damien says. "I don't think we should have sex."

"What?" Rome says. "Why?" His expression goes immediately calculating. "How are you defining sex?"

"Orgasms."

"What?" he repeats, whinier this time. "Why?"

Damien wants to say: *Because we've barely figured out how to be friends, and I don't want to fuck that up. Because you're in mourning, or something like it. Because I'm scared.*

Instead, he says, "Because, I'm not ready for that. I want to. Believe me; I've thought about it. Just not yet."

"Oh," Rome says. "Sorry." He starts to sit up

"No. Kissing is good. And I'd really like to take your shirt off. So I can kiss more of you. Would that be cool?"

Rome swallows. "I haven't taken a shower yet."

"I know," Damien says darkly.

Rome flushes further. "Will you take *your* shirt off?" he asks.

"You realize," Damien says conversationally, "that we're talking about kissing, right? That thing you said we couldn't talk about? And you're participating."

"Shut up. Fine. We can talk about kissing. Will you take your shirt off too?"

Damien grins, hooking his fingers into the back of the shirt in question. He pulls it over his head in one smooth movement. "Sure."

Rome seems a little frozen, so Damien goes ahead

and tugs Rome's shirt off, too, because he's helpful like that.

And then he pauses, trailing his fingers over Rome's darkly freckled shoulders, shadowed and beautiful and washed in sepia from the fairy lights on the bookshelf. He thumbs the softer, paler skin on the inside of Rome's biceps and then wraps his fingers around Rome's wrists, pulling his hands into the space between them.

He ducks to press a kiss to each of Rome's palms, grinning at the resulting wake of goosebumps that creep up his forearms, and then laces their fingers together.

"Does that mean we can talk about hand-holding now too?" Damien asks innocently.

"I'm going to fucking kill you," Rome says.

CHAPTER EIGHTEEN

PATRICK ROMAN'S FIRST crush was Amanda Kierne in the first grade. She had brown eyes, short curly hair, and could throw a dodgeball with vicious accuracy. She liked the color purple, arm wrestling, and had an ency-clopedic knowledge of butterflies.

Rome's second crush was Jason Maverick in the fourth grade. He was the center on Rome's mite hockey team: blue eyes, soft hands, and an even softer voice. Quiet and kind, he was taller than Rome but always seemed to take up less space. Sometimes, he would share his before-practice snacks.

Rome's third crush was Emily Greenspan, and it lasted through both seventh and eighth grades. Every-one called her Spanner. Spanner had hazel eyes, a dirty-blonde mohawk, an even dirtier mouth, and a wicked left hook. She played defense, the only girl on Rome's bantam hockey team, and she wore pink laces on her skates so no one would forget it. Spanner was the first time Rome ever looked at someone and thought: *I want to kiss you.* His crush on her lasted right up until he moved to a new team freshman year of high school and met Spanner's older brother.

Rome's fourth crush was Aaron Greenspan. The team called him Greenie. He was a lot like Spanner—hazel eyes, olive skin, gold-brown hair and a predilection for violence. But Greenie was bigger. Meaner. Louder. He was two years older than Rome and called him "kid," which Rome hated, but he also sat next to him on the bus and didn't pull away when Rome leaned against his shoulder, which Rome liked. Greenie would help him sort through the Lost and Found at various rinks to steal—*commandeer,* he called it—new equipment for Rome. And he carried around a jar of peanut butter in his hockey bag with a spoon he didn't mind sharing. Rome had a lot of fraught feelings about that shared spoon.

He never acted on any of his crushes, male or female. At first, it was because he was too young and too shy to do anything but pine from afar. Later, it was because he knew he couldn't. He couldn't date boys because his father was a homophobic asshole. But he couldn't date girls either because dating necessitated time and money and possibly nudity and talking, and Rome couldn't facilitate any of those things. He had no time and no money and secrets he wasn't willing to share—some of them visible under his clothes. Being alone was both safer and easier.

So. No dating.

His father never suspected he was gay. Or liked boys as well as girls, so bisexual? Pansexual? Whatever he is, his father never knew. Patrick Roman the First had ideas about what those kinds of boys looked like, and with his lean muscle and shaved head and beat-up thrift-store clothes, Rome didn't fit any of them.

He told Maura when he was sixteen because if there was anyone in the family it was safe to tell, it was her, and he wanted to tell *someone*.

It was a Friday in July. Both Uncle Bruce and Maura had docked at Port Winter to offload their catches, and then the two crews met up at a bar. Maura bought Rome his first beer, and within two minutes of her putting it in his hand, he quietly said, "I think I like boys the same way you like girls."

She turned her hat around backward and leaned her chin on her fist and said, "Well, isn't that something. You want to tell me about it?"

He didn't.

"You planning on telling other folks?" she asked.

They both knew what she meant: Are you planning to tell your father?

"No," he said. "Not yet. Maybe not ever."

She finished her beer before speaking again.

"You tell me if you do. I'll make sure nobody's a dick about it." She looked thoughtful. "Well. I can't promise that. But I can promise that if they are a dick about it, they'll be real sorry afterward."

He appreciated it then, and he appreciates it now.

The only difference is he didn't actually think he'd ever need to take her up on the offer. He always planned to turn eighteen and get the hell out of Port Marta and maybe, years later, find a girl to marry. Regardless of where he ended up in the world, that was the safest, the most normal option.

Now though.

Patrick Roman's fifth crush is Damien Raphael Bordeaux, and the word "crush" feels woefully inadequate. Damien has stupidly pretty brown eyes, a deep laugh, and a one-dimpled smile. He likes plants and poetry and Rome, apparently. He is strong and gentle, infuriating but kind, and words do not suit the things that Rome feels about him.

He is also, currently, in Rome's bed.

They're sort of awkwardly tangled because twin beds aren't meant to house two adult, or nearly adult, men. Rome isn't sure how they got here. How he went from exhaustion and uncertainty to slow kisses and warm skin.

It is a strange, tenuous place to exist, one that falls somewhere between wanting what he can't have and having what he shouldn't want, and he doesn't know how to navigate it.

Damien is awake, more on top of than next to him, ear pressed to the center of his chest, tracing gentle, barely-there fingertips over Rome's rose tattoo.

Rome's arms are loosely wrapped around him, deceptively casual, hands moving lazily up and down the broad expanse of Damien's back. While he was really hoping for sex, this is nice too. Rome thinks Damien probably has the most beautiful shoulder blades in existence, which he realizes is a ridiculous thing to fixate on, but it's also true.

He licks his lips, tender and chapped, and tries to focus. "So. About earlier."

"Earlier?" Damien says.

"Um. When you first came in. What did you want to talk to me about?"

"Oh. I want to get Piper a telescope. But I wanted to make sure it was okay first. And I'll need your uncle's address."

"A telescope," Rome repeats.

"Yeah. She asked for one for Christmas because she wants to be—"

"An astronaut. I know. But a telescope is a lot."

Damien shifts enough to meet his eyes, beseeching.

"I wouldn't get, like, a crazy fancy one. Just a starter one. Something basic but nice quality. Besides, I owe her. She snuck these into my bag."

He fishes in his back pocket and sets them just below Rome's collarbone.

Matching sparkly claw clips.

From Piper, a significant gift.

Rome touches the glittery wing of one of them.

"Yeah," he says. "Okay. I'll get you the address."

Pleased, Damien returns his treasure to his pocket, then flops back onto Rome's chest. He presses an absent kiss to Rome's sternum and then goes back to tracing Rome's tattoo.

Rome thinks about it. Damien was apparently upset

over not knowing where Rome was all day. That Damien would rather spend the afternoon keeping Rome company at the garage than being alone. That, while Damien was alone, he was thinking about Rome's cousin. Understanding the importance of her gift. Coming up with a way to encourage her huge, ridiculous dreams. Wanting to make her happy.

He thinks about it: the way Damien looks at him between kisses.

Like he's exceptional. Special. Worthy of awe.

He needs to know, Rome thinks. He needs to know exactly what he's getting into.

Exactly what Rome comes from.

He reaches out and pushes Damien's fingers, stark against the winter-pale skin of his ribcage, down to the space under his arm. He presses their hands flat to cup the date inked there over his ribs.

"You asked about this before. February eleventh."

Damien props himself up with his opposite elbow, just a few inches, enough to meet Rome's eyes. "You said you didn't want to talk about it."

"I do now."

"Okay."

Rome takes a slow breath. "February eleventh was the day I fought back."

It's a good start, but he's so focused on getting the initial sentence out that now he stalls, uncertain how to backtrack.

Damien waits.

"I'd come home from a hockey game late. Around 11:00 p.m. One of the other guys dropped me off. My stepmother was at her parents'—her mom was real sick then—and the girls were asleep. Dad was up. Drunk. Pissed about something. I didn't even mean to, really. I never had before. But he swung at me, and I was still so keyed up from the game. I'd nearly fought a defender that night, and it was automatic. To stop him. To *make* him stop. It hadn't ever occurred to me up until then that I'd gotten bigger than him, stronger than him. I didn't realize I could fight back until I caught his fist."

"Tell me you beat the shit out of him."

Rome laughs without humor. "Can't do that. I might have, but as soon as I got a punch in, he broke a bottle of scotch over my head. Once I'd passed out, he fucked up my ribs for good measure. Steel-toe boots, you know."

He pushes harder at Damien's hand. He pushes Damien's fingers against the rib that had taken the longest to heal. "This one here was the worst. Hurt every time I breathed. That's why I got the tattoo there."

"What happened? After."

"He left me in the kitchen. Went to go buy more scotch. He was at the liquor store when the cops arrested him. Ashley—my little sister—she called 911. She woke up and thought Dad had killed me."

Damien doesn't say anything but the muscles in his back have gone taught under Rome's left hand.

After several long seconds of silence, Damien kneels up, slides his hands down to bracket Rome's waist, and leans forward, head ducked, to press his mouth—gently, so fucking gently—to the arc of Rome's ribcage, following the inked line under his arm with a slow train of kisses.

When he sits back up, thumbs moving restlessly against the hollowed skin above Rome's hips, he looks furious in a way Rome would never have expected, considering the soft kindness of his actions.

"Where else?" Damien asks.

"What?" It comes out a little breathless, maybe.

"Where else did he hurt you?" Damien ducks and touches his lips briefly to the scar on Rome's chin. "Here, right?"

And Rome doesn't know if he's going to survive this. Whatever it is.

"Fuck you," he says, completely devoid of heat. "I can't—I don't know what to do when you're being like this."

"'Being like this.'" Damien's mouth curves up a little on one side. He kisses Rome's chin again. "Being nice? I'm always nice to you. Or recently, anyway."

"No. Being all...gentle. I'm not fucking breakable."

It doesn't sound true, the cracked way he says it, but Damien's eyebrows go serious and pinched.

"I know you're not," he says. "Obviously. I'm the only one on the team that outweighs you, and you've got me on height. In a year or two, you'll probably be one of the best up-and-coming players in the NHL. And you did it all yourself. Without the help you should have had. You're one of the strongest people I know."

One of his hands slides up to splay, palm down, over the center of Rome's chest. "But strong people need gentleness, too, sometimes."

Rome doesn't say anything because he doesn't know if he can without embarrassing himself.

Instead, he points to the crown of his head, above his temple and a little to the left.

"Here," he says.

It takes Damien a second.

And then he grins, both hands moving to cup Rome's jaw, to tip Rome's head forward so Damien can press his mouth to the soft bristly hair next to Rome's finger. He looks down, ducking a little to meet Rome's eyes, uncertain.

"There?"

"Yeah," Rome agrees.

"Where else?" Damien asks.

*

OLLY ARRIVES THE following morning at 10:00 a.m.

Damien is on a post-run walk around the lake, and Rome is freshly showered, vacuuming the rug in his room—they'd ended up watching a movie the night before and there might have been a popcorn fight.

Olly comes up the stairs, hauling his rolling suitcase behind him as Rome turns off the vacuum.

"Hey," Olly stops in Rome's open door. "How did things go?"

"Good. I'm emancipated."

Olly drops his things and tackles him in a hug. Olly still has snow on his shoulders and in his hair. He smells like airplane and cold air.

"And everything was okay with your family?" Olly asks, holding him at arm's length.

"Yeah. It was good. Damien actually went with me."

Olly's arms go slack. He takes a step back. "What?"

"I, uh, ended up spending Christmas in New York with Damien. And then he drove me home for court and stayed with me there a few days before we came back."

Olly's eyes are very, very wide. "Okay. Things have clearly happened. How did...all of that go?"

Rome shoves his hands in his pockets, looking down at his bare feet, knowing he can't do anything about the inevitable blush. "Good."

"Good," Olly repeats, maybe sounds a little strangled. "Are you two...?"

Rome shrugs. He doesn't know what they are. "He likes spending time with me."

For such an innocuous observation, the sentence— the truth of it—is weighty.

"Okay?" Olly doesn't understand.

"He likes to spend time with me. Not out of obligation or because he's going to get something out of it. Just because of me. I think."

And now Olly is looking a little damp around the eyes. "You know that's not just Damien, right?"

"What do you mean?" Rome says blankly.

"Why do you think I tell you whenever I'm trying to fix something around the dorm?"

"Because I'm the only one who knows the difference between a flathead and a Phillips head screwdriver?"

"Okay, true. But that's not the real reason."

Rome continues to look at him blankly.

"I like your company," Olly says slowly. "I like you. I'd rather spend time with you than be alone."

"Oh," Rome says.

And, objectively, that makes sense, but—

"And why do you think Kaner keeps finding things in her room that need fixing?" Olly continues. "Why do you think Justin invites you to run with him? Or Chai offers to stay late and practice with you? Or any of us try to help you with your homework?"

"Because," Rome says, "I'm good at fixing things. And I'm a top-performing player. I have to stay in shape and keep my grades up. And they want to make sure I can *keep* playing."

"Okay, no," Olly says, touching his elbow. "No. We don't care about you because of the things you do. Or because we want something from you. We care about you because you're you. Because you're smart and you work so damn hard—whether it's at hockey or your homework or just...trying to be a better person. I watched Chai intentionally pull his desk drawer out of alignment two weeks ago so he could ask you how your day was going and offer you a brownie while you were there looking it. And he was so disappointed you didn't take one, by the way. He took some from the caf just for you. Wrapped them in a napkin and everything."

Rome doesn't know what to do with this information.

"The point is that we love you," Olly says. "You. Period. And that's not just Damien. That's all of us."

"Oh."

"And maybe Damien loves you a little different from the rest of us," Olly muses, raising his eyebrows pointedly, "but that's none of my business."

Rome thinks he might need to sit down.

"Hey," Olly says. "Did I break you? Do you need some time alone? Or would you like to come help me cut up some peppers? I've already ordered a pizza."

"Peppers," Rome says. Because that's simple and uncomplicated, and also, he's pretty hungry. "Did you get the banana ones?"

"You mean Damien's favorite?" Olly observes casually.

Rome elects not to say anything.

Olly sighs. It's probably fond. "I did. Let me drop off my stuff, and I'll meet you downstairs."

He retrieves his things from the floor and heads off down the hall. "Don't forget to wash your hands!"

Rome goes downstairs and washes his hands.

He doesn't wait for the water to warm up.

He lets the winter chill of it splash sharp and shocking across his wrists.

We love you, Olly said.

Rome glances at the calendar, where Olly has penciled in everyone's estimated arrival times through the day. Next to the calendar, there are a handful of instant polaroid pictures Damien had taken with his stupid hipster camera the month before. None of the pictures are very good. But they kind of are anyway. Because it's the team. All of them. Including Rome. Blurry and yelling and laughing and fighting and squished onto the couch together and—

Maybe that's love.

He'd always thought the word love was dangerous, a thing more often used for coercion or justification than romance. And even if it was used kindly it was only kind

until it was taken away.
But this sort of love—
This doesn't feel nearly as dangerous.
Still just as scary though.

CHAPTER NINETEEN

DAMIEN RAPHAEL BORDEAUX'S first crush was Aladdin. He was four, which he feels is important to emphasize when his mother gleefully shares this information at dinner parties. And sure, Aladdin was an animated character, but he was cute and kindhearted and had a flying magic carpet. All good qualities in a prospective partner, really.

Damien's second crush was Adam Pope. Damien was six. Adam was eight. Adam had white-blond hair and big blue eyes, and he lived two floors below him at the London house. Their moms enjoyed taking them on "play dates" every weekend, which were really just coffee dates for their mothers at handy playgrounds or children's museums. Damien and Adam usually got in trouble, and it was usually Adam's fault because he was older and kind of bossy. But Adam was also sweet. He would help boost Damien into trees if he couldn't reach the bottom branches. He'd help him read instructions at the experiment lab in the science museum. He'd kiss Damien's skinned knees and give him piggyback rides, and when they had sleepovers, he didn't make fun of Damien's favorite stuffed cat. Adam moved two days before Damien's seventh birthday. He cried.

Damien's third crush was Richard West. Richard was a boy in his second-grade class with dark center-parted hair and a permanently serious expression who spent the first day of school studiously raising his hand every time the teacher asked a question. It was a short-lived crush, however, because the next day, Damien sat with Richard at lunch, and Richard said Percy Jackson was stupid. Obviously, that was unforgivable.

Damien's fourth crush was Yuri Takada. Yuri had black hair and a wide smile, and he was sitting on the opposite side of Damien when Richard West said Percy Jackson was stupid. Yuri called Richard "uncultured swine," and Damien fell briefly in love. Briefly, because a week later, Yuri said soccer was better than hockey, which was nearly as unforgivable as calling Percy Jackson stupid.

Damien's fifth and sixth and seventh and all of his subsequent crushes followed the same pattern. He'd see a cute boy. He'd like a cute boy. And then, inevitably, he'd find something wrong with them. His mother would sigh fondly over his proclamations each week that he'd found *the one* and then soothe him through the inevitable five-minute crisis a few days later when he realized that, no, maybe Benedict Ainsworth was not "the one." Maybe he was just a stupid straight boy with a nice accent and swoopy hair, which masked the fact that he was a massive dick.

Damien never thought to hide his attractions. He wasn't afraid to tell his parents he wanted to marry Aladdin or that he thought Yuri was the prettiest boy in the world. He has a pair of gay uncles, and one of his mom's best friends is a lesbian, and he's been going to Pride events dressed in rainbows since before he can remember. He didn't even realize there were people—places—in the world who had a problem with queer people until halfway through elementary school. He knows now that's a privilege a lot of kids don't have. Most gay thirteen-year-olds don't get to hold hands with their middle school crushes in the hallways without fear.

But this privilege, the confidence in his family's support, ensured his crush-related tendencies continued through high school, through moving from London preparatory schools to American boarding schools, through classroom flirtations and various hockey rosters and philanthropy events and dorm parties. Most of the time, his crushes turn out to be straight. But the sheer volume of them still means Damien has kissed a lot of boys and done rather more than kissing with several of them. He hasn't ever seriously dated one though. He decided, the summer before senior year, that he was going to change that. He was going to focus on hockey and poetry. No flirtations in stairwells. No make outs in the stacks. When he went to college, he would date properly and have a real relationship. But senior year would be about his future.

And then, two days before the semester started, he met Patrick Roman.

Damien's one hundredth-something crush is Patrick Roman. It lasts about five minutes. Because as attractive as he is, as compellingly sharp-edged and foul-mouthed and viciously pretty as he is, Patrick Roman is an asshole. He's an asshole teammate, though, so Damien plays nice. And he doesn't have any intention of doing anything with Rome aside from playing good hockey and maybe trying to educate him a little. Except.

Except, then one night, Damien gets sad and drunk and dances with Rome.

Except, somehow, he ends up shaving Rome's head.

And inviting him home.

And holding his hand.

And kissing him.

And now, Damien is sitting on his bed, knees tucked to his chest, having a small crisis. Not only has he returned to a crush for the first time in his life—not only has he maintained interest in the same person for weeks (months?)—but he's a little afraid the word "crush" is no longer adequate for the whole...Rome Situation. Entertaining other, perhaps more apt, words is something he's not willing to do yet.

Because it's been weeks. Close to a month, even, since their first volatile kiss. It's been weeks of lingering fingers on shoulders and wrists and lower backs. Weeks of ducked heads and nudged under-the-table feet and too-wide grins on the bench and *sustained eye contact*.

Which he didn't even know was a thing for him until now, but it sure as hell is.

It's been weeks of Damien slipping into Rome's single room at night and listening to Bon Iver and The Oh Hellos and Hozier and The Head and the Heart. Weeks of slow kisses with acoustic accompaniment. Of building piano crescendos, soft harmonies, and lingering guitar chords. Weeks of fighting off sleep in the heat of tangled limbs, of mouths against temples and ears on chests and thumbs rubbing over knuckles. Weeks of whispered conversations under the glow of fairy lights.

Weeks of leaving at midnight.

Returning to his own room.

Pressing his back to the wall that separates them.

Falling asleep alone.

It's been weeks.

And Rome won't talk about it.

He'll talk. About other things. Important things, even. Which Damien should probably be happy about. But any time Damien tries to talk about *them*, about whatever the hell they're doing and if maybe they can tell other people about it—if maybe, one night, Damien could stay—Rome gets still and quiet or changes the subject or kisses him.

So Damien takes the quiet moments, the secret affection and the lingering touches, and he tries to be cautious. He doesn't know how to, though, because he's in uncharted territory.

It's strange to know someone so intimately, to be so familiar with someone else's body, its likes and dislikes, its scars and its secrets, but still be so uncertain about the person inside it. To know someone but not know them.

He realizes, sitting in his bed with swollen lips and the smell of Rome pressed into his T-shirt, that he needs to talk to his mom.

Except he hasn't talked to his mom about a boy in over a year, and he doesn't even know where his parents are right now. Metaphorically or geographically.

He decides to send a text, agonizes over what to say, and then finally sends: "hey, are you free to talk?"

Two minutes later, without a response, he does what any self-respecting teenager with too many emotions would do and attempts to get spectacularly drunk.

It's easy enough to facilitate. The men's and women's hockey teams won their games the night before, and there's a small basement party in full swing. He and Rome snuck away, but then Rome cited an early morning working at the garage the following day and kicked him out to sleep. So Damien goes downstairs and finds some tequila.

He's not in the mood for dancing and, after a few shots, glaring broadly at all the fun that's being had, he ends up just taking the bottle back to his room. An unwise choice because Chai notices him skulking off and tries to talk to him, all concerned with his worried eyebrows and his gentle hands, and Damien just—

Can't.

He tucks himself into bed, pulls the duvet over his head to block out Chai's quiet "is there anything I can do?" and returns his attention to the tequila.

He checks his phone—nothing from his mom—and

takes another sip. He shoves his headphones on and pulls up his playlist of Rome's favorite songs because if he's going to be pathetic, he's going to do it really fucking thoroughly.

Some number of minutes later, probably not that many because he's uncomfortably warm in his duvet-tent rather than actively suffocating, someone slams the door to his room.

Chai doesn't slam doors.

"What the fuck are you doing?"

Rome does though.

Rome also rudely pulls apart duvet-tents.

And steals alcohol.

"Thought you were sleeping," Damien says, pushing down the headphones.

It sounds accusatory.

Maybe it is.

He realizes he might be a little belligerent.

Rome, delightfully furious, shirtless, and freckled, gestures wordlessly at him with the tequila bottle. "You were fine when you left my room. Why are you like this? What happened?"

"Nothing."

"Well, Chai was worried enough he came and woke me up, so obviously, something happened."

"I thought you had to work tomorrow," Damien says. "Thought you needed to sleep."

"I do. Which is why you need to tell me what the hell is the matter, so we can fix it, and I can go back to bed."

That's good. Sweet, even. Rome wanting to help. Wanting to fix whatever is wrong. But Damien doesn't even know what is wrong; he just knows he wants to talk to his mom, and he wants to hold hands with his boyfriend. And he wants to know if he even *has* a fucking boyfriend—

Damien sniffs.

"Hey," Rome says.

He sets the bottle on the desk. "Okay. I'm sorry." He drops his voice considerably. "Can you tell me what's wrong?"

"You always make me leave," Damien says.

He doesn't mean to say it, but—hey. Tequila.

It comes out embarrassingly plaintive.

"What?"

"And you won't talk to me. And I texted my mom because I don't know if I'm allowed to talk to anyone here about us and whether we even *are* an *us* because you won't talk to me when I try to talk to you about us. And I need to talk to someone. Except my mom didn't answer."

"Okay. I don't know if I really followed that, but— Are you crying?"

He might be. A little. It should probably be embarrassing.

"Shit. Don't cry. Please don't cry. I mean, cry if you need to, but— Oh my fucking god. No. I can't be responsible for making you cry, okay? So you need to stop."

"I'm sorry," Damien says wetly.

"For fuck's sake," Rome says, maybe a little desperately. He moves to sit on the bed next to Damien and awkwardly pulls him into a hug. "I'm sorry. For the not talking. Or whatever. What can I do to fix it?"

"I want to fall asleep with you."

"Okay?"

"And spend the whole night."

"Okay."

"And then go down to breakfast together and hold hands. I want people to know. That we're—us. I want us to be an us."

"Oh."

Rome's hand, his lovely, long-fingered hand that was rubbing gently up and down Damien's spine, goes still.

"But you don't want that," Damien says. "And I'm not going to give you an ultimatum. Because forcing you to out yourself would be a dick move. So I'll—"

"No. I do."

Damien blinks. "What?"

"I do want those things. I almost kissed you at practice this morning. Just automatically. Because you were being a little shit, and apparently instead of wanting to yell at you when you're being a little shit now, I want to kiss you. Which isn't the point. The point is that I want to do all that too. I just—I don't know how."

Damien doesn't say anything for several seconds.

His brain feels all warm and sloshy, but this is important, so he tries to rally.

"You'd be okay with coming out? To the team?"

"They won't care. Or they won't be dicks about it. Kaner is trans and bi. You're gay. No one is going to care that I'm—whatever I am."

"It's still a big deal. You're an NHL prospect. If it gets out—"

"I wouldn't be the first. My family won't care, and even if they did, I'm emancipated now. And you're upset, and that would make you...not upset."

"I'm not really upset." Damien rubs his palms over his eyes. "I'm just drunk."

"A. You are upset, you fucking liar. And B. That's actually something we should talk about. If we're talking about...things."

His head is starting to hurt. "What should we talk about?"

"The whole drinking thing."

"What drinking thing?"

"I don't like it. You drunk. A couple beers is fine, but I don't like this."

Oh.

Damien closes his eyes. "Because of your dad?"

"Because I don't fucking know. I just don't like it, okay?"

"Okay. I'm sorry."

"Whatever. We can talk about it in the morning."

"That's probably a good idea. We should just...table this until then, probably."

"Yeah."

Rome stands, and Damien swallows down a request for him to stay.

"Come on," Rome says.

"What?"

"You said you wanted to fall asleep with me, and I'm not cuddling you in the room you share with Chai. Let's go."

"Oh." Damien scrambles out of the bed, nearly

falling on his face when his foot gets hooked in the duvet. "Are you sure?"

"No. You're a mess. Come on before I change my mind."

Damien kisses the back of Rome's neck because Rome doesn't mean it. And Damien likes the back of his neck.

Rome shivers in a gratifying way and then grabs Damien's hand, pulling him into the hall.

It isn't fast or secretive or embarrassed.

He takes his time opening the door to his room one-handed.

There's no one in the hallway, but clearly, Rome doesn't care if anyone does show up, and that's nice.

Once inside, Rome pushes a water bottle into Damien's hands, makes him swallow a couple of Advil, and then pulls off his shirt and shoves him into the bed.

He fusses with the sheets for a minute before turning off his lamp and tucking himself right up into Damien's space.

"Hey," Damien says, mouth against Rome's forehead.

"Shut up," Rome says. "You wanted to sleep. We're sleeping."

"Okay," Damien says.

He knocks twice against Rome's spine.

Rome knocks back.

CHAPTER TWENTY

ROME WAKES UP to his phone trying to vibrate off the windowsill.

He can't reach it to turn off his alarm, however, because there's nearly 200 pounds of sleeping hockey player on top of him.

It's nice.

"Damien," he says, shoving at Damien's shoulder. "Move."

Damien does not move.

Rome has no choice but to hook a heel around Damien's calf and roll them.

They manage to stay on the bed, though it's a near thing, and Rome stretches his arm out, shoulder popping, to silence his phone.

Then he collapses back onto Damien's chest.

"Hey," Damien says, eyes slitted.

"Hey," Rome agrees.

Damien rolls them back over, away from the edge of the mattress, and presses his mouth to Rome's. Both of them have really terrible morning breath, but Rome isn't about to do something stupid like mention it.

Damien shifts a little to the side, propped up on one elbow so he's not actively crushing Rome anymore, and sighs, scratching at his stupidly toned belly. His nose is all wrinkled up in distaste at the early hour or maybe due to a hangover, but even with garbage breath and gunk in the corners of his eyes, Rome finds Damien outrageously attractive. He wants to do sappy shit like kiss Damien's eyelids.

"Get off me," he says instead. "I need to go."

"No," Damien whines.

"Yes," Rome says. "Come on. I can't be late. I have less than ten minutes before I need to leave."

Damien sits up, resigned, looking bleary and perfect in the shadowed just-after-dawn light, and Rome has to force himself to move. To get out of bed. To look away.

Rome shivers once he's left the warm cocoon of shared blankets. He pulls on the first pair of jeans he can find, a thick pair of socks, a tank top, a flannel shirt.

Damien grins happily at him as Rome rubs a little bit of sunscreen onto his cheeks and the back of his neck.

"Hey, so. We said we were going to talk," Damien says.

Rome rubs harder. "Can't that wait?"

"We said morning. It's morning. And if we wait,

then we won't get a chance until tonight. And we have team dinner tonight, so—"

Rome shoves his feet into his boots, then bends down to tie them. "Okay, but I have to go."

"You still have—" Damien digs his phone out of the sheets and squints at it. "—six minutes."

"And we're supposed to have a serious conversation in six minutes?"

"It doesn't need to be a long conversation. Just a sober one. Which I am, now. And I promise I will stay that way because you said it bothered you when I get drunk. See, that was quick. You also said you wanted to be together. Is that still true, or—"

Rome knots his laces with more force than is strictly necessary. "It's not that easy."

"Why is it not that easy?"

"Because I'm not *you*," Rome says, and his voice is suddenly too loud. "I can't just *want* things."

"Hey," Damien says, softer. "Come here."

Rome moves forward without really deciding to.

Damien reaches for his hand. Circles his wrist with warm fingers. Pulls him in until his hips hit the frame of the lifted bed.

"Why can't you want things?" he asks.

Rome exhales. "Because I don't know how. Because every fucking time I've ever wanted something, it was used against me or taken away. Except for hockey, maybe. But that wasn't a want so much as a need. Everything else—" He stops, horrified, because his throat is getting all hot and tight, and he's already cried on Damien once; he's not about to do it again.

"Rome," Damien says.

"Stop it," Rome snarls.

"I'm not doing anything," Damien points out.

The words are too gentle. Too kind.

He wants Damien to push back. To yell. Aggression and anger he can cope with, but this? He doesn't know how to handle quiet kindness. It's the same sort of uncertainty he experienced in the few months he lived with his aunt and uncle. When suddenly he didn't know how to navigate domestic conversations. Because the old scripts he used with his father and stepmother didn't work, but no one had bothered to give him a new manual.

"Stop it," he says again.

It comes out embarrassingly thready.

"I'm going to hug you now," Damien says. "Please don't punch me."

He lets it happen.

"I really do need to leave," he says a minute later.

He doesn't make any effort to pull away though.

"Okay." Damien sounds sad. He shifts, releasing Rome. He looks sad too.

Fuck.

"We can talk tonight," Damien says, leaning his weight back onto his hands.

"No. We can do stuff. If you want. I don't care if people know we're—whatever."

Rome turns away to collect his jacket from the desk chair. "I'm not comfortable with the idea of making out in the hallways or anything though."

Damien blinks at him. "I was thinking about just

telling the team for now. And we're not heathens. We'll make out in the stacks like civilized people."

"Of course. I really do need to go."

"You want me to drive you?"

Rome considers Damien, still sleep-rumpled and more than likely dehydrated and hungover. "I'm pretty sure that would be hazardous, so no."

"Your face is hazardous," Damien says. "At least take my car. It snowed last night."

"Damien—"

"Please. I don't need it today. The keys are on the hook by the door in my room, and Chai sleeps like the dead so just—"

"Okay." Rome catches Damien's face between his hands and ducks to roughly kiss his forehead. "Okay. Fine. Thank you. Shut the fuck up, and go back to sleep."

Damien grins. "Okay."

Rome pauses in the doorway, halfway into the hall, and just—takes a breath. Commits the moment to memory: Damien, warm and bleary and in his bed. Striped with pale gold early-morning light coming in the open blinds.

"Bye," he says.

*

ROME IS JUST finishing an oil change on a Subaru when his phone rings.

It's Elle, which immediately makes his stomach go clench-y.

There's no reason she should be calling him.

He doesn't want to answer, but he does anyway.

"Hello?" he says.

"Rome," Elle says.

Her voice is doing a thing he doesn't particularly like.

"Elle. Hey. What's going on?"

"I found your mother."

"Oh." He closes the hood. "Uh. Okay?"

"She's in a low-security prison serving a drug sentence."

It shouldn't be a surprise. It isn't, really. He remembers his dad yelling. His mom crying. The orange pill bottles scattered across the kitchen table.

Rome blinks. He sits down and leans back against the Subaru's front fender.

"I mean," he says, "that doesn't really matter though, does it? I'm already emancipated. She can't change that. Right? Especially if she's in jail."

"No, she can't. But Rome."

"But what?"

"You have a half-sister."

"I have two half-sisters," he responds automatically. "What do they have to do with anything?"

"No," she says. "You have another half-sister. Your mother had a child late last year, and she gave up parental rights to that child at birth. The paperwork just hit the system."

"Oh."

Rome feels like he's been punched in the stomach.

He shifts the phone to his other ear.

"The baby—what's its name? Does it have a name?"

"Finley." Elle's voice is very, very gentle. "She's eight weeks old."

"Finley," he repeats.

He closes his eyes, leaning his head back.

"Where is she? Has she been adopted?"

"No, not yet. She's at Boston Children's Hospital."

Boston. Close.

"Why is she still at the hospital? I thought that babies were in high demand for adoption."

"There were some complications. So the baby will have to stay in the hospital for a while. In the NICU."

"Is she okay? I mean, will she be okay or—"

"I don't have those details," Elle says. "I just found all this out a few minutes ago. I thought you would want to know."

"I want to meet her," Rome says. And he does. Urgently. In a way he can't explain. "Is that possible? Boston isn't very far."

"Easy," Elle says. "I don't know. I can find out for you, if you'd like."

"Please."

"Okay. Let me make some calls. I'll keep you posted."

"Thank you."

Rome details two cars on autopilot. He cleans up the garage, updates the books, locks up, and drives home in something like a daze. He manages to forget about the Damien situation until he gets back to the dorm. All the guys are camped in the common room, and Damien is in the kitchen talking to Olly. Suddenly, Rome remembers there's this whole other world full of problems unrelated to drug addict mothers and surprise infant sisters.

He bypasses the kitchen, despite Olly's cheerful invitation to join them, and goes right up the stairs.

"Uh," he hears Damien say, "I'm gonna go...deal with that."

"Yeah," Olly says. "He looks..."

Rome doesn't know how he looks, but he can guess.

He takes a shower because he's filthy and he hopes it will clear his head. It doesn't. Damien is waiting for him, sitting on Rome's bed, when he finishes, damp and cold and with no helpful shower epiphanies.

"Hey," Damien says.

"Hey," Rome agrees.

"Are you okay?"

Rome sits next to him. "I don't think so."

Damien looks stymied by that. "Okay, well. Points for honesty. Is this about us? I shouldn't have pushed you this morning."

"No. Elle called me." He isn't sure how to say it, so he just— "I have a sister. Or another sister, I guess."

Damien's face goes entirely blank. "What?"

"Yeah." The words come out steady and even and weirdly emotionless considering all the whatever that he's feeling. "Elle found my mom. She's in prison. She had a baby a couple weeks ago, but it's— The baby is still in the hospital because of complications. Her name is Finley."

"Holy shit."

"Yeah."

Damien shifts backward to lean against the wall, then pulls on Rome's arm until Rome follows him and tips against Damien's side, slouching, temple to shoulder, fingers tangled, both of them staring shell-shocked at the tidy rows of photographs opposite them.

"Will she be okay?" Damien asks. "The baby."

"Probably? It sounded like probably. Elle is going to see if they'll let me visit her."

"Where is she?"

"Children's."

"That's not far."

"I know."

Damien presses his mouth to the top of Rome's head and leaves it there. "I don't know what to say."

Rome makes a rough noise that might be a laugh. "Same."

Damien sighs, and his breath sends goosebumps down Rome's neck. "Is the father around?"

"Didn't sound like it. My mom gave up custody. I just— I can't believe my mom would do this again."

"Again?"

"Not the drugs. She didn't start that shit until I was, like, four or five. But the having a kid and then fucking abandoning it? Aren't you supposed to learn from your mistakes?"

Damien slides his arm over Rome's shoulders, cups his palm around Rome's elbow, and drags his hand up Rome's bicep.

It's annoyingly soothing.

"Yeah," Damien says. "That sucks. But now the baby has a chance at a good life, right? She'll get adopted by some couple who want a baby so bad. She'll be a tiny little miracle for them. And they'll love her and sign her up for ballet or hockey. And they'll let her paint her room any color she wants, even if it's a horrible purple that clashes with all the furniture. And they'll read her bedtime stories every night, and they'll give her stupidly OTT gifts."

"Like a Porsche for her sixteenth birthday?" Rome says wryly. "With the stipulation that she trade it for a Range Rover during the winter months? So she has four-wheel drive in the snow?"

Damien huffs out a soundless laugh against the top of Rome's head. "Exactly."

"That sounds pretty great," Rome allows. "Did you ever talk to your mom?"

"We're talking about *your* family drama right now," Damien says.

"Not anymore. Did you?"

"Yeah. Well, no. But she's planning to call in a few minutes. Should give me half an hour to talk to her before dinner."

"Good. You gonna tell her you miss her or whatever?"

"Yeah. I think so."

"Good."

Damien rocks them a little. Gently. Barely discernible. "You want me to sit with you until then?"

"I guess if you want to."

"Okay."

"Do you..." Rome pulls at a loose thread in the seam of his pajama pants. "Do you want me to sit with you while you talk to her?"

He can feel Damien swallow.

"I guess if you want to."
"Okay."

CHAPTER TWENTY-ONE

IT'S HARD TO talk to your mom about the boy you like when the boy you like is currently pressed right up against you.

Clearly, Damien didn't think this through.

"So tell me," his mom says after brief commentary on the weather (bad), his grades (good), and the hockey season (very good), "is everything okay? You had me a little worried when you asked to talk."

This is where he's supposed to say "I miss you," but the words stick in his mouth, lodged solidly between his tongue and teeth.

"There's this guy," he says instead.

And Rome goes very still beside him.

"Ah, *mon cœur*," his mom sighs, all warm and

dulcet and familiar. "It's been so long since we talked about boys. Tell me about this one, *dis-moi*."

"He's—" Damien swallows. "He's not just a...one. Or maybe he's—"

The one? He's not about to say that shit out loud. Regardless, he can't just lump Rome in with the rest of them.

"He's different."

"Oh." His mother sounds cautious. "Well, all right. Tell me about him. What's his name?"

"Rome. He's on the team with me. And he's going to go pro because he's so good, *Maman*. He's getting drafted for sure next year." Damien swallows again, his mouth suddenly dry. "He's kind of an asshole, but in a nice way? He's good at listening. And fixing things. And he cares a lot, even though he pretends he doesn't."

"*Mon chéri*," she says. "What does he look like?"

"Freckles," he says, blurts out, maybe. "He has a lot of freckles. Everywhere. And brown hair that would probably curl, but he keeps it buzzed short. And um...he's tall. About the same height as me. And he has really pretty eyes."

He glances askance at the boy in question, who's currently very, very pink.

"He blushes a lot too. It's cute."

Rome punches him in the thigh.

"And you're...dating?" his mom asks.

"Yeah. For a couple weeks now. But I've liked him for longer. He stayed with me in New York over Christmas. And then I went up to Maine with him after. Met his family."

"Damien," his mom says. And, yeah. He knows that's a big deal. Especially for him. "You really like this boy."

It isn't a question, but he answers it anyway. "I do," he says, and then more quietly, "It's kind of scary."

Rome's hand, still fisted against Damien's thigh, goes slack. He shifts so his palm cups Damien's leg instead; he squeezes gently, just above Damien's knee.

"Does he like you too?"

"Oh," Damien says, grinning sideways at Rome, "absolutely. He's totally gone on me."

Rome makes a face at him.

"Good," she says. "I'd like to meet him."

"Actually—" The words get stuck again.

Rome's hand moves on his leg. Slowly. Up and then down. A warm chafe against denim.

"Actually, I was wondering if you guys could come visit soon?" It's a little rushed, but Damien gets it out in one go. "I haven't seen you since summer and—"

Rome leans into him. Subtle. But heavy.

Damien leans back. "I miss you guys." It comes out a little thready.

It's silent for a beat, and then his mom sighs. "We miss you too."

"I mean, I know you guys are busy, but—"

"We're not too busy for you," she interrupts.

Except they have been.

"You missed my birthday," Damien says. And it's supposed to be a statement of fact, but the sheer amount of ugly pathos in his voice sort of overwhelms the intention. "And Thanksgiving. And Christmas. And I know you sent gifts and cards and stuff but...that's not the same."

It's silent for a significantly longer beat. Rome's hand keeps moving on his knee. And then—oh god—his mom sniffs.

"I'm sorry," she says.

Fantastic. He's made his mother cry.

"We didn't think you minded," she continues. "We know you're an adult now, and every time we visited last year, you seemed so embarrassed and you kept saying we didn't have to come."

Damien laughs a little wetly at that. "I'm a teenager. I'm supposed to be embarrassed when my mother is screaming she loves me from the stands at a hockey game or showing up at my dorm with a cake on my birthday. And you're supposed to do it anyway because I'm your kid. Maybe that's not fair, I just... I haven't seen you guys since summer, and it seems like I'm the only one who cares."

And that's more than he meant to say, really.

Rome's hand moves, abandoning his leg to slip around his lower back. It pauses, curled around Damien's opposite elbow for a minute, and then resumes traveling upward. His fingers cup Damien's bicep, palm against skin, thumb moving in slow circles. The length of Rome's arm, a warm *V* cupping his back, is reassuring and solid behind him.

"Damien," his mom says, and it kind of hurts, the way she says it. "We don't know what we're doing, you know? Your father and I. We're doing the best we can, but it's not like we've ever raised a teenager before.

We're lost here. So you have to *tell* us if we're doing something wrong, okay?"

"That's fair."

"I will get on a plane tonight if it means you stop thinking that we don't care. Your father is already planning a three-week family trip to Paris once your semester is over, and he's going to ban cell phones for a least a week of it so we can have family time and catch up without interruptions."

"Yeah?"

"Yes."

"Okay."

"Do I need to go book a ticket?"

He scrubs the heel of one hand over his eyes. "No. But spring break? Can we do something then?"

"I'm clearing our schedules right now."

"Okay."

She makes a considering noise. "Let's see. You have a game that Friday of spring break, so we can't all go somewhere, but your father and I can come to you. Stay in that charming little bed and breakfast north of campus. Maybe take a day trip or two? You could bring your young man with us, of course."

There are a couple things Damien has to work through there. First, his mother is assuming he and Rome will still be together two months from now. Second, she apparently knows his game schedule.

"You have my games in your calendar?"

"Of course we do." Her tone is judgmental. "We try to watch the stream online, if possible, but even if not, we always check the score. And your father proudly recites your stats to anyone who will listen."

"Oh."

"Now, how does your Rome feel about French food? We'll need to make reservations now if we want to eat at—"

Damien has to close his eyes for a minute and smile at nothing as she keeps talking.

He leans into Rome. "How do you feel about French food?"

"Um," Rome says. "Fine?"

"Mom," he interrupts. She's moved on to talking about wine. "Rome will eat pretty much anything. We're hockey players. We're always hungry. But, uh...we don't drink. Or, I'm not right now. And Rome probably won't."

Rome meets his eyes, wide and maybe a little shocked. He shakes his head.

"Yeah, he won't either."

His mother is quiet for several seconds. "Is this something we need to talk about?"

"No. It's not a problem. I'm just figuring some things out."

"Damien."

"Seriously, *Maman*. I'm fine. I promise."

She's probably going to push it, which actually makes him feel good, when Rome's phone rings.

They both jump.

"Hold on," he says, then shifts so Rome has the use of both arms again and can retrieve his phone from him pocket.

"It's Elle." Rome's eyes are wide and so damn blue and maybe a little scared.

"So answer it," Damien whispers.

"Right."

Rome stands and brings the phone to his ear. He ducks his head and cups the back of neck with his free hand. "Hey," he says lowly.

"Damien?" Damien's mom says.

"Hold on, one second," he whispers again.

"Yeah," Rome says. "I'm—oh? Oh. Okay. Yeah, that would be— No! That's totally fine. I can—I'll ask Damien." His fingers scratch absently at the short, bristly hairs at the nape of his neck. "Thank you so much. If you could text it to me, that'd be great. Thanks."

He straightens and slips the phone back in his pocket. "Can you drive me to Boston Children's?" he asks.

"What, now?"

"Visiting hours aren't over until eight, so we've still got time."

"Yeah, absolutely." Damien stands, then remembers the phone in his own hand. "Hey, *Maman*? I need to help Rome with a thing, but can I call you back later tonight?"

She sighs at him. It's delightfully familiar.

"Whenever you have time for me, I suppose," she says, feigning offense.

He laughs. He already feels lighter. Like he's just taken off a weight vest after a training run. "I love you."

"I love you too. Go see to your young man. And send me a picture of him at some point. I've pulled up your roster online, but these headshots are *so small*."

He laughs harder. "Okay."

By the time he's hung up, laced his boots, and retrieved his keys, Rome has his coat and backpack on and is struggling to get his left shoe on his right foot. Possibly because it's the left shoe and his right foot.

Damien sorts him out, still laughing, and then holds his hands for a minute in the hallway, forcing him into stillness. "Hey. You okay?"

"Yeah, I'm good. Shit. I just totally interrupted your heart-to-heart with your mom. We can wait, if you need to call her back. And did you want to stay for team dinner? I can figure out a bus if—"

"Shut up. Let's go."

He keeps one of Rome's hands, slots their fingers together as they descend the stairs, and yells cavalierly into the den, "Rome and I have a thing, so we're going to miss dinner! Save some dessert for us!"

"Please!" Rome adds, grinning, a slight edge of hysteria to his laughter as Damien pulls him out the door. He drops his voice, maybe giggling a little. And Rome giggling is something else. "Seriously. Manners, asshole."

He hears Brass say as the door slides shut behind them: "Wait. Were they holding hands?"

*

THIRTY MINUTES LATER, Damien smooths an adhesive paper visitor badge onto his chest and watches as Rome does the same. Rome is still holding Damien's hand. His skin is clammy.

"You good?" Damien asks.

"Yeah. Let's go."

They meet Amy Santana, NICU nurse extraordinaire at the NICU front desk. She's wearing scrubs with vintage motorcycles on them. Damien likes her immediately.

She does a double take when she sees them, and he almost lets go of Rome's hand, but then she grins, extending her own hand to Rome.

"You must be Finley's big brother. I can see the family resemblance."

Rome seems to have some emotions about that sentence.

"Hi," he manages. "Rome."

"Pardon?"

"Oh." Rome clears his throat. "My name. I go by Rome. This is my...Damien."

Damien maybe has some emotions about the way Rome carefully says his name.

Amy considers their joined fingers, then winks at Damien. "Well, I'd shake your hand too, Damien, but it seems to be occupied." Rome's ears go pink. "Are you two ready to meet Finley?"

"Yes," they say.

They get a rundown of the rules, wash their hands up to their elbows while humming the "Happy Birthday" song three times, tie on some paper gowns, and then, they meet Finley.

She's not in one of the clear plastic box things the tiny babies are in, but some sort of small, open-air, medical-grade crib. And there are monitors and wires and the usual kind of expected scary shit, but she still looks like a baby. A baby in a little patterned onesie gown thing with a little pink hat, her little eyelashes damp against little chubby cheeks.

Except the baby is—not white.

Or, not white-white, anyway. Her skin is maybe a shade lighter than Damien's. And sure, babies all kind of look the same but she's...

Well.

Not white.

"Uh," Damien says. "Are you sure that's the right baby?"

And then she opens her eyes, wiggles enough to dislodge the pink cap on her head and, yeah. Okay. She's got the same *blue*-blue eyes as Rome and wispy red-brown curls.

"Oh my god," Rome says.

Damien would make fun of him for how embarrassingly reverent the exhalation is, except a moment later, she flails her little fists. Damien—just sort of automatically—brushes a finger down the back of her tiny, soft hand (so soft, holy shit, he didn't know human skin could feel like that), and she shifts her attention over to him and yawns.

"Oh my god," Damien says.

"Do you want to hold her?" Amy asks.

"*Yes*," Rome and Damien both say.

Amy shows them how to pick her up without interfering with any of her trailing wires or the scary-looking tube-thing taped to her belly and then she just...leaves them. Goes to check on other babies or something. And Rome, sitting in the visitor chair, holding Finley like she's made of glass, watches Amy walk away in something like abject horror.

"Wait," he whispers.

Finley makes a little squeaky noise, and he immediately redirects his attention.

"Hey. You good?" he asks her. "You okay?" He glances frantically at the surrounding monitors and then at Damien. But it isn't like Damien knows what the red and green numbers surrounding them mean either.

Rome clearly wants to yell at Amy to come back but also clearly doesn't want to yell because he's holding the most beautiful infant that has ever existed, and he can't just *disturb* her like that.

Damien might be projecting.

It's fine.

"I can't believe she just left," Rome whispers.

Damien can't tell if he's talking to him or Finley.

"What if I drop her?"

"You're not going to drop her."

Damien scoots his own chair a little closer just in case though.

"What if I was a terrible person though?" Rome says. "I could be an axe murderer. And they're just letting me hold babies. Tiny, fragile, fucking, little babies. That seems irresponsible. Doesn't that seem irresponsible?"

"You're not an axe murderer. And Elle probably sent them your info. You're the most stand-up citizen that ever existed. Three-point eight GPA. Perfect attendance. Perfect athlete. Not even a parking ticket."

"I don't have a car," he hisses back. "It's hard to get

a parking ticket when you don't have a car."

"I'm sorry. Are we really arguing about whether or not you should be allowed to hold your own sister? Because I'll happily take her from you."

"No, you will not," Rome snarls, hunching himself protectively around her. "Wait your fucking turn."

"Okay."

Finley squeaks again, and he bounces her a little, looking concerned.

"God. She's so beautiful."

"Yeah," Damien agrees.

"Like. Holy shit. I love her already. Is that normal? *Look* at her."

"Yeah," Damien agrees.

Finley yawns again, and Rome grins down at her. At her little squinched-up face and her little chubby hand clenched firmly in both his paper gown and the green sweater under it, pulling the fabric low enough to expose the top of the rose tattoo under his collarbone.

And Rome is holding her like—

Looking at her like—

Damien needs a minute.

CHAPTER TWENTY-TWO

FINLEY HAS HETEROTAXY syndrome.

Amy explains that it's rare and complicated and means her heart has a couple of defects and is in the wrong place in her chest. It means her liver is a little underdeveloped, and she's already had two surgeries and will probably need several more as she grows. It means she's currently stable, but won't be able to leave the hospital for months. But it isn't a death sentence. And being at Children's means she has a shot at a more-or-less normal childhood. It means she's in the best hands possible.

What Finley doesn't have are any kind of drug-related complications.

"So my mom was clean?" Rome asks, a little startled, when Amy tells him. "I thought this was all because of her drug use."

"No. This is just down to bad luck. Your mother spent nearly her entire pregnancy clean in prison. So prison may have saved Finley's life, actually."

He gets a little lost in his head, thinking about that.

Because his mom...well, she was a good mom, from what he can remember. She'd read to him before bed and cuddled with him when he was sick and tucked him somewhere safe and quiet when his dad was drunk and angry. She would sing to him while he took his baths and cheer the loudest at his hockey games. She was the one who signed him up for his first team at five years old, who argued long and hard with his dad to justify the equipment fee. She was a good mom. Right up until she was gone.

Rome breathes in the baby smell from the top of Finley's head, presses a kiss to her tiny curls, and sways a little, listening as Amy tells him the plan for Finley's treatment. She asks if he'd like to be kept apprised of any changes. She asks if he'd like to speak with the hospital's social worker before he leaves.

He would.

He says he would without even really thinking about it. Rome wants— He thinks about Damien, eighteen and desperate for some sign that someone, at some point, loved him before his parents adopted him. That someone cared.

Rome wants Finley to have that.

He wants to visit whenever he can. He wants to be there for the surgeries. He wants to meet potential adopters. He wants to know her. Watch her grow up.

And if that's not possible, he wants to take pictures with her and add them to her file and leave every bit of contact information he has so she can find him again one day. Because she's small and helpless and a part of him. And even though he's only known about her for less than a day, he already feels fiercely, almost frighteningly, beholden to her.

When Rome sits down with the social worker, Damien leaves to go find them some food and doesn't come back for twenty minutes. His face—closed off, maybe even apprehensive?—when he does return with two wrapped sandwiches, makes something in Rome's gut clench.

"Visiting hours are almost over," Damien points out, not meeting Rome's eyes. "You want to go back and see her real quick before we have to leave?"

He does.

The car ride home is quiet.

They don't hold hands.

The dorm is weirdly still when they get back. There's no one in the den or kitchen, and Rome only spares a second to be grateful as he goes straight to his room and shuts the door. He wants to do some research on heterotaxy syndrome and look over his work, school, and hockey schedules to see when he can go back and visit again.

Damien slips inside a few minutes later with a protein bar. He sets it on the bed next to Rome's laptop. "So," he says.

"I was able to register with the hospital as being her family," Rome says. "Um...kin? So I can visit outside of

normal hours. I don't have any medical power or anything. But at least they'll keep me in the loop. They'd call
me if her condition changes. Things like that. And they'll
let me know when they choose a foster or adopter for her
to go home with and try to help keep me in contact with
her."

"That's cool," Damien says.

He still won't meet Rome's eyes.

Rome looks at the protein bar so he doesn't have to
look at Damien not looking at him. "Hey, so," he says,
and the words are quieter, sadder than he means them
to be, "I get it. It's a lot."

"No shit," Damien says.

"So, it's fine."

"What's fine?"

"I'm not going to hold it against you."

"Hold what against me? Rome. I have no idea what
you're talking about."

"You didn't sign up to deal with a kid when we
started this—whatever we are. And a kid is a big fucking
deal. Even just a normal kid. But a special-needs kid in
the hospital is something else. So, it's fine. I get it. You
don't want to spend all your free time hanging out with
a sick infant, and that's clearly all I'm going to want to
do right now. So, it's fine."

Damien makes a noise that Rome can't interpret at
all. He looks up, and Damien's face is—

Wow.

Damien's face is really, really angry.

"I'm sorry. Are you saying it's fine if I break up with
you?" Damien says. "Because you want to try and be part

of your tiny, beautiful, orphaned baby sister's life?"

"Is it a breakup if we were never together?" Rome says, and he regrets it before the sentence is even fully out of his mouth.

They both know the words are supposed to hurt, and they do; Rome can see that they do as they land. But Damien only moves closer instead of farther away.

"No," he interrupts, low and final. "I don't want to break up with you even though you're a colossal asshole. And I definitely don't want to break up with you because you're willing to take on the responsibility of showing the fuck up for your baby sister. And it *would* be a breakup because we *are* together and also *fuck you.*"

"Oh," Rome says. All the tightly wound aggression in him just falls away. "Then what? As soon as I said I wanted to see the social worker, you just left."

It sounds accusatory. It probably is.

"I left because I thought you might want some privacy, and I needed a minute to get my head on straight. I left because if I didn't, I was going to start saying the kind of stupid shit that would scare you off."

Rome swallows. "Like?"

"You don't want to know," Damien says, aggrieved. "That's the whole point."

"Damien." He swallows again. "Please."

Damien stills. He crosses his arms. "Finley has your eyes. And she'll probably get cute as shit freckles the minute she sees some sunlight."

"Yeah?" Rome says. "Our mom is, like, the most Irish person you'll ever meet. So?"

"So she's mixed race. And she's— And you—*fuck.*

You were standing there, looking at her like she was the best damn thing you'd ever seen, talking about how you loved her. It was like watching some fantasy of mine come to life. Just...look."

He pulls up a picture on his phone that Amy had taken right before they left. Of the three of them. Rome holding Finley, looking down at her, enraptured, while Finley reaches for Damien's grinning face.

"Oh," Rome says, and it feels a little like someone has hit him in the back of the head with a hockey stick. "She looks like us. A mix of the two of us."

"Yeah."

"Oh," he says again. "That's a fantasy of yours?"

Damien puts his phone back in his pocket. "Maybe," he says shortly. "Some day."

"Oh," Rome says a third time.

"So stop being a dumbass," Damien says. "We're not breaking up. Because we are together. And I'm going to call you my boyfriend, and you're going to deal with it."

He says it like a challenge.

He doesn't have to though. Rome has no desire to fight him.

"Whatever," Rome says.

"Hey." Damien clears his throat. "I'm going to need something more than 'whatever' for this one."

"No," Rome says, and then adds very quickly after Damien's face falls, "I mean, yeah. Sorry. I do. I want that too. Yes."

"Okay. Well, good."

"Do you—" Rome reaches for him, maybe a little desperate. "Can you come over here?"

"Here?" Damien asks, climbing onto the bed with him.

"No."

Rome hooks his fingers into Damien's shirt and pulls him closer.

"Here."

*

ROME WAKES UP to Olly's singing.

The bathroom is close enough down the hall that the Tim McGraw lyrics are clear above the sound of the shower, and Rome can't help grinning a little before opening his eyes and trying to extricate himself from Damien's various clinging limbs. Rome is beginning to build enough empirical evidence to confidently assert that Damien is part koala. Rome tries to generate some disdain about that, just for appearances, but finds himself utterly incapable. Because as he manages to wiggle from the circle of Damien's admittedly very nice biceps, Damien rolls onto his belly, frowning a little, and pushes his face into the pillow—Rome's Pillow—inhaling slowly and sort of like, burrowing his nose into it, smiling softly, and Rome can't—he's not equipped to—

Half of him wants to punch the fucking wall and the other half wants to curl around Damien and never leave. There is a fondness, now, that clings to Rome's ribs and makes it hard to breathe sometimes. There is a *want* in him. A want that grows a little each time he reminds himself he's allowed to *have*.

He wants Damien. All of him. All of the time. And

he only really lets himself think about this late at night or early in the morning when there is darkness and quiet and warmth to temper the clench in his gut.

He bends down, not to kiss Damien, not while he sleeps, that would be too much, but to cup a hand around his jaw for a moment. To push his hair back from his temple. To appreciate his stupid, shadowed face up close and still and without observation.

Damien blinks his eyes open, and Rome snatches his hand away, straightening.

"Hm?" Damien says.

"Nothing."

"You watching me sleep, Roman?"

"Fuck you," Rome says.

"You don't have to be a dick, you know," Damien says, slow and sleepy but still far too aware for comfort. "I won't tell anyone if you're sweet."

Rome crosses his arms. Because he's cold, not because he's feeling called out. "I don't know how to be sweet."

"Just—" Damien cuts himself off with a yawn. Rome despairs over how cute he finds Damien's wrinkled nose. "Just kiss me and tell me you'll be right back."

Rome uncrosses his arms. He leans forward in a series of halting movements. He kisses Damien's temple, dry and quick, and then immediately steps back, crossing his arms again.

Damien watches him patiently.

"Bathroom," Rome says roughly. "I'll be right back."

"'Kay," Damien agrees, beaming at him. He rubs his cheek against Rome's pillow. "Hurry."

Rome hurries.

They don't manage to fall back to sleep before Rome's alarm goes off, but they do get in a solid fifteen minutes of what Rome is unwilling to term "cuddling" but isn't sure what else to call it.

They get ready together, washing faces and brushing teeth in companionable silence, bumping elbows as they maneuver around each other.

It's frighteningly domestic.

They separate to get dressed, and then Rome waits outside Damien's door, trying and probably failing to look casual until Damien emerges. He takes a breath, holds out one hand, not looking at Damien—very intentionally not looking at Damien—and doesn't exhale until Damien accepts it. Damien does the thing Rome likes, where he pushes all of his fingers in between all of Rome's fingers, rubbing his thumb absently over Rome's first knuckle, and then nods toward the stairs. They can hear most of the guys in the common room already, waiting for the last few stragglers before they all head to breakfast together.

"You sure?" Damien asks, raising their joined hands.

Rome rolls his eyes and pulls Damien down the stairs.

CHAPTER TWENTY-THREE

HAVING A BOYFRIEND is great.

Having Patrick Roman as a boyfriend is a lot of other adjectives. Most of them are still synonyms for "great," but some are a little closer to "baffling," or "vexing," or "exasperating," or maybe just one of those long, teeth-clenched exhales that end more fond than angry.

For someone who writes a lot of poetry, Damien finds describing his relationship with Rome all but impossible.

His journal is full of trying though.

They fit, is the thing. Both physically—hands and bodies and mouths—but also generally. When Rome is having a loud-music-anxiety-spiral about a GM arriving for their next game, or he's spent too much time on the internet reading about Finley's next surgery, Damien can pull him out of his head with a little well-placed sarcasm softened by an invitation for pond hockey. When crumpled-up paper litters Damien's bed, and he should be working on his chemistry homework but can't until he gets the stupid fucking second stanza of this poem right, Rome will bully him into driving them to the store or ask for his help fixing something. By the time they've finished, Damien's brain has stopped running in circles, and he can breathe again.

They're good together. Even when they fuck up and yell at each other and slam doors and then have to apologize with actual honest words, or—more often than not—crossed arms and anxious, soft-spoken insults. Uncertain, reaching hands. Apologetic fingers.

The team doesn't really get it.

Mostly because Damien and Rome still act the same, but now, when Rome criticizes Damien's flagrant disregard for suggested daily sugar intake, he's sitting right next to Damien in the cafeteria, shoulders touching. When they're shoving each other on the bench or getting in each other's faces in a game, they're grinning. When they're arguing about plays on the bus, they're holding hands if they don't need both hands for pointed gesturing.

Now, when Damien misses a pass in practice, Rome can yell: "Distracted, Bordeaux?"

And Damien can answer: "By your beauty."

And Rome might tell him to shut the fuck up, and Justin might remind them they're there to play hockey, not flirt.

And if hearing their captain grouchily say the word "flirt" is enough to set them off into intermittent, lingering fits of laughter that make Damien miss a pass again, Rome can say: "Still distracted by my beautiful face?"

And Damien can answer: "Nah. This time it was your ass."

And Rome can say: "You can't even see my ass under all this shit."

And Damien can say: "I have a vivid imagination."

And Justin can say: "Hockey."

When, on Valentine's Day, Rome presents Damien with a homemade chocolate cake with an artfully rendered, if a little wobbly, icing dick on it, Damien kisses him and says thank you and declares that, from now on, he expects a dick-cake to celebrate every special occasion.

"Don't start having standards now," Rome mutters, ears pink.

"For you? Wouldn't dream of it, Roman."

"Are they flirting again?" Chai asks Olly, sotto voce, from the kitchen doorway. "Or are they fighting?"

"Hard to tell with them," Olly murmurs back.

"I think it's both," Kaner says helpfully.

And Brass and Olly and Chai and Kaner and Justin have all checked in with Damien, utilizing various levels of tact to make sure that Rome isn't being an actual dick to him. *Because he's definitely been better recently, but do you remember—* And of course, Damien remembers, he tells Brass. He can't forget what Rome was like. But that Rome isn't the Rome he's dating now.

The Rome he's dating makes him dick cakes and

shares his Gatorade during games, despite serious and frankly weird superstitions about personal water bottle use. The Rome he's dating notices when they stop at a convenience store for snacks and one of the employees chooses to shadow Damien as he browses the shelves. The Rome he's dating returns from the cold section with an arm full of drinks and says, "Afternoon, sir. I know my boyfriend looks like a real suspicious character in his floral shirt and velvet scrunchie, but he's got an Amex black card in his wallet and a Land Rover parked outside—a gift from his loving parents. I have six dollars and a borrowed bike. My parents are both in prison. So if you're going to follow someone around your fine establishment, it should probably be me."

The Rome he's dating loves babies. Especially babies named Finley. The Rome he's dating knows the names of all Finley's nurses and how to read all the monitors she's attached to. Sometimes, when Finley is upset or feverish, he'll sing to her in a soft raspy voice that does things to Damien's general chest region.

The Rome he's dating awkwardly kisses Damien's bruised fingers after a nasty slash and hesitantly asks if they can still hold hands or will it hurt too bad? The Rome he's dating likes cuddling, even if he won't admit it, playing with Damien's hair, and running at night together, no words, just steamed breathing.

Damien is still trying to be cautious, but the Rome he's dating now is nothing like the Rome he met in the administration office six months before.

Between his relationship with Rome, his recent publishing success, their team's current number-two standing in the league, and his improved communication with his parents, Damien feels like he has a solid grasp on happiness. He wishes he could feel like this forever.

And then he gets the email.

He's been waiting for it, is the thing.

Ever since he sent off the box with the little tube of his spit, he's been waiting for his results.

So it shouldn't be shocking when he receives them.

It is anyway.

He gets back from a run, checks his phone to see if Rome is done having dinner with the Hell Hounds GM (because as the season progresses, his boyfriend is now apparently being wooed by Important Hockey People), and then he absently thumbs over to his email.

A minute later, he's scrambling for his laptop.

Not only does he have his results, he also has an email from his—

Cousin.

Holy shit.

Thirty minutes and one FaceTime call later, Damien is standing in the basement, one hand on an open cabinet door, staring at a bottle of tequila.

Except he remembers the look on Rome's face when Damien pulled the scotch out of his hand the day before Christmas. He remembers the way Rome said, "Because I don't fucking know. I just don't like it, okay?" He thinks about Piper delivering a stuffed lobster to Rome on the couch. About the soft noises Rome makes sometimes in his sleep. He thinks about his mom's concerned voice on the phone. How she asks, every phone call now, if he's okay and if he's drinking.

Damien closes the cabinet and goes back upstairs.

Except Rome isn't here. Neither is Brass.

He goes to Kaner's room, but she's not there either.

He goes to Olly's next. But Olly isn't the one who answers the door.

It's Kaner.

"Oh," they both say.

"Um. Sorry," Kaner says, "I was just waiting for Olly, are you—"

"I was looking for you, actually."

Kaner smiles wanly, then frowns, taking a minute to really look at Damien. "Are you okay?"

Totally, Damien means to say. *Just wanted to see if you were free for some FIFA.*

His mouth doesn't say that though. It says, "I found my birth parents. Or...family. I guess."

"Oh. Wow. I didn't know you were looking for them."

"Yeah. Since I turned eighteen."

Kaner continues to study him. "Not what you hoped for?"

"No."

Kaner glances behind her at Olly's bed. She gestures to it. "Wanna sit?"

"No. It's fine. I'm—"

"Come sit."

Damien sits.

Kaner doesn't say anything, just waits, hands clasped loosely together, looking at him.

"I thought there might be a good reason," Damien

says finally, "that they gave me up and didn't leave contact info. Like, some sob story. *Whole family killed in terrible house fire. Only baby survived.* Or like, *Single mom killed in childbirth. No living relatives.* Something where it made sense, you know?"

Kaner says nothing, just continues to look at him expectantly.

"Except that's not what happened. What happened was two teenagers fooled around and got pregnant, and neither of their families wanted to deal with the social fallout of a baby under those circumstances. I got the story from one of my cousins. I talked to her a few minutes ago. She was in the database already, and after she got the email this morning, she went and confronted my birth mother about how, apparently, she had a baby at some point and never told anyone."

"Oh." Kaner says. "Wow."

"Yeah. So...I guess the secret's out to the extended family now. Whoops."

It's bitter.

He's bitter.

He thinks a little longingly about the tequila downstairs.

"That's a lot," Kaner says.

"And I get it. No judgement on not wanting to parent a kid as a teenager. Fine. They clearly made the right choice. But they just gave me up and then pretended I never existed. They could have at least— Rome isn't even Finley's *dad*, and he's trying really fucking hard to make sure he's part of her life. That there's a clear paper trail to find him if they get separated at some point in the future. She's going to know that he cared."

"Yeah," Kaner agrees. "He's really stepped up. And it sucks that your biological parents didn't. Are they at all interested in resuming contact now?"

Damien laughs without humor. "Not on my mom's side anyway. The cousin might be. She seems indignant on my behalf, you know? She's at Columbia. She said maybe we could meet up the next time I'm in New York. So that's cool."

"That is cool," she agrees.

"I guess I'm just pissed."

"You're allowed to be."

"And I know I have abandonment issues or whatever. Anxiety about stuff like that. Except usually, I just take a few shots and don't think about it anymore."

"I noticed you haven't been drinking the last few weeks," Kaner says slowly. "I didn't want to make assumptions, but if you're looking to talk to someone instead of getting drunk, that's a good thing. That's healthy."

"Yeah. I told Rome I would stop. Except usually if I start feeling like I want to, I just go find him or call him or whatever, and it distracts me. But he's meeting with the Hell Hounds GM right now, and I can't interrupt. And Brass isn't here."

"Ah, so I'm the backup emotional support person?"

He winces.

"No, I'm kidding," she says. "It'd be hypocritical of me, considering."

Damien opens his mouth and then immediately

closes it. He considers the slightly embarrassed hitch to her mouth. "What?" he asks.

"You know I have issues with anxiety. And...unhealthy ways of treating it."

He does.

"When it gets bad, I usually come to Olly, and he'll talk me down."

"What if he's not here?"

"Sometimes just sitting in his room helps."

"Oh."

Damien considers Kaner again.

Sitting on Olly's bed.

Waiting.

"Oh. Do you—"

"No, it's okay."

"Well. If you ever need someone, and Olly isn't there—"

"Thanks, Damien. But hey, did your genetic test have any interesting results? When my family did them, we found out my mom's side has Turkish ancestry, which was a surprise."

Damien laughs. "Actually, yeah. Apparently, I'm Chinese? The African and mixed-bag European wasn't a surprise, but the Chinese sure as hell was. God, I have so many questions. I need to pick Mandarin back up."

"No shit?" She considers his face. "Does that feel good, at least? To get some answers? Even if they give you more questions?"

"Yeah," he says. "You're right. That part does feel good."

The door downstairs slams, and the quick tread of

Olly's feet on the stairs interrupts them.

"Thanks." He stands and slips out the door just as Olly rounds the corner.

"Hey," Olly says, "did you need something?"

"Nah, I'm good. Just talking to Kaner."

Olly's face brightens. "Oh, I didn't know she was waiting for me."

Damien grins and retreats to his own room, except he still has Rome's key. He thinks of what Kaner said: "Sometimes just sitting in his room helps," and then suddenly, he's curled up on Rome's bed, arms wrapped around one of his pillows.

He breathes in.

And out.

And in.

And out.

The door opens an indeterminable amount of time later. It closes so softly that he props himself up on one elbow, confused. Rome doesn't do things softly.

"Hey," Rome says. His voice is soft too.

"Hey," Damien says, still confused.

Rome shrugs out of his jacket, presses toes to heels to remove his converse, and climbs onto the bed. He curls around Damien in a cocoon of winter-outside-smell and the warm press of green-sweater-fabric.

Rome wiggles a cold hand up the back of Damien's sweatshirt. "What are you doing?" he asks Damien's forehead.

"Feeling things."

"Ah. You want company?"

"You'll probably make it worse."

"That wasn't a 'no.'"

Damien makes a resigned noise. "Yeah, okay."

"Talk to me," Rome murmurs, breath warm against his face.

Damien does.

That night, his journal gets another damning entry:

> *people say 'i love you' like it's easy*
> *and maybe it is,*
> *for them*
>
> *but i am haunted by an anxious heart*
> *and i don't know how to explain*
> *that you are easy to love*
> *but i have only just started the project of loving*
> *   myself and*
> *i find it hard to believe that anyone else would*
> *   be willing*
> *to undertake the labor*
>
> *i want to say:*
> *if Pablo Neruda had seen your eyes*
> *he would have written twenty poems of love*
> *and one song of despair about them*
> *but people aren't supposed to say things like*
> *   that*
> *so i don't*
>
> *i want to say:*
> *please don't touch me if you don't mean it*
> *i'm scared the promises i'm hearing are just a*

poor translation
of what your hands are actually saying
but i'm too selfish or maybe too afraid
so i don't

i want to say:
i love you
so i don't

not because of the way you look at me
but because you might stop

because if i keep my love in my chest
and not in my mouth
then maybe it won't hurt so badly
when it is taken away

CHAPTER TWENTY-FOUR

WHEN ROME WAS fifteen, he slept next to another person for the first time.

Their hockey team was on a road trip and the shitty motel they were staying in had run out of rooms *and* extra rollaway beds. So the night before their game found him back-to-back with Aaron Greenspan in a full-sized bed. Marky and Boots were sharing the other bed, and Sebs was on a rollaway that mostly blocked the bathroom door.

Rome couldn't sleep.

Greenie was warm and solid and slow-breathing behind him, and he smelled like—well, Greenie. Except more than normal. Closer than normal.

Greenie chose him when they were all arguing about

who had to sleep with who. Greenie chose him, shouting *I've got Rome* as soon as Coach stopped talking. And then he threw his arm around Rome's shoulders as if to substantively stake his claim. As if Rome was something worth fighting over. As if he was a thing to be wanted.

They all ate a hasty dinner and piled into their rooms and wrestled over remote controls until their coaches yelled them all into silence and darkness.

The other boys in the room fell asleep quickly, but Rome couldn't. His brain kept telling him that Greenie was in the bed with him as if he wasn't perfectly aware of that fact. He kept remembering every time Greenie shared that damn peanut butter spoon with him. Every time Greenie loaned Rome his pill-y wool scarf. Every time Greenie crashed into him and shoved their helmets together, screaming through his mouth guard after a goal.

So he lay there and let himself pretend, just for a few minutes, that Greenie liked him back. That they were sharing a bed because they wanted to, not because they had to. And as Rome slipped sideways into sleep, he thought more abstractly about the future. That maybe, at some point, he would get to fall asleep next to someone who he loved, who also maybe loved him. That shared space and warmth and trust and love was something he could have one day.

Rome wakes up three years later to Damien's humid breath on the back of his neck, Damien's arms curled up between their bodies, knuckles pressed to the space between Rome's shoulder blades, Damien's outside leg thrown over Rome's hip.

He wakes up to grumbled discontent at the early hour, to reaching hands and the soft drag of palms down the terraced landscape of his ribs.

He wakes up to a persuasive mouth under his ear and slow kisses interspersed with laughter and what might very well be something close to *I love you* trying to force its way from behind his clenched teeth.

Damien—being with Damien—is everything he ever wanted. But now that he has it, he isn't sure what to do with it.

And he's desperately afraid he's going to fuck it up.

Damien knows how to do this. How to be a boy-friend. He knows when Rome needs to be left alone and when he needs to be distracted and when he needs quiet company. He edits Rome's papers and shaves Rome's head every two weeks and sneaks Rome's laundry in with his so everything Rome owns smells like Damien's detergent. Damien still messes up sometimes—less often than Rome does, obviously, because Rome is a disaster. But when Damien does mess up, when he pushes a friendly fight into unfriendly territory or turns down Rome's music before he's drowned out his thoughts enough or casually tries to pay for something that would take Rome months to save up for, Damien also knows how to apologize. He knows how to talk about his damn feelings in a way that makes Rome talk about his own feelings without even meaning to.

Damien knows Rome in a way no one else does. Because his father and stepmother hadn't wanted to know Rome. And in the shadow of their neglect, Rome had never given anyone else the opportunity. He knows his aunts and uncles have tried, especially Uncle Bruce and Maura. Only, for the longest time, he thought that vulnerability could only end in pain. But now, almost without meaning to, he's let Damien in. Damien, who wants to know Rome's weaknesses not so he can use those weaknesses against him, but so he can know how to love Rome better. Maybe. Or, maybe not love. He wonders if it is love though. He wants it to be love.

In return, Rome mostly tries to make sure Damien gets enough healthy food to eat and goes to sleep at a reasonable hour on school nights and doesn't make himself too crazy when he's writing. He reminds him that he's not bothering his parents if he asks them to FaceTime, and he stands in the audience when Damien does poetry readings and probably claps too loudly. Rome hopes that's enough.

It doesn't feel like enough, is the thing.

It doesn't feel like enough for all the whatever he feels when he watches Damien quietly carry on a full conversation with an enraptured Finley in his arms, head ducked, voice low, cadence soothing.

"Do you love him?" Kaner asked the night before.

She caught him staring at Damien in the den from the kitchen doorway like a creeper, something he's been getting worse and worse about because he doesn't have to hide it anymore.

"What kind of stupid question is that?" he snapped.

"An important one, assface. Is that a yes?"

"Shut the fuck up."

"I think that's a yes," she said, slapping the back of his head.

The slap turned into a noogie.

"Whatever," Rome said.

She just gave him a knowing look.

He's pretty sure it's a yes.

It's gotten to the point where the little things about Damien that used to infuriate Rome now only further endear him. His clumsiness off the ice. His seemingly innate political knowledge. His Opinions about everything from cream cheese to concussion protocols. Instead of finding Damien's bleary-eyed morning grumpiness obnoxious, Rome now sets his alarm five minutes early so he can let Damien pull him back into the bed a few times before they actually get up. So he can run his palms down Damien's clinging forearms. Slip his fingers through the divots of his knuckles. Trace the veins in the back of his hands.

"So do you have a hand kink, or what?" Damien mumbles into Rome's neck. "Don't think I haven't noticed you feeling up my knuckles every morning."

Rome is thankful for the semidarkness because his ears are undoubtedly going pink.

"No."

"No? It's okay if you do. No judgement. I've got a bit of a weird thing for your wrists myself, so."

Rome laughs and presses his mouth—not a kiss, just, whatever—to one of Damien's palms.

Rome's second alarm goes off.

"So," Damien says casually as they're brushing their teeth. "Spring break starts tomorrow."

"Mmm," Rome agrees.

"Maura is coming to the game on Friday. She'll get

here Thursday and stay for the weekend. And before you get mad about me paying for her to come or whatever, she paid her bus ticket and *asked* me to cover her hotel so she could visit. I'm taking her out to dinner Thursday night. You can come with us if you want."

Rome spits into the sink. "What the fuck?"

He is not awake enough to deal with this.

"Oh, and speaking of dinner," Damien continues. "You know my parents are here for the weekend as well? They were hoping you would come out to eat with us on Saturday. I know you're not working because we were going to see Finley, but would you mind if we did an early dinner before going to see her? My parents chose a restaurant right next to the hospital so we could do one and then the other."

Rome turns off the sink. "Your parents want to meet me? They want to meet Finley?"

"Well, yeah."

Damien is looking at him in the mirror like he's an idiot. "You and Finley are pretty much all I talk about on my calls with them now."

Rome is so distracted by the prospect of meeting Damien's parents, having dinner with Damien's parents, and then introducing Damien's parents to Finley that he forgets to be mad about the Maura thing.

"Wait. Can Maura come to dinner and the hospital too?" Rome asks, maybe a little desperate. "She'll still be here Saturday night, right?"

"I guess," Damien says with a smug little smile that means this has been his intention all along. "I mean, if you want, that's fine with me."

The conniving bastard.

"I hate you," Rome says.

Damien ignores him because they're both fully aware it isn't true.

*

ROME HAS TO work Thursday. He wouldn't have if he'd known about Maura's visit in advance. He might have called in sick anyway, except Benny really is sick and can only work for so long before he starts hacking up a lung. So Damien drops Rome off at the garage with a kiss through the open window and then goes to pick Maura up from the airport. Rome helps Benny finish an engine rebuild and sends him home to sleep. He then gets to work on all the things he can do by himself: fixing taillights and changing oil and putting on new tires and figuring out why the roof of a little Miata is leaking. It's good, simple work. Sweat and music and habitual movements. And, yeah, he wishes he could spend the day with Damien and Maura, but he's also stressed about the upcoming game as several scouts will be there. There's nothing like physical exertion to clear his head.

The only problem is that Damien has been a little worryingly uncommunicative after collecting Maura from the airport and taking her off to "explore." Whatever that meant.

After Kaner blackmailed Rome into letting her add him to her phone's unlimited family plan, Damien started sending him shit all the time. Photographs. Music. Dumb haikus. Passing observations. But his phone has been distinctly silent for hours.

Once the sun has set, Rome tries to decide if he should be worried or pissed.

Which is when a very familiar-sounding vehicle pulls up outside the garage.

By the time Rome manages to wiggle his way out from under the hood of the Chevy he's working on, Damien and Maura are ducking under the half-open bay.

"Hey, kid," Maura says.

She's still wearing her ever-present Habs hat, so clearly, Damien's campaign is ongoing.

She looks good. All plaid and work-worn jeans and a wide sharp smile.

And Damien has fucked him up with his casual touching and easy affection because his first instinct is to hug her. He gives her a fist bump instead. "Hey," he says.

"Told you he'd be pissed," Maura says to Damien. "You should have texted him."

"I'm not pissed," Rome argues.

"You are," they both say.

Rome rolls his eyes. He crosses his arms and kicks at the toes of Damien's boots. "I can't help it if this asshole usually texts me eighty times a day. It's weird when he goes silent."

"Aw," Damien says with a shit-eating grin. "Were you worried?"

"No."

Damien sidles up next to him in a way that means he wants a kiss, but he doesn't actually go for one. Rome realizes it's probably because Maura is there, and he's trying to gauge how comfortable Rome is with showing affection in front of her.

Which is sweet, but not necessary. Now it means that Rome has to be the one to initiate things, which is...not ideal.

"Oh for god's sake," Maura says, perceptive as always. "Just kiss him. I'm not a nun. Though, interesting story—"

"No," Rome says.

"Uh. Nun story? Yes," Damien says.

"It's not an interesting story," Rome says, ignoring Maura's affronted noise. "The woman wasn't a nun yet. You can't go around bragging that you've banged a nun when the vow of chastity was the next day."

"Wait. You were a nun's last hurrah?" Damien asks Maura. "That's almost more impressive. And negates any residual guilt for your listener in enjoying it."

"You think so?" she says.

"Definitely."

"Hm."

"Anyway," Rome says, throwing an elbow into Damien's side.

He also tips his head a little. Just to make his face more inviting. Available. Should Damien be interested in taking advantage of the easy access.

Damien obligingly leans in to kiss him.

Rome pretends this does not placate him. "Any reason why you're here?" he asks. "I thought you two were going to dinner. And ignoring me."

Damien grins, kissing him again in a way that seems more mocking than affectionate.

Rome allows it anyway.

"I was giving you distraction-free time to work as you so often request."

Rome can't really argue with that.

"I was also trying not to ruin the surprise."

"Surprise?"

"Well, if you couldn't go to dinner with us, we decided to bring dinner to you." Damien gestures with a flourish to the beat-up canvas bag over Maura's shoulder.

"Uh. Okay?"

"Oh shit," Maura says. "That was my cue. We probably should have practiced that."

She unzips her bag, and Rome is immediately hit with the gloriously unhealthy smell of hamburgers from the diner on the opposite side of the hardware store. The place has eternally sticky vinyl booths and the best strawberry milkshakes Rome has ever tasted.

"Milkshakes are in the car," Damien murmurs in his ear.

Rome tries to stifle a grin. "I don't think hamburgers are on our meal plan."

Maura throws a greasy paper-wrapped burger at his face.

Damien pulls Rome down to sit on a pair of recently removed tires. He passes him some fries while Maura goes to retrieve the shakes. When she returns, she unwraps her own burger and wanders around, poking at tool carts and ducking under the Chevy's hood with a considering noise.

"Shouldn't take us long to finish these up," she says.

"What's the Miata in for?"

Rome licks mustard off his fingers, then winces because his hands are not exactly clean. "Leak in the roof, and what do you mean 'us'?"

"Well, of the three of us, I'm the only one with ASE certification. I'm not about to leave my baby nephew to work the night away when, with my expertise, we could finish together in an hour or so."

"You're here on vacation," Rome argues.

"I'm not. I'm here to see you. Which I'll be doing."

"Damien said you're here to see him."

"Damien was lying. But if it makes you feel better, since Damien is the one that funded my trip, you can pay him back for my services." She raises an innocent eyebrow. "In whatever form of compensation you prefer."

Damien shoves a very large handful of french fries in his mouth. The subsequent choking noise he makes could either be from muffled laughter or actual choking.

"I think that's called prostitution," Rome says.

"Not if you'd do it for free anyway."

Rome can feel his ears going red.

"Why don't you tell your nun story," he says.

CHAPTER TWENTY-FIVE

DAMIEN'S PARENTS ARRIVE the following morning.

He drops Rome and Maura off at the garage after practice and then drives to the airport. His mother already has their morning planned out: brunch, shopping, sightseeing, lunch, and then back to the dorms for his pregame nap.

He offers his arm to her and carries her bags. He maybe talks too much and too long when she asks how Rome and Finley are doing, but she just smiles softly at him and makes him try on a shirt that brings out his eyes.

His father asks questions about his grades, his writing, the team, and where he plans to live for the next two years during the writer's workshop. Obviously, he'll stay at the house in Manhattan for the seminars once a month, but would he want to travel in between? Live in the Telluride house and commute to his seminars? Damien answers all but the last because he doesn't know.

Saying he wants to wait until after the draft—after he knows where Rome will be—to decide where *he* wants to be is a lot. More than he wants to admit to himself, much less to anyone else.

He drops his parents off at their hotel after lunch and then collects Rome from the garage.

Maura elects to stay a while longer to help Benny with his personal motorcycle project. Apparently, they've become best friends over the last few hours. Damien drives Rome back to the dorms in contented silence, their hands linked on top of the center console.

He doesn't ask if they're napping together because, of course, they're napping together. Rome waits as Damien leaves his shopping bags in his room, leaning against the wall between their doors in a way that is infuriatingly sexy. Mostly because he has no idea how sexy it is.

Damien waves to Chai, already in bed, and shuts the door.

Rome gets out his own key. "Hey, so," he says quietly, eyes on his hands, intentionally casual in a way that makes Damien immediately suspicious. "Can we revisit that orgasm conversation we had?"

Damien's brain goes offline for a hot second. "You realize we can't actually make a baby."

Rome pauses, blinking at the non sequitur. "What?"

Sometimes Damien forgets that Rome isn't in his

head. It's starting to feel like he is most days, is the thing.

He backtracks. "I'm just saying, you start spending all this time with an infant that looks like us, and suddenly, you're interested in making sweet sweet love to me?"

Rome makes a face that can only be called tormented. "Yeah, definitely not sudden, and please don't ever call it that again."

Damien considers this. "Not sudden?"

Rome shoves at the door a little and then jiggles the key in the lock. "Did you miss me trying to fucking jump you the first time we kissed?"

"Well, yeah, but you haven't tried to do anything more than kiss me since then, even though we're literally sleeping together, and half the time, I end up, like, sleep-humping you in the night."

"You said you weren't ready!" Rome whisper-shouts. He's turning a lovely shade of red. "And what you do in your sleep isn't a—a—" He gestures wordlessly for a second. "—an indication of consent!"

Damien is so proud.

Rome crosses his arms. "I was trying to respect your fucking boundaries or whatever."

"Thank you."

"You're welcome," he snaps.

"Okay. Just so it's clear," Damien says. "I'm on the same page as my dick. My sleeping dick. Well. I guess it's awake in this context, but—"

Olly comes around the corner. Kaner is on his back wearing light-up sunglasses and a pink cowboy hat.

They all just sort of stand there for a breath.

"I don't want to know," Olly says.

"I do," Kaner says, lowering the glasses to leer at him.

Rome viscously twists the key, and the door pops open.

"Uh," Damien says.

Rome pulls Damien into Rome's room and slams the door.

Rome face-plants onto the bed with an aggrieved noise.

Damien, uncertain of his welcome, takes off his sweater and shoes and waits for Rome to say something.

Rome rolls over after a minute, face still pink, scowling. "What are you doing? Get over here."

Damien joins him on the bed.

"So, that was mortifying," Rome says.

"If you recall, Kaner announced to the entire team that she thinks Olly's dick is perfect. This definitely ranks below that. Well below."

"Point."

Rome sits up, kicks off his shoes, and wiggles out of his jeans. He reaches for the hem of his henley and hikes it up over his head. "So," he says from the interior of the shirt. "Sex?"

And that's an unfair thing for Rome to ask when he's mostly naked and still delightfully flushed—flushed all down his freckled chest to winter-pale belly.

"Yes," Damien says. "Please."

Rome laughs at him, which, rude.

Damien takes off his own clothes in retaliation.

Rome stops laughing.

"I'm serious," Rome says. "I just want to make sure we're on the same page. So we don't fuck things up."

"Yeah. That's good. Do you know what you want to do, or—"

Rome shifts over, back to the wall, arms slung around his knees. "No? I think I'll like pretty much anything we do. Because it's you. But if not, we can figure it out together. I trust you."

Damien has to take a minute. He knows a declaration of love when he hears one.

"Is that cool?" Rome looks a little concerned. Probably because Damien is just sitting there like a potato. "I mean, you're still into me, right?"

Damien is so, so into him.

He wants to touch him everywhere all at once.

He wants to tattoo his name on the elegant line of Rome's scapula.

He wants to suck dark bruises onto the thin skin of his wrists, to mark the blue veins there as his.

He doesn't say that.

He says: "Yes."

"Okay. Good."

"Good. So. We'll do that, then," Damien confirms. "Sex things."

God. He's a disaster.

"Yeah." Rome bites his lip. "But not right now. We have a game tonight. And we need to nap."

"Right. Obviously."

Rome might be laughing at him.

*

THEY WIN THE game. Of course they do.

Because there are scouts in the stands, and Justin's and Chai's and Kaner's and Olly's parents are all there, as well as Damien's parents and Maura.

Kaner makes one goal.

Justin makes one goal.

Rome makes two. Both on assists by Damien.

When the final buzzer sounds, Damien and Rome are on the ice. They end up in the center of the team pile, Damien's face crammed awkwardly into Rome's sweaty neck, helmet no doubt pressing a hard indentation into his forehead.

He winces as someone's glove-heavy hand slaps the top of his helmet, listening to Chai yell about victory. He meets Rome's eyes through the cages of their face masks, grinning.

"Only two?" Damien asks Rome a minute later as they're skating for the exit. "Couldn't go for the hat trick when Maura came all this way?"

"Well maybe if you'd passed the puck to me instead of Kaner, asshole."

"Go fuck yourself," Damien says genially.

"Fuck me yourself, you coward."

Damien trips on his skates.

"Oh shit," Rome says. "Are you okay?"

"Fine," Damien says, scrambling back to his feet, helmet askew. "And, yeah. Maybe I will."

"Maybe you'll—? Oh. Well. Fine."

"Fine."

"Maybe revisit this conversation later," Justin suggests.

When they all emerge from the locker room, the atrium of the ice house is full of people. Damien watches as Rome finds Maura in the crowd—face lit up with pride.

"Holy shit, kid," Maura says, hitting his chest with the back of one hand. "You were good before but now..."

"It's all Damien."

"It's not. But it's cute you'd say that," Maura says.

"I'm not—no."

Damien decides to make his presence known, knocking his shoulder into Rome's. "Wow, Rome, what's got you all flushed?"

"My fault," Maura says.

Damien fist-bumps her. "Well thanks for that. I love it when he goes all pink." He tugs on one of Rome's ears. "It's cute."

"I am not," Rome says, slapping him away.

Damien smooshes a disgusting sloppy-wet kiss to his still-sweaty temple. "You are. Don't worry. It's cool. Oh, hey, there's my parents."

His parents change direction when they see Damien, his mom, literally, bouncing with excitement.

"*Mon chou!*" she says, throwing her arms around his neck. "You did so well!"

His dad goes for a less-exuberant shoulder pat.

"And you!" his mom says to Rome.

"Me?" Rome says.

"It's so wonderful to finally meet you. Come here and let me hug you."

Rome hunches a little to facilitate it, blinking, baffled, at Damien, his hands hovering over her back. "Uh," he says. "Hi. It's nice to meet you too?"

His mom steps back to beam at them both and then turns to address Damien.

"Oh," she says. "The pictures you sent didn't do him justice. You were right about the blushing; it's very cute." She turns to Damien's dad. "Isn't he cute, Elric?"

"So cute," he agrees stoically.

Rome makes a noise like a very small, very annoyed garbage disposal.

Damien slips his hand into Rome's and squeezes, trying not to laugh and failing spectacularly.

*

DINNER IS GOOD.

Maura and his dad bond over their love of shitty hockey teams, and then Maura and his mom bond over Maura's badass feminist boat crew. And his parents keep directing the conversation toward Rome—his grades, his interests, his plans for the future. Rome stutters his way through answering, anxious like it's a job interview and not a five-star dining experience. Damien keeps a steadying hand on his thigh and tries to run interference. By dessert, Maura has taken up the cause as well, regaling them with stories about Rome on his first summer crab haul. Stories about Rome's occasionally disastrous lessons in learning to cook in the months he lived with his aunt and uncle. About Rome playing Princess Star Warriors with Piper and Nicolaus Copernicus.

The hospital visit, afterward, is also good.

There's a line to get Damien's parents and Maura

visitor badges. Rome and Damien are a little spoiled with the freedom their permanent IDs give them. They proffer their lanyards more out of habit than necessity since the security officers know them by name now.

But once everyone is checked in, they talk them through the importance of handwashing and gown-wearing. Damien tells Maura seriously that she better take off her Habs cap just to be safe. Because germs.

Maura rolls her eyes at him but obeys, stowing it, brim down, in her back pocket. Damien nudges Rome, grinning, and Rome rolls his eyes too.

Rude.

Rome uses his badge to fob them into the cardiac NICU, and then they're in Finley's section. And there she is.

Damien's parents and Maura all have the same initial reactions to her as Damien and Rome, which is gratifying.

Amy comes over to introduce herself but mostly leaves them to their own devices. She shares a knowing look with Damien as Rome explains the rules about sitting down while holding Finley, navigating her various wires and tubes, and keeping her wrapped in the special phototherapy blanket that helps with her jaundice.

Finley sleeps through most of their visit.

Damien's mom gets a turn holding her first, Rome hovering close at her shoulder. He relaxes once it becomes clear that, A. she probably isn't going to suddenly yeet the baby across the room, and B. Finley is completely conked out.

Maura declines holding her, citing her preference

for tiny humans who are capable of speech, though she does run one knuckle very, very gently down the pudgy slope of Finley's cheek, smiling softly.

Damien's dad happily accepts her next, carefully tucking her blanket around her, eyeing the monitors suspiciously, before adjusting the little hat on her head and telling her a story about the first time he ever held Damien.

Damien is not a fan of this story.

It involves a lot of screaming and fecal matter.

Rome, however, is charmed.

Finley wakes briefly when another baby starts crying. The minute her little face squinches up, Damien moves forward automatically and pulls up another chair so he can take her from his dad in a series of well-practiced movements. He shifts her up so her face is in his neck and she can burrow in the way she likes, under his chin, one tiny hand bunched in the crinkly fabric of his gown.

She still can't seem to decide if she wants to yell for a bit or go back to sleep. Rome crouches next to them a moment later with a freshly sanitized pacifier and pops it into her mouth, careful around the cannula for her apnea—*she's been off the CPAP for a week now with no issues*, Damien tells his parents proudly. They all watch as her eyebrows lose their furrow and she settles. She bumps the crown of her head under Damien's chin a few times. She blinks slowly at Rome, who stays where he is, leaning back on his heels, braced with one hand on Damien's thigh.

"Maybe you should sing to her," Damien says. "That

always gets her back to sleep fast."

Rome flushes.

"You sing to her?" Maura asks, looking euphoric.

"Oh, how sweet," Damien's mom says. "Elric used to sing to Damien. He's no good, of course, but a little off-key Beatles would usually do the trick regardless."

Rome glances up at Damien, grinning, hand still on his thigh, squeezing a little. "Yeah? Maybe you should try some Beatles this time."

"Yeah, no."

Rome stands, and Damien misses him.

"Damien tried singing to her once," Rome tells his parents. "It didn't work out. There was vomit involved."

"Completely unrelated," Damien mutters, returning his attention to Finley. "Wasn't it, Finley? Say yes, completely."

She closes her eyes.

The soft glow from the phototherapy blanket makes her little face a study in shadows. Makes her look like a painting in blues. Everything about her is beautiful. The purse of her lips. The swoop of her nose. There's something completely captivating about her eyelashes that Damien has yet to manage to put into words, but he keeps trying.

He doesn't know how much time has passed when he glances back up, but Maura and his mother and Rome have moved on to discussing Finley's upcoming surgery.

His dad though.

His dad is looking at him, hands in the pockets of his slacks, head tipped a little, a completely uninterpretable expression on his face.

They leave shortly afterward, but instead of just dropping Maura and Damien's parents off at the hotel, his mother insists that Damien walk them up to their room.

So he hugs Maura and makes a judgmental comment about the return of her Habs hat and leaves Rome in the car knowing that his parents have Things to Discuss with him.

Up in their hotel room, he's expecting them to express support, or maybe gentle concern, about his relationship with Rome. After all, he's pretty sure it's abundantly clear how gone he is for Rome, and that's certainly not something that's happened before. What he's not expecting is for his mother to say:

"You didn't tell us Rome wanted to adopt Finley."

"He...doesn't?"

His mother raises an unimpressed eyebrow at him. "Rome looks at that baby girl like she's his. Talks about her like she's his. Treats her like she's his. She *is* his."

"What? No. He's—she's not. He knows that."

His mom lifts an eyebrow.

"He's *seventeen*," Damien says.

"He's almost eighteen," his dad points out. "And he's going to be a professional hockey player by this time next year."

"If anything, I think that makes him less qualified to be a parent," Damien says.

His mom sighs at him like he's intentionally vexing her. "Your father looked at you the exact same way that Rome looks at Finley. The exact same. From the day you were first put screaming into his arms. He still looks at you that way sometimes."

"*Chérie*," his dad says lowly.

"I'm just saying," she insists. "You might want to mention Nora to Rome."

And that gives Damien a pause. "Nora? But you guys didn't adopt Nora—oh. *Oh.*"

"And you might want to think about how serious you are about this. About him. Long-term serious, I mean," she says. "Dating-a-teenage-father serious, I mean."

"*Chérie*," his dad says again.

His parents do that thing where they have a conversation without any words.

"I'm going to go fill up the ice bucket," his mom says suddenly. "*Bonne nuit, mon ange.*"

She kisses his cheek and leaves the room a moment later.

"Damien," his dad says. And he's using his Dad Voice.

"Your mother might have been too busy spying on Rome and Finley to notice, but I pay attention too."

Damien honestly has no idea where he's going with this. "Okay?"

"You look at Finley the same way Rome does."

Damien swallows.

"I'm not going to say anything else about it now. You need to make decisions for yourself, and you've proven you're more than capable of doing so in the last few years. But before you let this go any further, you need to be certain. Or as certain as you can be in the circumstances. Not just for you, but for both of them too."

Damien doesn't say anything. He doesn't know what to say.

"Just know that we're here to support you. Whatever you might need. Or whatever you and Rome might need. If it comes to that."

His dad pulls him forward and kisses his forehead. "Regardless, I'm proud of you. Okay?"

"Okay."

"See you for breakfast tomorrow?"

"Uh. Yeah," Damien agrees. "Breakfast. Good."

He walks back to the car on autopilot, trying and failing to act normal on the ride home.

Because he doesn't want to be Finley's *father*.

Does he?

Sure, he loves her. And cares about her. And worries about her. But that's normal. She's a tiny baby. Tiny babies inspire those kinds of feelings. And she's a tiny, sick baby who's related to Rome, who looks weirdly like the two of them, so that's—that.

Watching Rome with Finley makes him feel some type of way.

A having-kids-with-Rome-one-day-might-be-nice type of way.

But that's a fantasy. A many-years-in-the-future kind of fantasy.

Sure, maybe his browser is currently half-full of YouTube tabs on easy styles and hair maintenance for toddlers with Finley's curl type. Even though it'll be another year before she even has enough hair for any of the styling videos and her hair type could very well change. But it's always good to be prepared. And what if she ends up getting adopted by white parents?

Damien could visit, maybe, and help them figure hair things out.

And maybe he's checked out more library books on infant development than books for his actual classes in the last month. That's only because he found a list of them scribbled on Rome's desk, and he knew Rome didn't have any extra time to read with his schedule. When Rome is at work, Damien does the reading for him, takes some notes, and later gives Rome the breakdown so they can know if Finley isn't meeting benchmarks. And they can talk to Amy about ways to increase her motor function despite the limitations she has and—

Oh god.

Okay.

He might get where his dad is coming from.

Shit.

He needs to talk to Rome about Nora.

CHAPTER TWENTY-SIX

THEY DON'T HAVE sex.

Rome doesn't know why, except that when Damien comes back to the car after dropping off his parents, he has a vacant look on his face that's concerning. He tells Rome his parents are supportive and approve. Then he bullies Rome into bed and wraps around him, even more constricting than usual, and keeps taking these long, careful breaths.

After submitting himself to fifteen minutes of anxious cuddling, Rome shoves Damien off of him and curls around his back. He pushes a hand up Damien's shirt and then pets his stomach in a way that Damien seems to find soothing.

Eventually, Damien's breathing evens out, and he

stops being a live wire of tension, and Rome can finally go the fuck to sleep.

In the morning, Damien acts like everything is fine and normal. They're meeting the guys, Kaner, and all of their parents for breakfast at the diner, so they don't have a chance to talk. Damien still seems normal. He keeps his arm slung over the back of the booth behind Rome's neck, leaning into him and stealing food off his plate.

After they eat, they pick up Maura to take her to the airport, and they hold hands on the center console while Maura makes faces at Rome in the rearview mirror.

It's worth it, the hand-holding.

Once they've pulled to the curb at departures and unloaded Maura's suitcase, Maura hugs Rome.

Rome just stands there. "Uh. What are you doing?"

"Damien says I should hug you more."

"Damien is—"

"The light of your life?" Damien supplies, joining the hug. "The fire in your loins?"

"Ugh," Maura quickly exits the hug.

"If you ever want me to touch your dick," Rome says lowly, "you will never say the word 'loins' to me again."

"Noted," Damien agrees.

They hold hands on the drive back to campus, too, and Damien keeps throwing him these sweet little half-smile glances. Rome doesn't know how to bring up that they said they were going to have sex and then didn't when everything else seems fine. What if it starts an argument? Or what if Damien is planning something fancy? What if he's one of those people who has romantic ideas about first times? What if there are rose petals or special playlists involved? That seems like the kind of ridiculous shit Damien would pull.

Then again, it's Rome's room.

Shit.

Should *he* be planning something?

Is Damien expecting him to pull ridiculous romantic shit?

What even goes on a sex playlist?

His mind is occupied with potential sex playlist contenders for most of the afternoon while they do some sightseeing with Damien's parents in Boston, visit Finley again, and then go to dinner.

Except only minutes after they've sat down and Damien is whisper-translating the French menu to him, his phone rings.

It's Amy.

He answers it at the table, immediately assuming the worst because he was just there—there's no reason for her to call him unless something is wrong.

"Is she okay?"

"Whoa, hey. No, she's fine."

Rome exhales, sitting from the half-standing position he'd been in. "Then why are you calling?"

"I just spoke to Finley's social worker. You only missed her by a few minutes or I would have grabbed you while you were still here."

"Oh. Okay."

"As you know, Finley's surgery next week should hopefully allow her to leave the hospital once she's recovered."

"Yeah."

"So her social worker has started the process of finding Finley a foster for when that happens."

"Oh."

"And," Amy says gently, "she's also started the process of finding Finley an adoptive family."

"Oh," he says again.

Or, he tries to say it. Except he doesn't make any noise. It feels like someone has a hand fisted around his throat.

"I know you'll want to be a part of the process, and considering the glowing assessment of you the hospital's social worker gave her, she's looking forward to hearing from you. She'll try to make sure you're as involved as possible."

He tries to swallow around the—panic? No. This isn't panic. This is something worse than that. Anger, maybe. Or jealousy, tempered by guilt because Finley getting out of the hospital is a good thing. Finley getting a family is a good thing. Except she fucking *has* a family, she has *him*.

"Rome?" Amy says. "Hey, you still there?"

"Yeah," he manages.

"Anyway. I told her I'd give you her number so you two can coordinate. Do you have a pen?"

He doesn't.

He records the number with disconcertingly steady hands in his phone's notepad.

He repeats it back to her blankly.

She confirms it is correct.

He should probably say thank you.

"Thank you."

"Rome?"

"Yeah."

"Are you okay?"

"Fine. This is—" He swallows again, and it's even harder this time. "This is good news."

"Rome."

"I've got to go."

He hangs up.

He stands.

"Sorry," he says, and Damien is looking up at him, eyes wide and concerned. "Sorry. Everything's fine. I just—need to go. I'm sorry."

Rome leaves.

He knows Damien is going to come after him. And that's gratifying, in its own way, but for once, he doesn't want Damien to try to make things better. He can't fix this. And Rome doesn't think—he can't—

Rome runs.

Like some kind of dramatic asshole in a film-festival drama.

He weaves his way through a few different streets by way of a few different back alleys until he has absolutely no idea where he is, and then he calls for an Uber.

Sitting in the back seat, spending money he doesn't have, he leans his head against the window and tries very hard not to cry.

He doesn't go back to the dorms; he doesn't want Damien to find him.

Or he doesn't for a couple hours, at least.

He starts wanting Damien to find him right around

the fourth shot of vodka at the seedy bar he finds.

Except he's done too good a job of disappearing.

And he's—well, he's drunk. For the first time ever.

He hates himself a little for that.

He breaks down and calls Damien, and he hates himself a little for that too.

"Where are you?" Damien says after the second ring. "Are you okay?" His voice is low and flinty.

Rome gives him the name of the shitty bar and then goes to sit on the curb by the dumpster in the alley.

He wishes he wasn't wasted because he knows the conversation they're about to have will be even shittier now than it would have been if he was sober.

He wishes, for once, that he looked his age. That he didn't have height and hockey muscle and the sharp edges of someone who's worked for every crumpled dollar bill they fish out of their pocket to buy shots. Maybe then, he'd just be a miserable, sober seventeen-year-old sitting on a curb having an existential crisis instead of a miserable drunk one.

Damien looks furious when he parks the Land Rover beside him a few minutes later. He slams the door. Definitely furious.

"I was so fucking worried about you," he says. "What the fuck?"

Rome tries to shrug.

He wobbles a little.

"You've been drinking," Damien points out. "You don't do that."

"I want to adopt Finley," Rome says.

Damien sits down next to him.

"I can drop out," Rome continues, voice even despite everything. "Start working more at the garage. Get a second job at a coffee shop or something. Find an apartment in town."

"No, you won't," Damien says.

"Funny how it's not your decision."

"First of all, the state isn't going to award custody of a disabled baby to a seventeen-year-old high school dropout, even if you are emancipated. But besides that, I know you don't want to raise Finley poor."

"The fuck is that supposed to mean."

"You want to raise her with plenty of money for specialists and therapy and private preschools. I know you do. You want to spoil her rotten. Give her everything you never had."

"Of course I do." Rome's voice breaks, and he doesn't even care. "But I don't see how that's an option."

"You're being projected as going early in the second round of the draft. And we all know you'd be higher if you'd been playing in juniors or had any kind of recognition before this year. You are going to make *actual real money* as a professional athlete."

The tears that have been building for hours, hot, behind Rome's eyes, finally push out into the open air. They cling to his lashes. They smear on his palms.

Playing hockey, making something of himself, is all he's ever wanted.

Until Finley.

"The draft isn't for another three months, though," he says, voice wrecked. "And the season won't start for another two months after that, and even then, I can't—"

Rome sniffs, rubbing the heels of his hands into his eyes again. "I can't take care of a baby as a rookie in the NHL."

Damien shifts so he's no longer on the curb but kneeling in front of Rome.

Rome resists the urge to tell him that he's ruining his jeans.

They're a pretty pale mustard color.

Rome likes them.

"Hey." Damien rests his hands, gentle and earnest, on Rome's bent knees. "Look at me."

Rome looks at Damien.

"If you're working two jobs to make ends meet, you're going to have even less time with her than you would as a professional hockey player," he says. "Even if the surgery goes perfectly, she still needs to be at the hospital for a couple more weeks, at least. And after that, long-term fosters are a thing, you know. And they're a thing for a reason. My parents fostered a kid before me."

Rome blinks. His brain feels slow and hot. "What?"

"My parents were long-term fosters for a little girl before me. Nora. They got her as an infant because her teenage mother was homeless. Kicked out for being pregnant. So they took care of Nora for nearly two years while her mother got her life together. And once she finished high school and got a job, they slowly transitioned Nora back. By the time she was three, she was living full-time with her mother. They got me shortly after."

"I don't—" Rome considers this. "Do they still keep in touch with her?"

"They do. They saw her in person once a month or

so until I was around four. They have pictures of us to-gether. But then her mom got married, and they moved. They're all still friends on Facebook. Talk on the phone. My parents paid for her college."

"Casual."

Damien rolls his eyes. "My point is. Talk to the case-worker. You're kin and have a good case for delayed guardianship. You can get a foster who will work with you until you've settled with a team, until you're through the first year or two and know you aren't going to be sent back down to the AHL, until you have a house. A room for her. Your options aren't *right now or not at all.*"

"Even then," Rome says, "even if I wait a year or two, that's— I can't be in the NHL and take care of a kid alone. Not when I'll be traveling a third of the year. That's not fair to her."

"Maybe not alone," Damien says. But it isn't agree-ment. It's something a lot bigger than that.

"Fuck you. You can't just—"

"I love you," Damien says, and it's like a punch to the gut. "I know it's probably a shitty way to say it for the first time, but I do. Love you. And I love her. I don't know what I want to do with my life, but I know I don't want to play professional hockey. I know I want to write. I ac-cepted the place in the writer's workshop, which means I'll need to spend a week in New York every month but for the rest of the month, I can write anywhere. And hopefully, when I'm finished with the workshop, I'll publish some shit and win some awards and just keep writing from wherever. And Finley— I know taking care of a kid is hard. Especially a kid with special needs. I'm not romanticizing it. But if this is something you want to do, and you do it smart, without killing yourself or throwing away your career or fucking off to drink yourself stupid..."

Rome winces.

"And maybe you talk to a therapist about it."

Rome winces harder.

"I guess I'm just saying that I know it's crazy. But I'm in. If you're in."

"So, what?" Rome says. "You're volunteering to follow me wherever I go in the draft? Maybe move a couple times while I bust my ass in the AHL and hope to be permanently called up somewhere? And even if I am, then you'll—what? Be a stay-at-home dad for a kid that isn't even yours?" It starts off abrasive as hell but ends almost plaintive.

"Yeah," Damien says. "That's exactly what I'm volunteering for. And she would be mine. If you'd let me have her."

Rome can't handle that right now. "You just want to be my kept man," he chokes out.

Damien laughs.

It sounds a little damp, but who is Rome to judge.

"It's true," Damien says. "I have dreams of lounging by the pool drinking mimosas while Finley is at kindergarten and you're off earning millions."

"Fuck you." It comes out as more of a sob than an expletive.

"I'm sorry. I think I may have misheard you. Was that a *thank*-you?"

"No."

"I think it was. I think it was a *thank you, Damien, you're right. I should stop being a martyr and let the people in my life who love me help me.*"

There's that word again.

"No," Rome says. He doesn't mean it.

"Yes?"

"No."

"Yes."

"Maybe."

Damien leans forward, weight still on his hands, hands still braced on Rome's knees. He kisses him softly. Barely even tangible.

"I'm sorry," Rome says.

"Don't do that shit again. You scared the hell out of me."

"I won't. I promise." He means it.

"Okay."

Damien stands and offers Rome his hands. "Home?"

Rome lets Damien pull him up to his feet and then just keeps going, falling into Damien with enough intention to telegraph his objective but not enough sobriety to make the movement elegant. He doesn't care. He tucks his face into Damien's neck and clings.

"Home," Rome agrees.

CHAPTER TWENTY-SEVEN

DAMIEN WAKES UP to his phone alarm going off and Rome staring at him.

Not in a creepy way. But a sleepy, bleary, horribly hungover for the first time ever and not handling it well kind of way.

After silencing his phone, Damien goes a little cross-eyed staring back.

"Hey," he says.

Rome grunts. It sounds pained.

"Tylenol?" Damien asks.

"Please," Rome whispers.

Damien hands over pills and a Gatorade, then brings him some scrambled eggs and toast. He lingers longer than he should to kiss the adorably anguished crease between Rome's eyebrows and zip him up in one of Damien's hoodies.

He's late for class. Damien finds he doesn't care.

Rome is sitting up in bed squinting at a textbook when Damien stops by the dorms at lunch. He leaves a chicken salad, a handful of cookies wrapped in a grease-spotted napkin, and another Gatorade.

After his last class, Damien returns to find Rome showered and dressed in the common room, and a dorm full of really good smells.

"Fuck me," Chai says, hanging up his coat. "I'm going to need whoever is cooking to marry me immediately."

"No," Rome says from the couch. "Though, technically, the Insta-Pot is the thing doing the cooking. And I can't speak for her."

Damien leans over the back of the couch to kiss Rome because he's cute and because he has just refused to marry someone else, an admirable quality in a boyfriend.

"Better ask her myself, then," Chai says, slicking back his hair and walking purposefully into the kitchen.

Rome laughs.

"So what's in the Insta-Pot?" Damien asks.

"Chili. Figured I'd make us something special for dinner since you—" Rome waves an embarrassed hand.

"Doted on you?" Damien supplies. "Cared for you? Played nursemaid? Saw to your every need?"

"Not my every need," Rome mutters and then goes abruptly pink. "Anyway. Whatever. Thank you."

"No problem."

"Also. I was wondering."

Damien raises his eyebrows. "Oh, I see. The chili isn't a thank-you; it's a bribe."

"It can be both," Rome says. "It's really good chili. And I got the stupid fancy ground beef you like, even though it costs twice as much."

"It's not stupid to want meat that was treated ethically, Roman. Happy, healthy, free-range cows taste better than sad, abused, antibiotic- and hormone-ridden—"

"Oh my god," Rome says. "Do not fucking start this again. A cow doesn't need to have a lullaby sung to it every night to be—"

"So what's that favor you wanted to ask me?" Damien interrupts.

Rome goes silent, glowering at him.

Damien smiles politely.

"I was wondering," Rome says, "if you would sit with me while I call Amy. To ask about adoption stuff."

"Oh. Yeah. Of course."

Neither of them says anything for a long, awkward moment.

"Now?" Damien asks.

"Sure. The Insta-Pot has two more hours, so we can wait a while if—"

"No, it's fine. Now is good."

They go upstairs and sit on the bed, backs to the wall, fingers laced together, phone on speaker bridging their thighs.

Amy doesn't answer at first, but she does call back a few minutes later.

"Hi, Rome. Are you okay?"

"Yeah. Yes. Hi. How are you?"

Damien can hear her smiling.

"I'm fine. I was just worried about you last night. You sounded a little off on the phone."

Rome swallows. "I was hoping I could talk to you about, um, adoption stuff."

Well. That's one way to introduce the topic.

Amy's pause is weighty. "Of course. Do you—"

"I know I wouldn't be able to take care of her now," Rome says, well, blurts out, really.

Amy exhales, and it sounds like relief.

Damien can tell that rankles a little.

"But I also know that longer term fosters are a thing," Rome says. "And I don't know how this is supposed to work or what channels I need to go through but... Do you think it might be possible for me to adopt her in a year or two? Start the process now, and then once I'm established take her full time? I know I'm young, but—"

"Oh, sweetheart. I'm glad you're being smart about this. That really shows maturity. I was afraid for a minute you wanted to adopt her *now*."

Rome glares briefly at Damien, who tries very hard to keep his expression blank.

Judging by Rome's subsequent eye roll, he's probably not successful.

"No," Rome says. "I want to"—he throws Damien another look—"be smart about it."

"Well, good. There is a process for what you're describing, and we'll need to talk to our social worker as well as Finley's caseworker and child services if this is something you want to work toward. But I think it's feasible. I'd be happy to explain what that might look like and the things you need to do the next time you visit. Or I can have Sonja—that's Finley's caseworker—contact you directly and walk you through things."

Rome exhales. "Thank you. I'd like to talk to Sonja as soon as possible. But we have next weekend off, and I haven't made my work schedule yet. Can I talk to you then, too, or—"

"Of course. Also, if the surgery next week goes as planned, Finley will be cleared for short adventures two weekends from now. So if you want to ask for some time off now, you could start planning to take her for her first-ever trip outside the hospital. No more than an hour or two, but still a big milestone. Maybe to the botanical garden next door or something?"

Rome looks horrified by this prospect. "Are you sure that's safe? So soon after heart surgery?"

"Oh, look," she says dryly, "you're parenting already."

"That sounds good," Damien says when it's clear Rome is too busy having an existential crisis to respond.

"Oh, hello, Damien," Amy says. She doesn't sound surprised to hear his voice. "How's the baby-wearing research going? Did you find a wrap you like?"

Traitor, he thinks uncharitably.

"The what research?" Rome says.

"I did," Damien says stoically. "I went with the ERGO Baby for now while she's small. But, uh. I think the Wrapsody one would be a good option for when she's bigger."

Wrapsody, Rome mouths.

"Sounds like you're prepared," Amy says. "Maybe you should teach Rome how the ERGO Baby works, and you can bring it to try after Finley's surgery."

Damien can do that. Thanks to YouTube tutorials and practicing with Kaner's stuffed tiger, he's basically a pro. "Sure thing," he says.

Amy and Rome talk more about arranging a meeting time and that Rome can't actually "adopt" her as a sibling, but rather, he'd be applying for "guardianship," which is legally the same thing.

Damien tunes them out because he's thought before, abstractly, about carrying Finley. Against his chest. Out in the world. But now he has a date, in the near future, when it will actually happen. But the world is such a big, loud, dangerous place. And she's so small. He kind of gets why Rome's first response to the idea was caution. Is this what being a father is like? Constant worry?

"Hey," Rome says, and Damien realizes the phone's screen is dark. "You okay?"

"Yeah."

They should probably talk before things go any further. Both legally and in terms of baby-wearing and Damien's poor, hopeful, anxious heart.

"Do you really have a wrap?" Rome asks.

"Yeah," Damien admits. "Back of my closet. I've been practicing with Kaner's tiger."

He probably could have done without sharing that part.

Rome's sudden, face-splitting grin is worth the embarrassment. "Seriously?"

"Well. Her shark wouldn't work."

"The tail," Rome agrees sagely.

His grin fades.

"We should probably, uh—"

"Yeah." Damien says.

They both look away.

The silence stretches past the point of comfort.

One of them is going to have to be brave, and Damien is really hoping it's not him.

"So," Damien says.

"So," Rome agrees.

Shit. Okay. It's going to have to be him.

He opens his mouth, but nothing happens.

"I know," Rome says.

"What?"

"I know we need to talk. About last night. "

"We do," Damien agrees.

Rome licks his lips. "Feel free to start," he says, a little sheepishly, and Damien tries to laugh but doesn't quite manage it.

"I know I said—"

"I'm not—"

They both start and then stop again with a lurch.

"It's okay if you didn't mean it," Rome says, more exhale than sentence. "Or if you did then but aren't sure now. Or you need time to think about it."

"I did," Damien says. "Do. But it doesn't have to be me. If you don't want me, for you or for Finley, that's—fine."

It isn't fine.

For someone who hadn't even realized he was in love or wanted to be a father until the day before, the words are overwhelmingly, wrenchingly terrible.

"We're new. And we're young. And there are awesome live-in nannies, you know?" Damien continues. "And you'll be able to afford one once you're signed. Whatever team you end up with can probably even help you find a good one. So if *we* aren't something you want, you can still have Finley. But you've gotta tell me now because I'm already— If this isn't serious for you, I need to—"

"I am," Rome interrupts. "I mean, I love you. I'm pretty sure."

Rome's mouth seems uncomfortable around the word.

"You're pretty sure," Damien repeats.

From anyone else, Damien might find that inadequate. But from Rome—

"I haven't associated love with...good things. Historically. But I realize my perspective is fucked up. And I know good things are supposed to be associated with love. I've seen it with my aunts and uncles and the kids. So, I think I do. Love you. Because you're...good things."

He scrubs his fingers over his face, making an annoyed noise.

"I'm good things?" Damien

"The best," Rome mutters.

Damien tries to stifle a grin.

"Shut the fuck up," Rome says. "I'm trying."

"I know. I see that."

"The closest model to a healthy relationship I have is my aunt and uncle, and I only lived with them for a couple months. But I think this may be endgame for me."

"I'll take it."

"I guess I don't understand. Why you even—"

Damien thinks he wants to say *love me* but can't quite make himself go there.

"You can do better," Rome says. "So much better than me. You're you. And I'm just..." He shrugs as if that's all he needs to say.

"You're just?" Damien repeats, incredulous. "What the fuck. There's nothing *just* about you."

The words are woefully inadequate.

Rome goes very, very red. He clears his throat, standing suddenly. "I was going to make some corn-bread to go with the chili. You want to help?"

"I—sure?"

"Great. Let's go."

Rome more or less flees the room, and Damien follows, catching his arm as they descend the stairs. He pulls Rome to a stop so he can tuck down the tag in the back of his shirt and kiss his neck for good measure while he's there.

"Your hair is getting long again," Damien notes. "You want me to cut it tonight, or are you finally going to give in and let your ringlets grow?"

"I hate you," Rome says.

"You love me," Damien says. And he's pretty sure it's true now.

"I tolerate you."

"You already admitted it." he says, commandeering Rome's hand as they enter the common room. "No take-backs."

"No takebacks? Are you twelve?"

"Twelve inches."

"You wish."

"I don't, actually. That would be really inconvenient."

"Yeah? Probably true, right, Olly?" Rome asks, rounding the corner into the kitchen.

"Hmm?" Olly says.

"Having a monster dick," Rome says. "It's inconvenient, right?"

Olly throws a chip clip at them.

*

THAT NIGHT, DAMIEN leaves Rome to his make-up work and goes to have dessert with his parents. They order room service and lounge on the king-sized bed dipping forks and spoons into various shared dishes, occasionally devolving briefly into silverware warfare.

Damien tells his parents about Rome's decision.

His decision.

His parents are very quiet afterward.

They do that thing where they have a whole conversation through raised eyebrows, quirked lips, and subtle utensil gestures.

"Well," his mother says, "I can't say it's a surprise, really. Though I certainly thought I had more time be- fore— Oh my goodness—" She interrupts herself with sudden, urgent ferocity. "I'm going to have a grandbaby. What is she going to call me?! I didn't think I was going to have to decide this until much later. Okay. This is fine. We can figure it out right now. What do you think?" She drops her spoon to grab Damien's hands in both of hers. "Do I look like a grandma? A grammy? A nana?"

"You look far too young to be any of those things," his dad says around a forkful of tiramisu.

"Points for charm, love," she says fondly. "But that's not actually helpful."

"You realize Finley isn't going to start speaking any time soon, right?" Damien points out. "And it's not like *I'm* adopting her. I'm just—dating her potential future dad."

And planning a life with the two of them.

And having daydreams about teaching Finley to skate.

And maybe, sort of, very abstractly, thinking about what she'll call Rome ("Dad"?) and wondering then if she might call Damien "Papa" or something else.

Damien needs to take a few deep breaths.

His parents ignore him.

"I'm rather partial to *grand-père* myself," his dad says thoughtfully.

"Oh," his mother says. "Oh, that's perfect. *Grand-mère* and *grand-père*. Are you wanting to teach her French?" She turns to Damien. "We can certainly help with that. It's served you so well, *chéri*."

"Oh. I mean, I'll have to ask Rome, but that's prob-ably— All the books say the sooner you teach kids differ-ent languages, the better. And multilingual children tend to have better social, analytical, and academic skills than monolingual kids. I probably need to read up some more, but—"

"Just something to think about," his dad interrupts. "Deep breaths."

Damien finds that advisable. He clears his throat. "Speaking of languages, there's something I've been meaning to talk to you about."

Both of his parents sit up a little straighter.

"I did a DNA test a couple months back. And I found out why I took to Mandarin so quickly."

He knows that's not how it works. Probably. But it's the closest thing he's found to use as a segue into a conversation he feels ill-equipped to have.

His mother drops her fork. "You didn't tell us."

"It was a personal thing, at first. But I'd like to talk about it now? I've also been in contact with one of my cousins."

Her hand curls around his wrist and squeezes.

"Of course," she says. "Tell us everything."

*

AN HOUR LATER, Damien returns to the dorm feeling a little overwhelmed.

Rome is already in bed and mostly asleep, though his laptop is open on the mattress beside him.

"Hey," he says.

"Hey," Damien agrees.

"Did you apologize to your parents for me?"

"I did. You're forgiven. They also sent me back with

the name and info for the lawyer they used when they adopted me. Just in case you wanted it. And they want to help us teach Finley French."

"Oh. Okay? They really must forgive me, then."

"Yeah."

Damien strips out of his clothes, moves Rome's laptop to the desk, and tucks himself right into Rome's space.

"I know you're calling the shots and everything, but I think it'd be a good idea to teach her a few other languages as early as possible. French and Spanish for sure. Maybe Mandarin?"

"I don't know any of those languages," Rome says. "Do you?"

"Yeah. My Mandarin is a little rusty, but I've started using the Murder Owl app again. I know basic Italian too."

"Jesus," Rome says. "You should probably start teaching me now, then. Can't have you two off using secret languages and leaving me out."

Damien's chest goes tight with what feels like an excessive amount of affection. "Please tell me you're freaking out a little about this, too," he mumbles into Rome's warm, Rome-smelling neck.

"I'm freaking out a little about this, too," he confirms.

"Okay, good."

"Second thoughts?" Rome asks.

"None."

"Okay," Rome says again. "Good." He reaches to turn off the light. "Did you brush your teeth?"

"Nope. And I'm not going to."

"Heathen."

"That's me."

Rome pushes his mouth briefly, brusquely, against Damien's forehead. He still hasn't figured out sweet, gentle kisses yet. But they're working on it.

Damien wiggles one hand up the back of Rome's shirt and exhales, long and slow. "Night."

"Night," Rome agrees.

Several minutes later, when Damien is more asleep than awake, Rome shifts, dragging his hand down Damien's outside arm.

"Hey," he says. "You don't still write sad poetry about me, do you?"

"No. I do write about you though."

"Happy shit?"

Damien grins. "Sure."

"Do one."

"You want me to make up a poem about you...right now?"

"Yeah," Rome says, sleep-slow. "Happy one."

Damien considers for a moment. Runs his fingers up and down the terraced landscape of Rome's ribs.

There was a time when Rome was untouchable. Too sharp for physical affection. Damien can't imagine going back to that now.

"You are," he says, mouth under Rome's ear. "The happiest accident."

He kisses Rome's jaw. "A book left on the wrong shelf."

He runs his nose down the tendon of his neck.

"Found by the right hands."

He exhales, damp breath on hot skin. "An accidental allurement I never want to stop reading."

Rome swallows, and Damien can feel it. "Thank you," he whispers.

"I love you," Damien says. And it isn't particularly poetic, but it is true, and it feels necessary to remind him.

"Love you," Rome answers.

It's quiet and rough and still more than a little awkward, like he's preparing to have to defend himself for being briefly vulnerable, but it lacks the uncertainty of before.

Damien continues to drag his fingers in aimless patterns up and down Rome's back as little fragments of poetry, now that they've started forming, continue to crowd in his head. He traces words down the margin of Rome's spine:

Maybe my happiness will not be counted in days.
Maybe I deserve a soft epilogue.
Maybe you are mine.

CHAPTER TWENTY-EIGHT

TWO DAYS AFTER Damien's parents have left, Rome sits on his bed pretending to do homework, waiting for Damien to come home.

Damien had a meeting with his poetry teacher after his final class, and they have—Rome checks his phone—eleven minutes before they're supposed to meet the rest of the guys at the gym.

"Hey," Damien says, shouldering open the door. "Olly and Kaner were leaving as I came in, and I didn't see anyone else downstairs, so it looks like we're walking over alone."

"Ok," Rome says.

Damien crouches and starts to unload his laptop, charger, two textbooks, and journal on the chair. He'll leave them there until after dinner and then hog all of Rome's desk space while Rome does his own homework on the bed.

It's a good routine.

He likes it.

"So," Rome says brightly because it's now or never. "I think we should have sex."

Damien drops a handful of highlighters. "What?"

"Sex," Rome repeats. "We should do it. Or, like, start the process."

Damien blinks at him. "We should start the...sex process?"

"Fuck you. I don't know the terminology for it. It's just with the last couple of days, Finley and the social workers and everything— We're planning our future together, and I've never even touched your dick."

He glances at the door suddenly, as if he's expecting Kaner might barge in at any moment to chastise him. "Not that that's a requirement or whatever. If you don't want to do sex things...well, it would suck. Or not suck as the case may be—ha. Um. But I would get over it. Except I'm pretty sure you do want to do sex things, so feel free to make me stop talking at any point here so I can stop saying the fucking phrase *sex things*—"

"Rome."

"Yes," Rome says, relieved.

"I would like to do sex things with you," Damien says solemnly.

"Great."

Damien finishes emptying his bag and stands. He gestures vaguely to his crotch. "Right now, or—"

"What? No. We've got to go work out and eat and finish our homework. Tonight though?"

"Yes. Sex Things. Tonight," Damien agrees. "After working out and eating and homework. I'll put it on my calendar."

Rome glowers at him.

"Oh, and I can add it to yours too." Damien uncaps the Expo marker velcroed to the wall and writes his name on Rome's whiteboard "To Do" list.

To Do, it reads. *Damien Raphael Bordeaux.*

"I will choke you," Rome says.

"Not one of my kinks, but thanks for asking."

Rome makes a noise that can only be called a squeak. He throws his pillow at Damien's face. "Go change," he says. "Gym."

Damien tosses the pillow back and salutes, laughing his way into the hall, "Yes, sir."

"Not one of my kinks, but thanks for asking," Rome shouts after him.

"I don't want to know," Justin calls from the hall-way.

Rome maybe screams a little and slams the door.

They walk to the gym together, gloved hands linked and tucked into Damien's anorak pocket like a giant fucking cliche.

He likes that too.

"So, I'm seeing someone," Rome says.

"You better be talking about me," Damien says.

"No, I mean, a therapist. Here. I started today. This morning during my free period."

"Oh." Damien squeezes Rome's hand. "Can I ask

why? Why now?"

"Because I'm hopefully going to be responsible for a kid. Making sure she's happy and loved and shit. And I don't know how to do that. I didn't have an example of how to do that right until I moved in with my aunt and uncle. And I only had a couple months with them. I think it'd be good if I start figuring all that out now. So I can do things right if I get her. *When* I get her. And I want *us* to be good too. So, I'm going to talk to the guy about, like, relationship shit as well as baby shit."

"Oh."

"If you make a big deal out of this, I will punch you. I just wanted you to know."

"Okay." Damien squeezes his hand again. "FYI, threatening to punch your partner is probably frowned upon. Like, therapeutically. Free tip."

"Shut up." Rome abruptly sobers. "You know I wouldn't, though, right?"

"What?"

"Hit you." The words are urgent, almost embarrassingly earnest. "I wouldn't. Ever. I fucking swear."

"I do," Damien says. "I do know."

They go quiet for several seconds.

"Also," Damien says, "if you're going to have a kid, you'll have to clean up your language. Or you're going to be getting some calls from irate kindergarten teachers in a few years."

"Oh," Rome says. "Fuck."

"Yes, exactly," Damien agrees. "I'm, uh, also going to start seeing my therapist more often. The one from home, not here. I emailed and asked if we could start talking once a week again. Over video chat."

"Oh?" Rome prompts carefully.

"Yeah. I figured it would be smart, considering everything. And I talked to my parents last night. Like, really talked to them. About—" He waves a hand at his general self.

"Your abandonment issues?" Rome quips.

Damien winces. "Funny you should say that."

"Oh. Shit. Sorry."

"It's true though. Ever since I was little, I was always really sensitive, always afraid of being left out or left behind. And objectively, I know that's common for kids who are adopted, but apparently it doesn't just go away once you're an adult. So back to regular therapy I go."

"Look at us," Rome mutters, "being so mature and shit."

"Who would have thought."

"Not me."

Damien squeezes his hand.

They mostly ignore each other once they get to the gym. Rome needs silence and focus and prefers to attack his training routine with something akin to malice, while Damien likes to play his bouncy hype music and dance a little between sets and talk with whoever is on the machine next to him. Rome and Kaner and Justin tend to work out together in stoic silence while Damien joins Chai and Olly in laughing their way through the following hour.

It works.

They're mostly on the opposite sides of the room, so that means Rome can glance up from his hunched position on the exercise bike and watch Damien shimmy his spandex-clad ass between sets without anyone noticing.

Well.

Kaner probably notices. She blessedly doesn't say anything though. Maybe because she's too busy similarly staring at Olly. But that's none of Rome's business.

After showering, they all go to the cafeteria and then walk back to the dorm in a group. Damien and Rome's hands are tucked together again in Damien's pocket, and it's so normal, so ordinary, that no one says anything. Kaner and Damien carry on a conversation for the duration of the walk while Olly tells Rome about a new pepper-related recipe he wants to try. It isn't even noteworthy, this thing Rome always imagined would be too big and unwieldy to ever act on. He ducks his head, tucking his chin into his scarf so no one can see him smile.

He's happy.

"So," Rome says once they're back in his room, and Damien is trying to sort out his icy, snowed-on hair.

"So," Damien agrees.

"You know your cousin Devon? The, uh, biological one?"

Damien turns away from the mirror on the back of the door. "...Yes."

"I friended her on IG."

"You have an IG? Rome. It's like I don't even know you." Damien digs for his phone in his pocket. "What is it?"

"I haven't posted any pictures; I just used it to find her. Can you focus for a minute?"

"Right, sorry." Damien widens his eyes, faux complacent, and moves to sit next to him on the bed. "My cousin," he prompts Rome.

"Her spring break is next week."

"Okay?"

"And I invited her to our Friday game. It's only a three-hour drive for her, and the game is a matinee, so she could come see it and then maybe we could all get an early dinner before she has to go back. Or at least that's what I suggested. And she said that sounded cool. Fuck. Should I have asked you first? I wanted it to be a surprise, but then I started thinking maybe this isn't the kind of thing to surprise someone with and—"

"Rome," Damien says.

"Yeah."

"Thank you. "

He exhales, sagging. "Okay. Good. You're not mad."

"No. I'm glad you told me though. Do you think she'd want to spend the night? I could get her a hotel room. And then we could all visit Finley on Saturday. I've sent Devon a bunch of pictures, but they don't do Finley justice."

Rome grins. "That sounds nice."

He nudges Damien with his elbow because he's still not very good at initiating kisses.

Damien, thank god, knows him well enough to nudge him back and then press his smiling mouth to Rome's. It isn't a very good kiss—too many teeth involved, and subsequently too much laughter, but it's still good.

"So," Rome says. "Have you...talked to anyone else

biologically related to you?"

"No. Just Devon. Though I did find a couple links to my dad's side of the family. One lives in Taiwan, which is cool. But I haven't messaged any of them yet."

"Well," Rome says, resisting the urge to pull out the notes he made after his therapy appointment. "If you ever need support. Or whatever. I'm here for you."

Damien toys with the cuff of Rome's sweater sleeve. His hands are warm and familiar, and he probably doesn't even realize he's doing it. These days, Damien touches Rome like his limbs are an extension of Damien's own body. It's bafflingly pleasant.

"I know," Damien says. "Thanks for telling me though. And thanks for inviting Devon. Is there— You know the same thing goes for me, right? Do you want to visit your mom? Because I'd go with you. If that was something you wanted."

Rome doesn't answer for several long seconds.

"I don't think so. Not now, anyway. I'm good with the family I have."

"Yeah," Damien agrees, and it seems significant. "Me too."

Rome doesn't think he can handle it if things get any sweeter. "So," he says, definitely at normal volume. "Sex?"

Damien laughs, tipping forward to plant his face into Rome's neck. There's still melting snow in his hair, and it's startlingly cold against Rome's jaw.

"Wait," Rome says, pushing Damien away. "Wait. Hold on."

He flips the light switch, closes the curtains, makes

sure the door is locked, and turns on the fairy lights. Then he plugs in his phone to the speaker's aux cable and pulls up the playlist Olly helped him make the day before.

"Okay," he says, returning to the bed. "Continue."

Damien hauls Rome into his lap, still laughing a little, but his hands are too gentle, too reverent—slipping up the back of Rome's shirt, pulling their hips together—for Rome to take offense.

"Did you make a *sex playlist*?"

Rome's face flushes hot. "I was trying to be romantic, asshole. I can turn it off."

"Don't you dare," Damien says.

"Great. Take off your fucking pants."

Damien just looks at him for a minute. Like Rome is something important. Like maybe Damien really does think he's worth several million dollars.

"Oh my god," Damien says. "I love you so much."

He stands and pulls Rome's shirt most of the way off, leaving it wrapped around his head. Rome kicks blindly at him, trying to free himself, but Damien catches his foot and drags him off the bed. It turns into a bit of a wrestling match before Damien gets sidetracked, thighs bracketing Rome's waist, one hand pushing Rome's face to the side because it's imperative that he pause to touch the newly exposed freckles on Rome's shoulder.

He follows his fingers with his mouth.

Rome rolls them a few minutes later and scrambles back up onto the bed, mostly as an excuse to catch his breath. He refuses to let Damien join him unless he *gets fucking naked already, honestly*, and Damien acquiesces easily enough.

Rome watches him, skin cast in sepia starburst patterns from the fairy lights, his grinning mouth a slash of white in the darkness as he struggles to shove his skinny jeans down over the bulk of his thighs. Rome watches the flex of his naked back as he bends to pull at one pant leg, and Rome thinks, suddenly, about the dozens of times he played make believe with Piper. There was usually a *true love* involved. Piper's true love almost always lived in space and was often in need of rescuing. She tried to get Rome to play along, but that was one game he'd never been any good at. The very idea of it, that there was someone out there, just for him, who would love him despite all his faults and who he would love in return—that kind of fantasy was too unbelievable.

It isn't so unbelievable now.

"Fucking stupid things," Damien curses.

His jeans are hobbling his ankles, blocked by his thick winter socks, and he's hopping around a little, trying to pull the jeans up enough to get the socks off first.

It gives Rome a very nice view of his ass.

Rome grins and bites his already tender bottom lip and thinks about fantasy and science.

He'd learned all about stars and space in the few months he lived with Piper. He knows that people are made of star dust. He remembers watching *Cosmos*, hearing Carl Sagan say that humans' matter was composed of long-ago exploded stars.

Rome also knows that attraction is down to chemicals and pheromones and biological imperatives. He knows there are scientific reasons for elevated heart rates, for lust and love and feelings of affection.

But he's started to think—he wonders if maybe it isn't a little bit of both. Fantasy and science. Maybe there are people who are made of the same sort of dust. People who used to be part of the same star that's trying to find its way back together again.

He looks at Damien, still struggling with his socks, and leans forward, reaching for him.

A hand on his hip.

Hot skin and cool air.

"Here," he says, "let me help you."

Maybe that's what this is.

EPILOGUE

THREE MONTHS LATER

With the final pick of the first round in the draft, the Houston Hellhounds select Patrick Roman.

Rome doesn't remember much of the following minutes because he's too busy thinking: *What the fuck, what the fuck, what the fuck.*

He remembers pulling the jersey on over his head, probably looking like an idiot. He remembers posing for pictures.

"You'll have to win a cup straightaway, you know," Damien says, one arm around his shoulders after rescuing Rome from the press.

"Uh. Okay?" Obviously, that's the goal.

"Finley won't be small enough to sit in it past, like, three years old," Damien continues seriously.

"And Finley sitting in the cup is necessary?"

Damien looks perturbed by this. "Of course it is."

"Right."

And then, while he's tucked in an alcove with Damien, playing with his phone and considering how long he can pretend he's talking to important people before returning the media circus—

His phone lights up.

And it's Alexander Fucking Price.

His new captain.

He doesn't remember much about that conversation either, but thankfully, Damien takes over. They've been joking that Damien will be his agent, but he should find an actual agent now. Because he was just drafted in the *first round*. Right at the end, sure, but still. First round. And there are a lot of people who want to talk to him, and he has no idea what to say to them. Jesus.

"Once more into the breach?" Damien asks.

"Yeah," Rome sighs. "Summon up the blood, or whatever."

"Oh my god," Damien says. "You're quoting Shakespeare with me. I'm rubbing off on you."

"You're not, but you could be if you help me sneak out of here and back to the hotel."

"See, this is why you need a real agent," Damien says, steering him down the hall and toward the noise. "Someone you can't bribe with sexual favors."

When they finally get back to the hotel that night, they FaceTime Finley, who lounges in her Bobby, poking at the iPad screen with visibly sticky fingers, screaming happily as they wave at her. Screaming is her favorite thing at the moment.

Her foster, Michael, tells them she rolled over unassisted for the first time that morning, and Damien cries some more while Rome hurriedly opens his laptop to add that to her milestone spreadsheet. She loses interest in them a few minutes later, and they say goodbye.

They order room service for the first time in Rome's life and sit squished together in the center of the king-sized bed, sharing a plate, laptops open, elbowing each other companionably.

Rome has several real estate tabs open, looking at the available apartment units. He knows Damien has tabs open looking at houses for sale that are so outside Rome's budget—even his soon-to-be, admittedly generous budget—it's unreal. Rome will insist on an apartment for the first year, at least until they know for sure that he's not going to be sent down. But he also knows they'll probably end up compromising eventually. They'll find a small house, and Rome will let Damien buy it with the stipulation that Rome pays the utilities and the rest of their living costs. Damien will probably argue, but the thought of it is—

Damien made Rome's dorm a home. And if Damien can make cinder block cube feel warm and safe, Rome can only imagine what he'd do with a house of his own. With a kitchen. With a nursery.

"You know," Damien says later, when they're brushing their teeth, "if we got married, you might be able to move the whole petition for guardianship thing along faster. Not to take her full-time sooner. But just to have the paperwork done. So we could take her full-time as soon as we wanted. Without having to deal with red tape then."

"Yeah?" Rome says, spitting in the sink. "How do you figure that?"

"Well, you wouldn't have to wait until you're settled with the team to prove you have a reliable form of housing and income and a stable home life. If we got married, we'd have my trust fund, and I'd be a stable parent regardless of your"—he gestures with this toothbrush, flecking the mirror—"hockey shit. I mean my writing program schedule is easy enough to plan around, especially if we get a nanny."

Rome grins, wiping his mouth on his arm. "While I appreciate your continued willingness to throw your trust fund at my problems, I think we'll stick with the route we're on now. Seeing as we've been dating for less than six months and are literal teenagers."

He sobers. "But I could ask about officially adding you as a supportive party? I'm sure there's a word for it. For partners of adopters. You're making a face. Why are you making a face?"

Damien stalls by rinsing his mouth twice as long as usual.

"She's yours," he says finally. "Or she will be. I get that. I want that. But I think, not, like, right now or anything, but eventually? I want her to be mine, too, you know? Down the line. In a few years if everything works out."

Oh.

Oh.

Rome barely resists clutching his chest like a romantic idiot. "Of course. We'd need to talk about it. But yeah."

"Well," Damien says, slinging his arms around Rome's waist. "We're getting better at that. The Talking."

"We are."

Damien rests his chin on Rome's shoulder, and they consider their joined reflections in the mirror.

"Okay," Rome says. "So we'll talk about it."

"Okay," Damien agrees.

"Also," Rome says. "Would you stop trying to marry me?"

"No," Damien says, kissing the shell of his ear. "No, I will not."

*

TWO YEARS LATER

"Did you know," the interviewer—he's pretty sure she said her name was Chelsea, but he's nervous—says, "that you're the second-youngest person to ever win the Yale Younger Poets Prize?"

"Am I really?" Damien asks. He's suddenly forgotten how to sit like a normal person. "Who was the youngest?"

"Edward Weismiller. In 1936. And he only beat you by a few months. He was also twenty."

"Wow. I had no idea." He crosses his legs. Then uncrosses them.

They're at Damien's parents' place in New York City, and this is the first of three interviews he's supposed to do in the next two weeks. Because he's won the Yale Younger Poets Prize. It's the oldest annual literary prize in the US in which Yale University Press publishes a first-time writer's debut collection of poetry and, typically, cements their place within the literary world for life. And he's won it. Rome explained the prize to Maura as "the poet version of winning *American Idol*," which was a terrible comparison but not...entirely inaccurate.

Damien's manuscript, *Formation*, was published the week before, and it still doesn't quite feel real. Maybe it will after he's had a few more interviews and done a few more signings. But now he's nervous, sitting in his parents' apartment with a glass of water on the side table next to him and a copy of his book—his *book*—beside the water, and his hands awkwardly folded in his lap. He's wearing Rome's green sweater because it smells like him, and it quiets his nerves. He knows when Rome gets home and sees him, their evening will assuredly end on a high note.

But for now, he needs to focus.

"So, Damien," probably-Chelsea says, "your collection transitions drastically in terms of content and tone as it progresses. Would you say the dichotomy between the beginning and ending pieces tells a personal story? Or what was your intention with that significant change?"

"Well—" He clears his throat. "—Chelsea."

She nods encouragingly and doesn't correct him, so he gives himself a mental pat on the back.

"It was organic," he says. "Nearly every poem is in chronological order. The first, I wrote when I was a senior in high school, two years ago now. And I was writing about identity, my perception of my identity, and my place in the world from the start. But I don't think I'd call it a change or a transition, if you'll excuse me getting picky about words."

"I'd expect nothing less," she says, gesturing for him to explain.

"See, I considered titling the collection *Transformation*, at first. But the word 'transformation' has this connotation of changing from one thing to another. Where the new form replaces or leaves behind the old one. *Formation* means to create or to build upon. I like to think of personal discovery and developing your perception of self that way, a process of building that needs all the difficult and unsavory experiences at its foundation. I mean, the confusion and anger and pain that influenced the earlier pieces in *Formation* are all a part of and visible in the discovery and catharsis and relief of the end pieces. Just like my past self is still intrinsic to and visible in what I've become today, not something that was discarded or left behind."

"I love that distinction," she says, consulting her notepad. "Okay, you say that *Formation* is about identity. But only two poems actually use the word 'identity,' and they look like mirror images as they appear on the page, using the same allegory, even. But they're drastically different in composition and tone otherwise, even contradictory in message."

"You mean 'Bell Jar' and 'Broken Glass'?"

"Yes. Exactly. Can you talk about the conflict that occurs between those pieces within this conversation about identity?"

He has to think about that for a moment. "A lot of people treat writing like it's a form of therapy, and sure, in some ways it is. But there's this assumption I've encountered a lot—people think you have to be unhappy to create truly compelling art. That evocative writing comes from dark places full of pain and angst. And I was one of those people. I was most inspired by uncertainty and grief. And I actually—as I became healthier and happier, I stopped writing for a while. There were months between 'Bell Jar' and 'Broken Glass' where I didn't write hardly anything at all. Because I was happy. And I didn't know how to create when I was happy. Or, I guess I didn't think anything I created when I was happy was...worthwhile. You know?"

"Wow."

"Yeah. I was on this fantastic personal journey. I was adopted and, only within the last few years, started looking into my genealogy. During that period, I spent two weeks with my biological family here in the US and then flew to Taiwan to meet my grandparents and a bunch of aunts and uncles and cousins. It was one of the happiest experiences of my life. And I was journaling the whole time, but I also felt like I couldn't write seriously about it. I didn't know how."

"So 'Bell Jar' preceded those visits?"

"Yeah, and 'Broken Glass,' I finally wrote...god, four months later? I just had to learn, or maybe rediscover, how to draw inspiration from joy and contentment and—"

"Love?"

"Yeah." He plays with one of the sweater's cuffs. "Definitely love. And that's what the rest of *Formation* is about. Building happiness on top of fear and pain. Not in a way that covers it but in a way that...includes it. I guess. Maybe even appreciates it."

Chelsea clears her throat. "Pivoting a little to the topic of love, there isn't typically a lot of overlap with the literary world and professional hockey."

"No there is not," he agrees.

"But your partner is one of a small subset of out NHL players. I'm sure that hasn't been an easy journey for him, or you supporting him. Has your relationship, or being forced into the public eye because of your relationship, influenced *Formation*?"

"I think it's pretty obvious that 'Pollock's Muse' was

written about Rome if you've ever seen a picture of him. And 'Cosmos.' I wrote those while we were apart, and I was missing him pretty badly. He's on the road a lot for games, and I've been traveling between Houston and New York for the workshop I recently completed. He's the first person I ever wrote love poetry for. The *only* person I'll ever write love poetry for."

"Aw," she says quietly.

Damien clears his throat. "But, yeah. A huge influence of *Formation* was making those family connections I mentioned. Rome is part of that because he's part of my family now. Another big part of that is our daughter. We try to keep her off our social media for privacy reasons, but 'Half-Size Handprints' is about the pride and terror of loving a child who is endlessly brave but has no sense of self-preservation."

"Yes, that one resonated with me," she agrees dryly. "I have to say, for someone so young, you've developed a very distinct voice in your writing, and you've clearly been navigating challenging personal circumstances. To what do you attribute your maturity?"

Damien is stymied. He has no idea. His eyes drift around the room: clean counters, Rome's hoodie on one of the bar stools. A pile of rollerblades and sticks by the door. He eyes come to rest on the chest-high hole in the wall across from him. He decides to sidestep the question.

"I don't think I am that mature, if I'm being honest. I know I'm responsible for my age, but I'm still twenty, you know? You see that hole in the wall?"

She glances behind her. "Yes?"

Damien taps his elbow. "We were playing roller hockey last night."

"Indoors?"

"Indoors," he agrees. "And sometimes things happen when you're playing roller hockey with your competitive NHL boyfriend. And sometimes the downstairs neighbors call the doorman to complain. And the doorman calls you and, knowing it's just you and your boyfriend there, informs you that the downstairs neighbors have complained about 'the children playing loudly' in your unit."

She laughs, no longer looking at her notepad. "Point taken. Have you or do you think you'll ever use hockey as an inspiration for your writing?"

"Well, I promised Rome I'd write him a six-stanza limerick celebrating his on-ice prowess when the Hellhounds win another Stanley Cup. And I'll post it online. So you have that to look forward to."

"I can't wait."

Neither can he.

*

THREE YEARS LATER

They win the Stanley Cup Rome's third year with the Hellhounds.

It's the second in franchise history.

Rome is twenty-two and has an *A* on his jersey, and he feels like it's too good to be true.

Alex passes the cup to Matts, who passes it to Rome, and Rome kisses it with his eyes closed and too much everything in his chest.

Rome's entire family is in the stands except for Piper. She's at a summer camp hosted by JPL and messaged him, *I love you, Patrick, but NASA.* Damien's father pulled some strings to get her in the camp, and Rome wasn't even mad about it. He's probably biased, but Piper is brilliant. Like, already-skipped-one-grade and is still talking about how bored she is brilliant. If Damien's dad is willing to bring that brilliance to important people's attention, and it makes Piper happy, well, he's not going to complain.

Though Piper was far too busy doing genius things in California, she *had* sent along Nicolaus Copernicus with Maura as a stand-in for her. The picture Rome posted on Instagram that morning of the beat-up stuffed lobster wearing a Hellhounds bandana and matching hair scrunchies around his pinchers had over 25,000 hits already.

So Nicolaus Copernicus is somewhere in the stands with Maura and most of Rome's family and Damien's parents. Devon is there, too, using Finley's old ERGO Baby carrier and bulbous baby headphones with her own eight-month-old boy. Damien isn't in the stands though. Damien is walking out onto the ice with all the close family members of other players—wives and kids and parents. He's holding Finley's hand, walking slower than he clearly wants to, making sure she doesn't slip. She does anyway, and Damien swings her up onto his hip instead.

"Alex, Matts," Rome says. "Can I borrow the cup for a minute?"

They wave away the photographer who's been taking pictures of them holding the cup together, and they hand it over with no argument, possibly because Alex's husband and Matts's girlfriend are running toward them, and they want their hands free to deal with that.

So Rome takes the cup.

And he waits until Damien is close enough to hear him.

And he goes down on one knee, holding the cup up toward Damien with a shit-eating grin. "Hey, Damien. How would you feel about marrying me?"

Damien just stares at him, narrow-eyed for a moment. "Are you seriously proposing to me with the Stanley Cup right now?"

"Well, you won't be allowed to keep it—"

"Cheapskate."

"But I figured it's the gesture that's important. I also have a ring in my bag if that's more your style."

Damien shifts Finley from his hip to his back in a practiced movement. "Hey baby, can you hang on real tight for a minute?" he asks her.

She wraps her arms around his neck. He chokes a

little. It's fine.

"I don't want to rush you," Rome says, "but this is kinda heavy and my shoulder is definitely fucked, so—"

"Stand up, asshole."

He abruptly remembers the four-year-old clinging to his back and winces.

They've improved a lot of things over the years, but their language is not one of them.

"Is that a yes?"

Damien reaches for the cup, hauling Rome to his feet by proxy. "You want to kiss under the cup, don't you?"

"I really do." Rome rolls his eyes, but he does it, pushing the cup above their heads, fingers curled tight around the bowl.

He kisses Rome and doesn't stop.

Alex pointedly clears his throat, and they both laugh, separating. They hand the cup back to him.

Finley takes this opportunity to launch herself into Rome's arms, and he catches her, pretending to almost drop her purely so she'll shriek with laughter.

"Just as a point of clarification," Rome says, once she's propped upright on his hip, "that was a yes, right? On the marriage...thing."

Finley pokes his cheek, and Rome catches her hand, smacking an absent kiss to her palm out of habit.

"That's a yes," Damien says. "I've had a ring for you in my sock drawer for over a year now."

Rome leans forward to kiss Damien again.

"Ew," Finley says.

*

DAMIEN WAKES UP the following morning to sunlight coming through the partially opened curtains.

His head hurts, but in a dull, well-deserved kind of way.

Rome is asleep beside him, a rumpled riot of tanned skin and freckles against white sheets. His left hand, fingers lax and sleep-curled in the space between them, has Damien's ring on it.

Damien takes a moment to admire the band on his own finger.

He's happy.

It is a quiet joy. Not the vibrant, noisy celebration of on-ice success but the soft hush of content, early-morning quiet. It isn't stadium echoes and rattling sticks and shouted expletives but soft outside noises: birds and wind-in-leaves nearly hidden under the familiar hum of the air conditioning inside.

He hears footsteps in the hall.

Finley pushes open their bedroom door, the cat in a fireman's carry over one shoulder.

The cat's name is Galileo—Piper's influence. He's a grumpy orange tabby who showed up on the back porch the previous year, and Finley fell immediately in love with him. He has three legs, is missing half an ear, and is an absolute dick to everyone who isn't Finley.

"Daddy," she says somberly, coming to stand at Damien's side of the bed. "We're late for swimming."

He squints at the clock.

So they are.

"It's okay. We're skipping today."

"Are we sick?" she asks, going up on her toes to try to see Rome.

"Nah, but Stanley Cup champions get to sleep in."

"Are we Stanley Cup champions?"

"We are, baby."

She's wearing footie Christmas pajamas, even though it's June.

She yawns, and it's still the cutest thing ever.

"Are you hungry for breakfast?" he asks. "Or do you want to come cuddle?"

"Cuddle," she says decisively. She hefts Galileo onto the bed and then climbs over Damien, inserting herself with practiced ease in the space between him and Rome.

"Dad," she whispers, patting Rome's cheek. "Dad, we're cuddling."

"Oh good," he murmurs, "thanks for letting me know."

She arranges Rome's arm over her to her liking and then looks over her shoulder at Damien expectantly. He drapes his arm over them both, tucking his hand up the back of Rome's sleep shirt, palm against morning-warm skin.

Finley nods approvingly and returns her attention to Rome.

"We're not swimming today," she informs him. "We're sleeping in because we're Stanley Cup champions."

Rome opens his eyes.

He meets Damien's, grinning.

He kisses Finley's forehead, then leans closer to kiss

Damien.

"We are," he agrees.

ACKNOWLEDGEMENTS

I dedicated this book to my mom. When I say she's read everything I've ever written, I mean it. From my first short story in elementary school, to the (terrible) first full-length novel created in middle school, to the (actually not bad) first 100k word piece of fan fiction I wrote in high school. She's a VP at a fortune 500 company with Many Important Responsibilities, yet she was the first person to finish reading the ARC for this book and send me a list of copyedits she found. The woman is a marvel and without her encouragement I have no idea if I'd be writing today. Thanks, mom.

In addition to my mother, I'd like to shout out to B, Deacon, my dad, and my Uncle R for their endless support. To Elizabetta, my editor, for her endless patience. To Chelsea, Ishita, Byron, and David who were there to help cultivate some vibes and a couple pages of banter into an actual story with a plot. Shout out to David and Jay, the OG betas, and everyone on Tumblr and Discord who have continued their vendetta against my ever-present imposter syndrome over the last several years. To the hundreds (thousands, now??) of folks who have followed me from fic to fiction and back again, who ordered signed copies of LRPD and LYNLTP, who've posted about my books on social media, who've sent me (and Deacon!) mail and silly gifts and generally remind me daily that fandom is a community and one I am privileged to be a part of. I'm so lucky to have made so many friends online. I love you guys.

About E.L. Massey

E. L. Massey is a human. Probably. She lives in Austin, Texas, with her partner, the best dog in the world (an unbiased assessment), and a frankly excessive collection of books. She spends her holidays climbing mountains and writing fan fiction, occasionally at the same time.

Email
elmasseywrites@gmail.com

Facebook
www.facebook.com/ericalyn.massey

Twitter
@el_masseyy

Website
www.elmassey.substack.com

Instagram
el_massey

Tumblr
www.xiaq.tumblr.com

Other NineStar books by this author

Breakaway Series

Like Real People Do
Like You've Nothing Left to Prove

Coming Soon from E.L. Massey

Free from Falling

Breakaway Series, Book Four

"Hey, Matty. Are you petting a dog in some back room at a party again?"

He almost hangs up the phone. Because yes, Justin Edward Matthews—Matts to anyone who matters and Matty to his asshole stepbrother—is hiding in a back room at a party petting a dog. Again.

"I hate you," Matts says.

"You don't. What's the dog's name?"

"It's Hawk, Eli's dog."

"Give her a kiss for me."

He does. He's sitting on a fancy bench thing at the base of an equally fancy bed in one of the dozen bedrooms at the house where the party is taking place. He doesn't know if Hawk is allowed on the furniture or not, but he figures if she's mostly in his lap, they're good either way. He leans into Hawk's warm bulk and briefly buries his face in her neck.

"So," his stepbrother says, "the gay kid talked you

into going out and socializing, huh?"

"Don't say it like that," Matts says, straightening.

"I'm not saying it like anything. I'm stating a fact. He's a kid. He's gay."

"He's twenty-one, and he's married to my captain. He's not a kid. And he's one of my best fucking friends. Use his name."

"Fine. Whatever."

Matts is regretting calling Aaron already. They used to do it all the time—calling each other whenever they got drunk. It was the way they bonded as teenagers when their families were recklessly combined. Matts was off at boarding school, so lonely it was hard to breathe sometimes, and Aaron was unceremoniously uprooted from the only town he ever knew, suddenly expected to call a stranger "Dad." Their relationship was easier then, born out of isolation and a shared resentment for the people they called parents. But in recent years, their conversations have gotten more and more stilted. Exhibit A: this conversation.

"Hey," Aaron says, like he can hear what Matts is thinking. "I'm trying. You know I'm trying."

"Try harder."

"Okay," he says quietly. There's an extremely awkward pause. "Well. Why are you hanging out with Hawk and not a less furry lady?"

Aaron has a point. The only good thing about going to parties is that sometimes girls will recognize him and he can get laid without having to stumble his way through a conversation first.

"I came upstairs to use the bathroom. And it's time for Eli to check in anyway. I'll go back downstairs when he does."

Hawk is Eli's service dog. Eli doesn't go to parties much, but when he does, he brings her with him and keeps her somewhere quiet where he can have her sniff him or whatever she does to predict his seizures every so often. And he always has someone with him as human backup too. Tonight, Matts is the human backup. Because he's still doing PT for another week and isn't cleared to travel with the team yet. He made the mistake of having dinner with Eli, and afterward, Eli *looked* at him with his big stupid sad eyes and asked him to *please* go with him, and Matts is a pushover.

He doesn't like parties in general, but he especially doesn't like them when he keeps having to explain that no, he's not Eli's professional-hockey-playing-husband. He's Eli's professional-hockey-playing-husband's injured alternate captain. Which is weird. Not because people are assuming he's gay. That's fine. That's whatever. But people are assuming he's *married*. Twenty-one-year-olds should not be married. Even if it seems to be working for Eli and Alex.

"The drinks are all colorful and sparkly," Matts says. Making fun of rich people's alcohol preferences is always a safe topic with his family.

"No," Aaron gasps with faux outrage. "*Sparkly*?"

"No beer cans in sight."

"The horror. Not even a bougie IPA?"

"There's a tended bar, and the menu is all cock-tails."

"Gross. What color did you go with?"

Matts sighs in the direction of his drink on the nightstand. "Green. And then purple. And the worst thing is that I'm drunk after two of them."

He regularly goes shot-for-shot with Russian NHL players. A neon drink should not be laying him out. He tries to look at his tongue to see if it's changed color and is unsuccessful.

"Are you still on meds?"

"No, *Mom*, I'm off everything as of two days ago. Healing great. Should be playing again in another week. And I can't even celebrate with a beer."

"What a brave little soldier you are," Aaron says. "Hey, speaking of moms. Are you coming home for Christmas or not?"

"I don't know. Maybe. Is my dad…" He flips Hawk's ears inside out. One will stay that way. The other won't. He boops her nose, and she sneezes.

"You're gonna need to finish the question if you want me to answer it."

Matts sighs. "I don't know. Just...you think he'll ever apologize?"

"I think those would be hell-freezes-over type odds."

"Yeah."

"Come home anyway."

"I'll think about it."

The door opens, and Eli slips inside, music from downstairs bleeding through before he shuts it again.

"Hey," Matts says, "I gotta go. I'll call you Friday, and we'll talk about Christmas, okay?"

"Sure. Say hi to Eli for me."

"Yeah," Matts says, "I will." The word "thanks" gets a little stuck in his throat, but he mumbles it out and follows it with "bye."

He slides his phone back into his pocket as Eli slides onto the bench beside him.

"You okay?" Eli asks. He's a perceptive little shit.

"Fine." Matts gestures toward the door. "It's just a lot. Do you always have to be so damn good at social shit? You're making me look bad."

"Oh, no," Eli says, "you do that on your own." He gives him a second look and gentles his tone. "You do look a little rough though. You want to go outside? Or we can call it early."

"Outside works."

They sit with Hawk for a few more minutes, and when she remains calm and sleepy, they bid her good-bye and head downstairs toward the backyard.

But halfway through the living room, Matts stops.

Because there's a girl in the kitchen.

Well, there are a lot of girls in the kitchen. But this girl is wearing black ripped skinny jeans, and her equally black ripped shirt—advertising some incomprehensible metal band on the front—has no sleeves or collar. The shirt's sides have been cut from arm to hem and reattached with long lines of glittering safety pins. Her lips are full. Her hair is a wild riot of brown curls.

She looks like the unholy offspring of '80s hair-metal-era Bon Jovi and '70s Joan Jett, and her whole vibe is...unexpectedly but thoroughly doing it for him.

"Who," he asks, "is *she*?"

"Absolutely not," Eli answers. "You are not ready for Sydney."

"Sydney," he repeats.

"No," Eli says again, forcefully steering them toward the back porch. For someone so lean, he's surprisingly strong. Sydney also looks lean and strong. Her

glutes and thighs are particularly nice. She could probably squat him. He'd be happy to let her try.

"I thought the whole point of me coming tonight
was that I needed to…expand my social realm or whatever," Matts says.

"Social *repertoire* is the phrase I used." Eli is still
pushing him. Matts is still resisting.

"Repertoire. Right." He cranes his neck to keep
Sydney in sight. She's completely flat-chested, but her
ass is something else. He wonders if she plays hockey.

"And yes, it was," Eli agrees. "Except I know that
look, Matthew."

"Not my name."

"I know that look, *Justin Edward Matthews*."

That is, admittedly, his name.

"You don't want to meet her," Eli says. "You want
to hook up with her."

"And that's…bad?"

"Have you ever even *spoken* with a trans woman before?"

"Trans…as in transgender?"

"No, as in transformer. Yes, transgender, *idiota*.
And clearly, your taste in music is worse than I thought
if you don't already know who she is."

"Wait, she's a boy? Or—used to be a boy?" She
doesn't look like a boy. Though that might explain the

boob thing. Is that bad to think? Eli would probably hit him if he said it out loud.

"And this is why you're not allowed to talk to Sydney," Eli says. "She would eat you alive."

Sydney catches him staring, and Matts waves as Eli finally, successfully, shoves him around the corner and through the sliding doors to the porch.

Sydney appears again, moments later, from the opposite side of the open-concept kitchen, and purposefully makes her way toward them.

"Oh, fuck me," Eli mutters.

"No thanks."

"Eli," Sydney says, stepping over the threshold to join them. "Who's your friend?"

"Hi," Matts says. "I'm Matts. I play hockey with Eli's husband. Eli says I'm not allowed to talk to you because you'll eat me alive."

She gives him a considering once-over. "Eli is likely correct, but I'm sure we'd both enjoy the experience."

Eli throws up his hands.

"Don't let him fool you though," she says conspiratorially, bowing with a flourish that somehow doesn't spill her drink. "I am but a humble bard, at your service."

"Bard, sure," Eli mutters. "*Humble* though—"

"You look like you need alcohol, Eli," Sydney interrupts.

He sighs. "I do. Syd, behave. Matts, good luck."

"Wait," Matts says, "aren't I supposed to be…monitoring you?"

"Monitor me with your eyes while I go acquire a beverage. I promise to swoon obviously if I need your attention."

He throws one wrist against his forehead and falls briefly to one side before straightening and making his way back inside.

"So you're Hawk's understudy tonight?" Sydney asks.

She has dimples. It takes him a beat longer than it should to respond because of them.

"That's me. Temporary service human. Not as cute as the A-team upstairs, I know."

She gives him another leisurely assessment, and he suddenly wishes he was wearing something more edgy than khakis and boat shoes.

"I wouldn't say that," she murmurs over the rim of her glass.

He watches her drink; he watches the light from the hanging lanterns on the porch glint off the rings on her hand; he watches her tongue slide over her drink-stained lips. He realizes he's staring.

"So how do you know Eli?" he asks, only a little desperately.

She tips her head, expression suddenly assessing. It's an oddly predatory look for someone whose curl-augmented height barely comes up to his chin.

"You have no idea who I am, do you?" she says.

"I—no." He squints at her, remembering Eli's assertion about his taste in music. "Should I?"

She reaches out to flick the collar of his button-down. "I guess not. Though one of our songs *is* on syndicated radio currently."

"You're a musician?" That makes sense. That makes a lot of sense. "What's your band called?"

"Red Right Hand."

She looks like she's braced for something as she says it, but the name means nothing to him.

"Is that, like, a Twister reference?"

She coughs on a laugh, then hides her smile with the back of her wrist, her long fingers—guitarist fingers?—splayed over the mouth of her cup.

"It's a *Paradise Lost* reference," she says:

"What if the breath that kindled those grim fires,
Awaked, should blow them into sevenfold rage,
And plunge us in the flames; or from above
Should intermitted vengeance arm again

His red right hand to plague us?"

The cadence of her voice, the tone, is almost unbearably musical. She's not a guitarist, he thinks with sudden certainty. She's a *singer*.

"Math was more my thing than English," he says. "You're going to need to explain that."

She kicks one of his shoes with the toe of her boot, like they're sharing a secret. "See that's the fun part. There's no easy explanation. Because the red right hand is meant to be some kind of divine vengeance against the rebellious demons. But the *form* that vengeance will take is uncertain. Maybe the red right hand is God himself. Maybe it's Jesus since he sits at the right hand of God. But also, the mark of the beast is supposed to be on the right hand. So maybe it's the antichrist."

Matts thinks this is the most interesting conversation involving God he's ever had. If sermons were more like this, his mother wouldn't have had to poke him awake with her Bible highlighter so often during Sunday services growing up.

"So…you wanted to imply that you're a divine tool, but no one knows if you're good or evil? That's why you chose the name?"

"Mostly, we just thought it sounded badass. But it makes me look cooler if I say I appreciate the complexity of its literary origins."

It startles a laugh out of him, and she looks pleased.

Her whole face changes when she smiles. Though she quickly ducks to hide her smile behind the curtain of her hair. It's an odd, habitual gesture. Shy in a way that seems at odds with the rest of her.

"You met Eli through YouTube stuff then?" he asks.

Eli is a popular vlogger who started with videos about cooking but now talks about skincare and skating and service dog stuff too.

"Yeah." She considers him for a long moment and then seems to make a decision. "I'm a singer."

He *knew* it.

"And I'm trans. I started a vlog when I was fourteen to document my transition. But I ended up posting a lot of videos of me singing covers too, just for fun. By the time I was sixteen, I had a pretty solid following and decided to share some original songs. And then I started doing short form stuff. A couple went viral. Got the band noticed. We signed a record deal last year, and now we're touring and making a living doing it. So—living the dream."

She pauses for a beat. He tries to look attentive and supportive and not like he's wondering what exactly the whole gender changing process entailed. He doesn't need Eli to tell him that'd be a wildly offensive thing to ask.

She narrows her eyes at him, and for a brief, drunken moment, he's afraid she can read his mind.

Pink Elephant, he thinks quickly. *Pink Elephant Pink Elephant Pink—*

"Anyway," she says. "There was this Texas influencer meetup thing downtown last year, and Eli and I ended up hiding on the roof together for an hour. We've been friends ever since."

"Eli is pretty great. Though he did try to keep us from meeting."

"Point deduction, for sure." She studies him over her cup, taking a leisurely sip. "You handled that better than I expected," she says finally.

"Handled what?"

"Realizing you were hitting on a trans girl. Worst case, guys like you, they get angry. Best case, they fall into a mental spiral about the Schrödinger's dick situation. You at least made an effort not to immediately look at my crotch."

He redoubles that effort, now.

"Schrödinger's—wait. 'Guys like me'? What does that mean? And what does 'angry' mean? Have people *hurt* you?"

"Clearly, I can handle myself. And I just mean that

most straight dudes typically need an adjustment period to be comfortable with the idea of sleeping with a trans girl. Or even the idea that they *want* to sleep with a trans girl."

"I guess," Matts allows. "But at least dicks are straightforward. I'd for sure know how to get a girl off if she had a dick. That's, you know, not always the case the other way around."

He can't believe he's saying this out loud. He's never drinking again. Or talking to another human. This is why he doesn't go to parties.

She's full-on grinning at him now, wide and completely unobstructed by her hair.

"Full disclosure—if you *are* looking for a hookup tonight, I am not your girl. I'm just flirting."

He can't decide if he's relieved by that or not. "Ouch. Am I not your type?"

Someone pushes past them, and she shifts to stand beside Matts rather than in front of him. She nudges him in the ribs with a pointy elbow.

"Consenting humans are my type," she says. "But I don't do one-night stands. Which I'm guessing is what you're angling for. If you're angling for anything."

He considers being insulted by that.

"No judgment," she adds. "If I was a twenty-some-thing professional athlete, I probably wouldn't want to settle down yet either. Well…" She glances across the room at Eli. "Unless I was Alexander Price and found my soulmate at nineteen."

"Do you do friends?" Matts asks. "Or— Shit, not— I didn't mean—"

He tries to find a different way to say it other than "do you want to be my friend" like a five-year-old. Fuck, maybe that's his best option. "Do you want to be my friend?"

She studies him, bottom lip tucked between her teeth. "You know, weirdly, I think I do."

"Cool."

"I also *do* my friends sometimes, too, just FYI."

Matts chokes a little.

"But only the really good ones. They have to have tenure."

"Something to aspire to," he manages.

"Something to which to aspire," she corrects, "if you want to be grammatically correct."

"I've never wanted to be grammatically correct in my life."

She laughs and gestures to the room at large. "Since *I'm* not an option, do you want me to introduce you to some cute ladies with absolutely no interest in marriage, kids, and a white picket fence?"

"Do they have legs like yours?"

She nods contemplatively as if she's taking the question seriously. "How do you feel about horses?"

"Uh. Generally positive?"

"Good enough. Let me introduce you to our resident rodeo queen. I have personal hands-on experience with her legs, and they're not *quite* as nice as mine, but few are. Hey now. Don't bluescreen on me. You okay, bud?"

"Sorry. You two have, uh… Are you—?"

"I told you; I sleep with my friends sometimes."

She did say that.

"So she…has tenure."

"That she does."

"Would she be interested in *me*?"

She looks at him like he's an idiot. "A six-foot-three professional athlete? Yeah, I think so."

"Okay. But I don't look anything like you. So if she's attracted to you—"

"Her type is also consenting human."

"Oh, good."

"Though, fair warning, she will want to talk about horses before, after, and possibly during sex."

"Weird, but not a deal-breaker."

He grew up on a ranch. His first vaguely sexual experience was under the bleachers during a rodeo. Horse girls are familiar territory, at least.

"I need to keep an eye on Eli though," he realizes.

She pats him on the back. "Well, they're currently both in the kitchen, which makes that easy. Let's go."

They go.

Connect with NineStar Press

www.ninestarpress.com

www.facebook.com/ninestarpress

www.facebook.com/groups/NineStarNiche

www.twitter.com/ninestarpress

www.instagram.com/ninestarpress

Printed in the USA
CPSIA information can be obtained
at www.ICGtesting.com
LVHW021622160923
758255LV00028B/178

9 781648 906855